For Mara
Happy Flying.
—Hope

Deceptive Perfection

Hope E. Davis

ISBN: 1722390204
ISBN-13: 978-1722390204

For Ms. Quinn, Ms. Graham, and Ms. Shellhorn

ACKNOWLEDGMENTS

Cover Photo by Faith Culler
Edited by Laurie Aames, Alijah Hinson, and Alyxandra Battaglia

Part One

ELDALYN

OCTOBER 2012

      Dropping a dish into the soapy water, Eldalyn dodged the droplets that splashed towards her face in retaliation. While she was mostly successful, the crumbling wall behind the sink was not so lucky. Eldalyn lived in a small worn out house on the wrong side of town. Not only did the drywall barely keep out the weather, the aging windows also had needed to be replaced long ago, but she had neither the ability nor the funds to see it done. The yard was in a perpetual state of complete disarray with weeds overtaking the sills of the windows and scaling the sides of the house. Eldalyn had tried to keep up at first, but then found her efforts to be futile as the weeds seemed to be a sort of hydra, two growing for every single one she picked. The grass and vegetable garden had both died long ago, and there was no longer a hose to allow her to do any watering.

      The neighborhood was one of color—in fact, the neighbors referred to her as "the white girl," as if there were no others. Eldalyn didn't get out enough to be sure, but often assumed it to be true. Although she was ostracized, the neighbors often came to check up on her, as they were concerned that there never seemed to be anyone else living in the house, and she seemed so young.

      Small in stature—but what she lacked for in size she made up for in determination—Eldalyn was a quiet girl, often receding into the depths of her mind for days at a time. She knew she wasn't a model, and seriously doubted anyone would take interest in her average brown hair and boring brown eyes. She was thin, sometimes from lack of food, but more often from the vigorous exercise she completed as part of her job. Not that she minded working, in fact she never had. A job kept her mind busy and on task, and she often found that she felt useless when she had days off from work. Her talents were few, but Eldalyn knew she had a good work ethic, and she hoped that someday that would be enough to improve her manner of living.

Eldalyn sighed as she washed the dishes carefully, using as little water as possible. She wasn't sure if the dishwater really made a huge effect on the water bill anyways, but every little bit of cash she could save helped her maintain what little sanity she figured she had left. Dipping her dried hands into the hot, soapy water again, Eldalyn fished around for the fork she knew was in there. She'd bought two packs of two forks at the dollar store over a year ago, and somehow, one had gone missing, leaving her with only three. There was no way she wanted to lose another. Even the cost of a dollar was something she couldn't afford right now.

Wiping a soapy hand across her brow, she wondered how long things had been like this, how she had let time get away. Her mom had died years ago—lung cancer, thanks to her pack-a-day smoking habit. Eldalyn had been young, but old enough to understand her mom wouldn't be coming back. She remembered the beginning, when at first her mom just seemed to cough a lot. Then she remembered the middle, mostly her mother in bed. And then, she also remembered the end. The end was the most difficult for Eldalyn to bring to the front of her mind. She remembered the hospital, the way it had a certain scent—one of what she would call a "clean decay." It smelled sanitary, but not in a good way. Her mother's room hadn't been like the others in the hall—it wasn't full of laughter of other children, or flowers, or even old relatives come to say goodbye—it was just Eldalyn and her father.

Eldalyn's hand finally encountered the fork wedged beneath the edge of the drain cover she had placed in the sink for the purpose of preserving the water. It was a good thing she hadn't turned on the barely functional garbage disposal. or it could have been disastrous for both the fork and the deteriorating appliance.

Eldalyn thought about her father in the days before her mother had died. He had been supportive, going to the hospital almost every day. In fact, he'd often picked Eldalyn up from school— something neither of her parents had ever done—and driven her to see her mother. And he'd been there when her mother had breathed her final breath and exited Eldalyn's life forever.

That was the past. Her father's current absence was a different, much less excusable, story. When Eldalyn turned fifteen, she began to notice her father had a drinking habit, or perhaps she was just finally old enough to understand. And over the next four years, it grew—from two beers a night, to half a handle starting most days at sunrise. Sometime just before she turned nineteen, he began to go out often, and come home late. And one day, he didn't come back at all. Not that Eldalyn minded—in fact, things were almost better with him gone. He'd lost his job long ago, transferring the house into Eldalyn's name once she turned eighteen so he wouldn't lose it when he declared bankruptcy, and she had been paying what she could of the bills ever since. At least this way. her father wasn't breaking things of value or eating food that Eldalyn couldn't afford to purchase.

Eldalyn pulled the plug to drain the rest of the water in the sink, glancing at the calendar as she felt the water rushing by her hands. There was a big red circle on the following day, reminding her the electricity bill was due.

The bills were barely covered by her part-time job, but she did what she could, slowly selling off any items left in the house with value that hadn't been smashed to smithereens. At first it had been easy, selling off her mother's china and old clothing. But then Eldalyn began to have to sell things she was attached to, such as her grandmother's jewelry and the oil paintings that had been on the house walls since the 1950s. Now, there was almost nothing left to sell. The house was paid off at least, but the utilities often totaled two to three hundred dollars a month. Eldalyn barely made two hundred dollars a week working as a dog walker for a pet hotel. It wasn't glamorous, but she loved dogs, and it had been one of the few jobs that hadn't asked for a GED, which Eldalyn had never managed to complete.

She'd attended school, almost every day. But then, during her senior year, her father's alcoholism had peaked, and he'd been fired from his job as an accountant for one too many absences. And Eldalyn had started working more and attending school less.

She really didn't have many friends toward the end anyways. At twelve, she was the only girl in her class to lose her mother, and she often found that other kids didn't understand. And when her father started drinking, she found the two close friends she did have could no longer come over to her house. At the time she hadn't understood why their parents forbade them to come see her, but now she knew; her father had been an utter disgrace in his clothes that had gone unwashed for months and breath that smelled like alcohol twenty-four seven.

Kids in high school hadn't really wanted to be her friend anyways. There was a reputation surrounding kids that came from her side of town. The babies born there weren't smart, and only went to school to get a job at the local fast food joint, if they even finished school to begin with. Everyone knew that nothing good could come of hanging out with a girl of her background. And she couldn't argue; she had not done much better.

Eldalyn finished draining the sink and walked around her small house. Perhaps when her grandparents had bought it in 1948, it had been a nice place. Maybe it had looked better when her father had redone the bathroom in the early eighties. But now, thirty some years later, it was more of a liability than a luxury. There were two small rooms facing each other directly adjacent to the small living room. Behind that was the kitchen, which had a bathroom located at the rear. The house was small, barely thirteen hundred square feet.

When her mother and father had both lived here, it had seemed even smaller. Her mother had often mentioned having other children, but for whatever reason that never happened. And if it had, Eldalyn wasn't sure where they would've put them; her room wasn't much larger than a walk-in closet.

Entering the bathroom, Eldalyn grabbed her toothbrush and the near-empty tube of toothpaste. There was only enough left for maybe two brushings. She would stretch it to last six. She'd been a lucky girl, having nearly straight teeth without the braces most of her classmates had required. Not that her parents could have afforded it on her father's measly accountant salary.

Even before she'd been diagnosed with cancer, Eldalyn's mother had been ill, often taking to her bed with coughing fits and headaches that she claimed wouldn't go away. By the time Eldalyn was eight, she could do her own laundry, clean the portions of the house she could reach, and cook simple meals for her mother and herself.

Eldalyn finished brushing her teeth and looked in the mirror. She was only twenty, but she felt so old. Her shoulders felt weighed down, her heart heavy with stress; it was only a matter of time before it started to show on her face. Although she was mature for her age, she was still a twenty-year-old girl and couldn't help but try to smooth the worry line that was starting to form on her brow.

Walking back into the kitchen, Eldalyn jotted *toothpaste* down on her grocery list. The list was long, payday was days away, and she knew she wouldn't be able to afford it all. She always took her father's old work calculator to the store with her, calculating the cost of each item with tax included. She often ended up with cases of ramen noodles, easy mac, and whatever items she could find on the past date sale shelf. Occasionally she would get lucky, and there would be sales on shampoo, toilet paper, and cleaning products. Eldalyn had learned to cut coupons when she could, walking the neighborhood on trash days to grab old newspapers from her neighbors' recycle bins.

Eldalyn felt as if she lived in a dark hole, but she wouldn't say she was unhappy. But she couldn't say she was happy either. She sort of just existed. A state of being without even feeling—because Eldalyn knew if she allowed herself to feel for just one moment, she would most certainly fall apart.

Rolling her shoulders to try to relieve the stress, Eldalyn walked towards the door grabbing her only jacket on the way out. Time for work.

JOSHUA

OCTOBER 2012

"No, it's my turn!"

"But I was here first!"

"I'm older. Back off!"

"It's whoever gets here first, and you know it!"

Joshua sighed and removed his headphones. This could go on forever. He rolled his eyes and spun around in his father's large leather office chair. "Miki, Marc, cut it out! I'm trying to work!"

"But Miki is hogging the microwave!" Marc whined in a high-pitched voice. At nine, it had yet to deepen.

"Miki hurry up and finish and let Marc have his turn!" Josh slipped his headphones back on, fully intending on returning to the paper he was writing for his biology class. He was interrupted by a yell.

"Marc bit me!" Miki squealed, suddenly appearing in front of Joshua. He sighed, realizing this would never resolve itself, and followed his seven-year-old sister into the kitchen. Why couldn't they just behave for five minutes without fighting? Joshua was so tired of staying home and babysitting his siblings every day while his parents played saviors of the city. His mother was an attorney, working odd and often long hours to help clients out. His father was a doctor at the local hospital, always picking up an extra shift when they needed him. This left Joshua home with the kids, pretty much around the clock.

Twice a week, Joshua attended classes at the local university. His current degree was pre-med, but it was his third year and he wanted to change it to something different. He found he didn't like to deal with patients as much as he thought he would. In fact, he'd rather work in a lab studying the effect of diseases on rats. But his father so desperately wanted him to be a doctor like himself that Joshua was unsure how to break the news that he wanted to change his major.

Turning the corner into the kitchen, Joshua felt his mouth drop open. There was spiral pasta everywhere—all over the floor, the counter, and the table. And sitting on the floor in the middle of the mess was Juni, Joshua's three-year-old sister, and she was clearly enjoying the floor rotini. "Marc, Miki, what have you guys done? You were supposed to put the pasta in the microwave and press the 'add 30 second' button." Josh bent down and picked Juni up, placing her in a chair at the table, where she happily transitioned from eating floor rotini to table rotini. At least it was less dirty, Joshua figured.

"I was going to! But then Miki was using the microwave and wouldn't let me have a turn!" Marc whined as Joshua leaned down to start picking up the mess.

"I was cooking my chicken nuggets! Mom told me what buttons to push!" Miki argued back, putting her hands on her hips just as their mother did when she was mad. Joshua could just tell she'd be a huge diva in a few years.

"I don't care who did what! Both of you need to help me clean up!" Joshua shouted over the whining to put it to a stop. Marc and Miki were forever fighting. As the closest in age, they seemed to grind personalities the most, and Joshua was sure that wouldn't change as they aged.

Joshua had wanted to get a job and move out on his own, but his parents had insisted they pay for his college and that he attend, no matter what he wanted. Joshua had a suspicion they just didn't want their full-time babysitter to get away. His parents were the kind who had kids, and then proceeded to pass them off to someone else. He remembered his grandfather caring for him more in his childhood than his parents had. He wasn't sure how the mechanics had happened, but Josh was twelve years older than his closest sibling, becoming the built-in babysitter by the time his mom had returned to work after having Marc. Miki had come soon after. Joshua had assumed his parents, the workaholics they were, would stop there. But then Juni came along four years later, much to Joshua's surprise and annoyance. The last thing a high school senior boy wanted to do was admit he had to go home right after school to take care of a toddler.

Joshua had to admit, though—Juni was the easy one. To his parents' concern, she had not yet started to talk even though she was three. But as far as Joshua was concerned, this was a godsend, considering how Miki and Marc never seemed to shut up.

Finally, all the pasta had been collected off the floor and deposited into the trash. Joshua stood up, dusted himself off, and grabbed the partially open bag of chicken nuggets off the counter, dumping its entire contents onto a plate and putting it in the microwave.

Marc pouted. "But I wanted leftover pasta from last night!"

"Well that was an option before you two spilled it all over the kitchen." Joshua remained calm and grabbed down three plastic multicolored plates and began filling plastic glasses half full with milk. If he filled them all the way up, he just knew there would be spilled milk everywhere.

The microwave dinged, and he removed the chicken nuggets, placing five on two of the plates, and three on the last plate. Performing a sort of balancing act, he carried the plates and the glasses of milk to the table, putting them down in front of each child. When they all began happily munching, he returned to the paper he was writing. *It would be so much easier to study if I didn't have to babysit*, Joshua huffed to himself.

He knew he shouldn't complain too much; babysitting now was easier than it had been a couple years ago. At least Juni was past the stage where she was either eating or destroying everything that crossed her path. And Marc and Miki could usually microwave their own lunches (whatever leftovers or frozen food their mom bought) and look after themselves. They were also well trained to yell for Joshua when Juni got into something she wasn't supposed to.

But Joshua felt lost. His parents barely saw him as more than a babysitter, and he didn't like the profession his father wanted him to pursue. His only redemption was the occasional night when his parents would come home and feel like being parents. Then Joshua would get the rare luxury of riding his bike. Often times he would just ride until his legs hurt, but every now and then he would ride to this place he found. It was some sort of flood-control channel, but there was rarely any water in it. It was in a valley, hidden in the middle of suburbia, where concrete walls rose eight feet high around an assortment of bridges, stairs, and pillars. The concrete was covered with some of the most beautiful graffiti he had ever seen, though he was unsure how the art got there—as he'd never seen another soul around while he'd been there. And he tended to visit about once a week. Sometimes, he would take his iPod and sit there and listen to music for hours on end. If his parents noticed his extended absences, they never said anything.

Joshua finished up his paper and pushed *PRINT.* As the printer started spitting out his document, Joshua sighed; he doubted his parents even cared about him anymore. He stacked his paper, stapled it together, and was about to slip it in his backpack when he simultaneously heard the doorbell ring and an "Ow! Miki bit me!" with a corresponding scream from the kitchen. Joshua rolled his eyes and then closed them, leaving them that way for a second so as to allow himself one last moment of peace before he stood up and headed for the door. No rest for the wicked.

ELDALYN

OCTOBER 2012

The bell on the door jingled as Eldalyn stepped into the pet boarding business where she worked. She was immediately assaulted by the smell of dog shampoo and the overwhelming sound of dogs barking excitedly. Bernice, the middle-aged manager, looked up from where she sat reading her newspaper, giving Eldalyn a small smile.

"Morning Bernice." It was barely a mumble, but Bernice had learned not to expect much from Eldalyn. She was a quiet girl, but she was punctual—and great with the dogs.

Eldalyn stepped through the back doors to the kennel, glancing at the whiteboard on the wall adjacent to the door. Only five dogs today, not nearly her normal load. Most days she could have anywhere from ten to fifteen dogs to walk, maybe even more if it was during a peak travel season such as holidays and ski weekends. Eldalyn popped her head through the door back into the front room that Bernice was occupying, "Really? Just five today?"

"Yeah, it's back to school season. People just aren't boarding their dogs this time of year," Bernice answered without looking up from the dinosaur of a computer that occupied the majority of the check-in desk. Eldalyn bit her lip and shut the door.

Bernice and her partner, Millie, who was a well-known dog trainer, owned the pet boarding company, aptly named *Pet Palace*. Millie had spent most of her twenties and thirties training dogs for both agility contests and show. Once she turned forty, she decided the running was too difficult on her joints, and instead put all her hard-earned money into Pet Palace, a boarding and dog training facility. The facility could house up to thirty dogs in separate kennels (as well as a few cats if requested); it had two yards for the dogs to play—one for the smaller dogs and one for the larger ones. There was also an agility courtyard for those pet owners who wanted to teach their dogs to compete.

Millie and Bernice had quickly realized they had their work cut out for them when they had twenty-five dogs their first week. The two of them worked day and night for almost a month before acknowledging they needed to hire help. First, they hired Trevor, a full-time janitor who also had a passion for dogs and usually took the nightshift—a time when they needed someone to take care of the dogs but not the front desk, though he would occasionally if asked. Bernice usually manned the desk during the daytime hours. Millie did all the training and helped at the desk when needed. Even with Trevor, the ladies soon realized they needed a little more help feeding the dogs in a timely manner, as well as exercising the ones which required longer walks than the small shop allowed. That's where Eldalyn came in. She helped exercise and feed the dogs as needed, oftentimes only getting twenty-five to thirty hours a week. Since she was paid minimum wage, her checks amounted to nothing. Bernice and Millie never asked, but seemed to understand she needed the hours, occasionally having her come in to relieve one of them an hour or so early.

Eldalyn couldn't complain though. She loved her job, and they had been willing to hire her without experience or a GED. And the best part … unless she had to cover the desk for a lunch break, she didn't have to talk to anyone other than the dogs.

Eldalyn re-checked the whiteboard to see which dogs needed to be walked. Below each name were kennel numbers with instructions on how to feed, walk, and treat each dog. There were also notes on temperament. Eldalyn was often assigned the larger dogs that didn't get along with other dogs well enough to put them out for group play time but still needed their exercise. Eldalyn grabbed a blue leash from the hook below the unit five box.

Turning to the kennel right behind her, she kneeled down and gently attached the leash to the hefty lab laying by the door. "Hello Shane, how are you today?" she murmured while considering the route she was going to take. She knew almost the entire west side of the city like the back of her hand, often trying new routes whenever she could. Pulling gently on the leash, the lab slowly rose to his feet. "Come on boy." Eldalyn opened the door to the lobby with Shane in tow, waving to Bernice on her way out.

Shane was a well-behaved and sweet dog; however, he was astronomically overweight—somewhat resembling a small bear. Therefore, his elderly owners paid extra for Eldalyn to walk him a mile a day. Shane loved to walk, but sometimes he'd get tired from the amount of weight he had to carry, forcing Eldalyn to turn back early or risk being stuck with a 150-pound dog that refused to move.

Outside in the chilly October air, Eldalyn took a deep breath, feeling the air fill her lungs. Something about this time of year was sad. Maybe it was the leaves dying on the trees as the seasons changed. Maybe it was the kids all going back to school and to college as Eldalyn often wished she could. But more often than not, she knew she didn't like this time of year because of the memories.

Eldalyn walked towards the north portion of the west side of town, around a small pond and down a path that led through what Eldalyn liked to refer to as "the heart of suburbia." Every house was an exact cookie cutter of one another with matching families residing inside. All the moms had the same haircut, and the same two kids, who played in the street, with the same friends, riding their same razor scooters. Granted, they all had different colors, but there was no individuality. Yet, society felt this was the *right* side of town.

The only redeeming structure in this neighborhood was the library. Built of brown bricks and only one story tall, it was the most magical building of all. The library on Eldalyn's side of town was outdated and picked through, but this library—it was modern and always well stocked.

Eldalyn couldn't go inside today though, not while she had a dog with her. So without a word, she turned to her right and began the slow trek back to Pet Palace with the overweight black lab. Only four dogs to go after this.

JOSHUA

OCTOBER 2012

"—And I expect all of your papers to have at least three sources, though you'll need five to get an *A*. Make sure you pick a disease you're passionate about, otherwise writing this paper is going to be really difficult for you—" Joshua's professor droned on as the students quickly scribbled as many notes as they could.

Joshua was exhausted. Poor Juni was sick and had been requiring more of his attention than usual. So another paper on top of his current workload was not helping his stress level any.

With a few last scribbles on the board, the professor dismissed the class, letting them know they had two weeks to complete the twenty-five-page research paper. Joshua sighed in dismay; two weeks was hardly any time at all when you had three kids to corral at home.

As he turned to walk out the door, a blond-haired, baby-faced guy he knew only as Liam who sat behind him in class stepped in front of him. "Hey, Joshua, right? A bunch of us guys are getting together to play soccer at four today. You want to join us?"

Joshua was surprised anyone was talking to him. He had a couple friends from high school, but they had all gone off to different universities. He hadn't really bothered making friends and was shocked someone had approached him. As fast as his shock came, it faded away as he thought of what lie to tell his parents as to why he didn't relieve their part-time nanny on time. *Oh well*, he thought, *this is a one-time opportunity.*

"Sure, where at?" Josh responded after what felt like too long, though in actuality only a few seconds later.

"Ralston Park—see you there." Liam put out his fist for Joshua to bump. The whole thing seemed very juvenile to Joshua all of the sudden, but at least it was getting him out of the house for one night.

Joshua picked up his backpack and tossed it over his shoulder. With a glance at his watch he confirmed it was 2 p.m. and that he had time to start his paper in the library, as well as time to call the nanny and let her know she would need to stay a few more hours. She wouldn't mind; Joshua's parents had cut back her hours ever since Joshua had started college. While he'd been in high school, it had been a much more regular gig. In fact, she'd been telling his parents if they didn't give her more hours she would have to find a second job, and who knows if those hours would work with her current ones. So from Joshua's perspective, he was actually helping his parents—in a roundabout way they may or may not like. But either way, he was an adult and had earned some time off.

He found a quiet corner near the back of the school library, pulling out his laptop and cell phone. He quickly placed the call to the nanny, and as he guessed, she was happy to stay a few hours longer; in fact, she was ecstatic. After he hung up with her, he put his phone away and began researching diseases to write his paper on. At least this was something he was somewhat passionate about. He just couldn't get into some of the biology and anatomy classes he was being forced to take.

Before he knew it, Joshua glanced at his watch and it was ten till four. He quickly gathered up his computer and notes and dashed out to his car. Tossing the books into the back of his black BMW 325xi, he climbed in swiftly and started the engine. He knew he should be grateful that his parents bought him such a nice car, but sometimes he wondered at what cost. How long did they think they could buy his affections and keep him home?

Resolving to ponder the problem more later, he flipped the car into reverse and headed to Ralston Park. He hadn't played soccer in forever and he couldn't lie—he was a little nervous he might have lost all the athleticism he'd had in high school. He hadn't had time to work out since starting college, but luckily, he had a high metabolism and a three-year old to keep him trim.

As he pulled up at the park, he immediately noticed a group of about ten college guys surrounding a soccer ball. As he stepped out of the car, he spotted Liam who was waving him over. Joshua recognized two other guys from his Biology class: one was named Ben, and he had no idea the other guy's name. Joshua walked over and stood next to Liam as they began dividing up into teams. Joshua was put on the "skins" team and stripped off his shirt, heading to the far side of the field. There was no other way to put it—he was glad to be playing sports again.

ELDALYN

OCTOBER 2012

It was almost ten by the time Eldalyn finished feeding and walking all the dogs. Bernice had headed home for the night around eight, asking Eldalyn to keep an eye on the desk for the last two hours they were open. No one usually came in that late anyways, so Eldalyn didn't mind.

She was just finishing filling the dogs' water dishes when she heard the sound of the bell on the door. Must be Trevor coming to relieve her. She double checked all the locks on the kennels and exited into the lobby.

She stopped dead in her tracks when she saw a gorgeous blonde standing there with a small dog tucked under her arm.

Eldalyn mumbled a quick "sorry" and made her way behind the counter. This wasn't her forte. "Are you dropping your dog off?" she asked hesitantly, looking up to evaluate the woman's flawless face.

"Yeah. This is Buster. I'll be back for him in two days." The blonde smacked on her gum while pulling food and dog toys out of her Gucci purse with her perfectly manicured diamond studded nails and putting them on the counter. She looked to be about Eldalyn's age but so much prettier.

"Are you a new customer?" Eldalyn asked as she shuffled through papers looking for anything with the name *Buster*.

"Yes, I know I need to fill out paperwork." As Eldalyn handed her a clipboard, the blonde smiled a wide smile with perfectly white teeth. Eldalyn couldn't help but notice the woman's large bust and perfect hourglass figure. She wondered if the woman worked out or had surgery; she was willing to bet on the latter. Something about the woman was incredibly familiar, but Eldalyn just couldn't put her finger on it. Perhaps the lady had come in before but not taken the time to fill out paperwork? Or maybe Eldalyn had seen her on the street. However, that was highly unlikely as Eldalyn sensed the woman had plenty of money to buy a car and park it wherever she pleased. Her clothes were some of the most attractive workout clothes Eldalyn had ever seen, and they fit the woman perfectly. "Here." The blonde slid the finished paperwork across the counter, while quickly shoving the Chihuahua into Eldalyn's arms. "Sorry, I'm in a hurry." And with that she quickly kissed the dog's head and left, nearly knocking over Trevor on her way out.

Trevor, also a bit of a recluse, seemed shocked at the sight of such a beautiful and perfectly proportionate woman exiting the building. He turned to watch her ass as she walked away, blushing when he turned back and his eyes met Eldalyn's. She gave a small smile. There was no need to explain—she'd been guilty of looking at the woman's ass too. She quickly deposited Buster into Trevor's arms while she grabbed all his belongings and took them to kennel 12 where he would be residing. Trevor followed, placing the dog on the standard issue dog pillow they kept in every kennel.

"Hey Eldalyn."

"Trevor." Eldalyn pushed past Trevor to finish setting up the kennel.

"How are you?" Trevor leaned down to pet Buster, not looking at Eldalyn while she answered.

"I'm fine. You?"

Trevor nodded, "Good, can't complain." This was actually one of their longer conversations, but now there was nothing more for Eldalyn to say.

With a wave and a quick "see you later," Eldalyn grabbed her backpack and headed out the door to start the long walk home. Usually she would take the bus, but funds were short this month, so it was a two and half hour walk for her. Not that it mattered, not like she had anything better to do.

Often times, when she would get off early, she would walk through the suburbs to the west of downtown before heading back to her home on the east. She knew it wasn't practical, but the library on the west of town was so much nicer than the ones on the east. There was a much more complete book selection, the computers were always free, and there were no homeless people begging her for change she didn't have.

Tonight it was too late—the library was already closed, so with a sigh Eldalyn turned and headed east. Pet Palace was in a great location. Just on the edge of the west side of town, it drew in most of its business from the very rich transplants who spent over half a million on their foothill mansions. To the east was a moderate middle class community. Although they couldn't afford the pricey training service offered at Pet Palace, there wasn't really another dog boarding place for miles, so they too used the boarding services.

The middle class community went on for almost five miles. Then past that, the homes began to deteriorate from moderate three bedrooms to doublewide trailers and homes built as far back as the early 1900s. In the middle of this mess, on an acre of land, was Eldalyn's home. There were two parks on the way home, the first being a nicely furnished place to play and pass the time. The second, well, it was right next to the eastside library and more of a journey through what could only be called a homeless slum. Often Eldalyn would walk around the second park, but she could still hear the catcalls and begging as she did. She hoped she would never have to join their ranks.

Tonight, she was so tired that she was debating running through the second park—the direct route other than going around. Just as she was weighing her options she heard a distinct "Eldalyn!" from off to her left.

Her hand tightened on her backpack strap and she turned with caution to see who it was.

"Hey Terrance!" Eldalyn recognized one of the homeless men she had befriended. She wasn't sure where he slept, but she knew he worked as a dishwasher at one of the nice restaurants near the first park.

"How are things going Eldalyn?" Terrance ran his hand through his barely-there, greying hair, his bike resting at his side. Terrance had a daughter or two around Eldalyn's age. Terrance was only forty years of age, but Eldalyn noticed he looked older and older every day.

"They're going okay. Work is the same as always." Eldalyn managed a half smile. His teeth showed signs of possible drug use of some sort. While she felt like she knew Terrance, she still felt a little nervous speaking with him alone after dark.

"That's good, still walking dogs?" Terrance fell into step with Eldalyn as she continued walking.

"Yeah, how are the dishes treating you?" Eldalyn wished she wore a watch so she could look at it and at least pretend she was late. But she figured chatting a few more minutes wouldn't hurt.

"Not good. I, uh … I got fired. I'm looking for a new job now." Terrance placed his cap back on his head and started to mount his bike.

Eldalyn wanted to ask what happened, but she didn't dare. "I'm sorry to hear that."

"It is what it is. I'll find a new job soon. See you around Eldalyn." And with a wave, Terrance was headed off the way Eldalyn had just come. Although she didn't have much, Eldalyn was glad she wasn't homeless like Terrance.

A bit on edge since their conversation, Eldalyn came to the second park and took the slow way around. Better safe than sorry.

JOSHUA

OCTOBER 2012

Trying to be as quiet as possible, Joshua slipped his key into the lock and turned slowly. But it was no use—he opened the door to find two munchkins staring at him. The minute he was fully inside they began their ambush.

"Joshy! You're home!"

"Joshy! Joshy! Joshy!" It was Marc and Miki, apparently ecstatic to see him. Juni wasn't in the immediate vicinity. Then again, it was after eight; she was probably in bed. "Joshy! Read me a story!" Miki tugged Joshua towards the couch at the same time Marc tried to pull him in the kitchen.

"No Josh, make me a snack!"

Joshua rolled his eyes and detached himself from both children's grasps. "Miki, go pick out a book, read it once by yourself, and then I'll be up to read it to you. Marc, you should've eaten more dinner. If you want a snack, I can get you some carrots or an apple—those are your choices." Marc pouted while Miki ran off to get a book. Chances were she would forget all about it by the time Joshua got there.

Joshua heard the creak of the stairs and turned behind him to find the nanny standing on the bottom step. At only five foot four, she was much shorter than Joshua's six foot one frame. Often times she'd have to leave some of the dishes on the counter for Joshua to put away when he got home—some of the cupboards were up too high.

"Ah Joshua, you're back." She laughed at her joke. How could anyone miss hearing the chorus of "Joshy"s that had just been squealed about the house.

"Yeah, I see the house is still standing and you're not tied up, so that's a plus." Joshua smiled. The nanny wasn't always his favorite person, but she did have a great sense of humor.

"Well, Juni is in bed. I was just about to tuck Miki in before I headed out. They ate fish sticks and rice for dinner. Or more painted the table with it. Juni had a bath. Same ol' same ol'." With a quick smile she headed back up the stairs to Miki's room. Joshua stood there for a moment, and just as he turned to head to the kitchen, the nanny reemerged from Miki's room. "Guess she fell asleep. There's a book open on her lap and everything."

Joshua laughed as she descended the stairs; that's exactly what he'd banked on happening. He loved when his plans worked out like this.

The nanny grabbed her purse and headed out the door. "See you on Tuesday Joshua. Let me know if you need me to cover any time before then."

"No problem, will do." With a small wave he closed the door and locked it. He leaned against it for just a moment before he turned and headed to the kitchen only to find Marc standing by the stove with an open bag of frozen French fries.

"Marc, I said carrots or an apple, *not* French fries!" Joshua snatched the open bag of fries and tied it with a rubber band before placing it back in the freezer. Marc pouted.

"But… But, Joshy!"

"No, your options are carrots, an apple, or bed. Now pick; I don't have all night" In fact, Joshua had a hell of a paper to get started.

Marc huffed out of the kitchen and up the stairs to his bedroom. Joshua was just too good at this.

Joshua slowly sank down into a kitchen chair, using his left hand to try and massage some of the stress out of his shoulders. He was just so tired all the time; between parenting non-stop and school, he had no time to plan his adult life—which he figured is what his parents wanted. Soccer had been a blast tonight, and the guys had invited him to play with them every Thursday and Sunday. Joshua had told them he was unsure about this Sunday, but he would be there next Thursday for sure.

Joshua didn't know how he was going to do it, but he was going to talk to his parents. Well, whichever parent happened to be home tonight, so more likely his mother. He just couldn't do this full time parenting anymore. He needed at least one day to focus solely on homework. He wasn't going to tell his mom about the soccer—just say that he needed Sundays off for homework—and hopefully, she would agree.

Glancing at his watch he decided he would wait up for one of his parents tomorrow; tonight he was just too tired. With one last look at the dirty kitchen, he picked up his backpack and headed down the stairs to his room. At least he had a little privacy in the basement, and he had his own bathroom, which was a huge plus.

Their house was a moderate six-bedroom, four-bathroom house on the west side of town. The basement had two bedrooms connected by a Jack-and-Jill bathroom. Joshua knew that he had to move out soon before his parents decided Marc was old enough to have the other room. For now, the second basement room was his dad's man cave, complete with a big screen TV and reclining couch. The younger kids weren't allowed in there, but Joshua's dad often let him watch movies—though the beer mini fridge had been off limits until Joshua turned twenty-one this past year. The rest of the family lived on the second floor—his parents in the master suite, his siblings each with their own rooms. All three had to share a bathroom though, which worked now, but he was sure would be an issue the minute Miki hit puberty.

Joshua tossed his backpack on his desk and flopped down on his queen-size bed. At least he had some peace and quiet down here.

He quickly realized he was too tired to do homework tonight, deciding instead to brush his teeth and head straight to bed. The homework would be there in the morning.

ELDALYN

OCTOBER 2012

The next morning Eldalyn rolled out of bed and ran a brush quickly through her dark brown hair, tying her long tresses in a fold over bun on the back of her head. She glanced in the mirror over the sink while she splashed warm water on her face. For some reason, the sleep did not want to leave her eyes this morning. Eldalyn slipped her purple Pet Palace polo over her head and smoothed out the wrinkles with her hand. The iron had broken a couple weeks ago and she had yet to find another. Eldalyn made a mental note to put this shirt in the dryer tonight when she arrived home.

Grabbing her backpack on the way out the door, Eldalyn rolled her head from one side to the other trying to stretch out her neck. The night had been too short, but Bernice had a lot of dogs checking in today and had wanted extra help.

As she walked through the park, Eldalyn noticed Terrance leaning up against the wall with his beanie hat pulled low over his eyes.

"Hey Terrance!" Eldalyn shouted and waved in his direction. Terrance moved one of his dark hands to his hat, peeling it up just enough to look at Eldalyn. Upon seeing who it was shouting his name at this ungodly hour of the morning, he cracked a smile that showed all his missing teeth. Then he put his hat back down and closed his eyes.

Eldalyn continued on her way past all the other bums sleeping in the park. They seemed much less menacing in the daylight, probably because they weren't as high on drugs and the crevices where they stored their things seemed much less daunting.

The bell on the door jingled as Eldalyn walked in Pet Palace to start what would probably be her longest work day of the week.

"Ah, Eldalyn! Can you take Snickers here back to his room?" Eldalyn

looked up to see the lobby was already occupie
various owners waiting to check in. Bernice wa
help.

Eldalyn nodded and smiled at the first cust
husky mix back to the rear area with the kennels.
note in Eldalyn's hand as she passed—it had Snic
information written on it.

While she was getting Snickers settled in his kennel, Bernice brought
back the second dog, a smaller Chihuahua named Oreo. Bernice quickly
placed him in the kennel next to Snickers and handed Eldalyn another post-
it with Oreo's information. Bernice closed and locked the door on Oreo's
kennel, then headed back to the front to collect the third dog. Eldalyn
began writing both dogs' information on the white board with their
corresponding kennel numbers.

Bernice returned a moment later with the third dog just as Millie came
in from the back door which connected to the outdoor, fenced-in dog run.

"Eldalyn, what a pleasure to see you this morning!" Millie said in her
perpetually peppy voice. Eldalyn knew she just had to have been a
cheerleader at some point.

"Hi Millie," Eldalyn answered as she took the third post-it from
Bernice and began writing the information on the whiteboard.

"Eldalyn, would you mind manning the desk this afternoon? I have a
doctor's appointment and Bernice already asked for the evening off."

"Sure, no problem." Eldalyn turned and smiled at Millie. Any money
was good money.

Scouring the white board and brushing back the few strands of hair
that had fallen in her eyes, Eldalyn grabbed the first leash. Now that she
had to man the desk this afternoon, Eldalyn had half the usual time to walk
the dogs. Rubbing her neck one last time to try to relieve the stress, Eldalyn
turned and headed for the kennel where Shane was housed.

...day night when Bernice asked Eldalyn to man the desk ...ith a sigh, Eldalyn put down her broom and agreed. She ...say no to a boss who had given her a chance when she really had ...ason to. Eldalyn quickly finished putting the gear away and feeding the ...ogs before she headed out front.

It was already close to eight in the evening and the neighborhood was quiet. Eldalyn took Bernice's stool behind the desk as the older woman grabbed her purse and headed out. "Thanks again Eldalyn! We will see you on Monday!"

"No problem. Have a good night." Eldalyn smiled, waiting until Bernice was out of sight to slump over the desk. She hadn't been sleeping well lately and she was unsure why. It may have something to do with the fact she had turned the thermostat down to save some money. It was only fall, but already the nights were falling below freezing. This winter would be rough.

Eldalyn began flipping through paperwork trying to get a sense of organization. If there's one thing at which Bernice did not excel, it was keeping the paperwork in an orderly manner.

The bell above the door jingled and Eldalyn looked up to find the gorgeous blonde who had dropped off her Chihuahua only two nights before.

"Hey, I'm here to pick up Buster." She breezed in stopping right in front of the counter. Eldalyn was sure she was staring but couldn't seem to stop.

"I remember." Eldalyn stood up and turned towards the door to the back.

"Hey, wait!" Eldalyn spun back around in confusion. "You used to go to West High, right?" The blonde was inspecting Eldalyn in a peculiar manner that made her slightly self-conscious.

"Um yeah, but I didn't finish. I went to work instead." Eldalyn continued to look at the blonde with questions in the back of her mind.

"I remember you. I don't know if you remember me, but we went to middle school together too. We were both in the fall musical together. I look a lot different now but—"

Suddenly something clicked in her mind; she knew where she'd seen this woman before. "Cassie?" Eldalyn said with a gasp. Gone was the skinny, nerdy blonde girl, and instead, this busty model had taken her place.

"Yeah." The woman smiled a friendly smile. "So what happened? Why didn't you finish school? You were always so much smarter than me."

Eldalyn smiled at the girl who had once been her childhood friend. "There, uh, just wasn't money. And I've been working here to save up, but they only employ me part-time, and they don't have enough business to make me full-time yet."

Cassie seemed to think for a second, then she gave Eldalyn a look up and down. "Well, I know of a job. I'm not sure if it's something you would be interested in, but I'm … friends … with the manager, and I feel sure he'd let you have a shot if you were." She emphasized the word *friend,* and Eldalyn wasn't naïve enough to miss the implication. She was desperate though, and willing to give any job a shot.

"What kind of job is it?" Eldalyn knew her skills were limited, and most jobs didn't want to hire someone who only had household skills on their resume. In fact, most jobs didn't care that you could cook a mean beef stew; they wanted to hear that you had at least five years of experience in their field.

Cassie smiled in a way that was almost apologetic, as if slightly embarrassed by what she was about to say. "Well, it's a bar, but the girls you know, dance and stuff. No nudity, but about as close as you can legally get without being a strip club. But you would be a cocktail server, Mike usually leaves the dancing to the pros." Cassie ran a hand confidently through her hair.

For some reason, the answer didn't surprise Eldalyn at all; her subconscious must've seen it coming. "Um, I have—I mean I don't really know—"

"Don't worry about experience. The manager is willing to train, and I can help you off the books if you need. You might find you had the skills all along." Cassie's voice was smooth and reassuring. Eldalyn wondered what had happened to her passion for acting. Cassie should've been famous by now.

Still, Eldalyn hesitated. She'd never done anything like that before. In fact, she'd never even worn a bikini in high school. Then again, she'd never had a reason to buy one.

Cassie must have sensed her hesitation. "Trust me—you'll make way more than you do here. Even on a 'bad' night I bring home at least two hundred dollars."

Eldalyn felt her eyes go wide. *Two hundred dollars?? In* one *night?!* That was half a week's pay at the Pet Palace. She quickly calculated how long it would take her to catch up on bills.

"So what do you say?" Cassie was patiently waiting for her response.

"That would be great. When would I be able to start?" Eldalyn figured she had absolutely nothing to lose. If it didn't work out, she could always come back here.

"Come in tomorrow morning around eight. Wear something that shows a lot of skin." Cassie smiled as Eldalyn turned to finish collecting Buster. What luck that she had run into Cassie these years.

Returning to the front room, Eldalyn had never been very confrontational or outgoing, but she couldn't hold back the question bubbling on her lips: "What happened to your dreams of being an actress?"

Cassie sighed, giving Eldalyn a sad smile. "Turns out I wasn't good enough. My mom took me to a couple auditions when I was sixteen, but they're looking for some real talent. The manager told me to go out for modeling instead."

"And?" Eldalyn had no idea why she was suddenly so curious.

"I did, for a little while. But the market is so saturated and competitive, it was stressful. I couldn't take the fighting for jobs anymore. And not only that, I would work one job for a couple thousand then have to make that stretch three months till I could land another job. And I'd have to pay to keep up my hair and nails and skin the whole time." Cassie looked down at Buster who was content in her arms. "I was so unhappy. It wasn't worth it. Maybe someday I'll try again for acting, but I have a feeling it would be the same as the modeling market."

Ella nodded in understanding; she had no experience in the field of acting or modeling, "Makes sense. How's your mom?" Eldalyn felt awkward, asking but felt she should have a polite conversation, especially if Cassie was going to help her get a job.

"Better actually. She did round two of chemotherapy while we were in high school and has been cancer free since." Cassie's mom had also had cancer, but unlike Eldalyn's mom, she'd responded well to treatment.

Cassie snuggled and baby talked to the dog while Eldalyn felt a sense of relief at the prospect of having another job. She would be able to turn the heat up this winter and finally get the water company off her back about the stack of unpaid bills sitting at home on the table. This was the chance she'd been hoping for.

As Cassie turned to walk out the door, Eldalyn suddenly remembered something she forgot to ask. "Hey Cassie, wait!" Cassie turned back around. "Where do I meet you tomorrow?"

Cassie smiled once more. "Oh right, almost forgot. It's a bar downtown called The Wolf Pack. And seriously, wear something hot. A bikini if you have nothing else. It was good to see you again Eldalyn." And with a swish of blonde hair, Cassie was gone.

Eldalyn began to gather her stuff and close everything down for the night. She'd never heard of The Wolf Pack, so she decided to Google it on Bernice's computer real quick. As she printed out the map complete with the bus routes she would have to take, Eldalyn pondered what she would wear the next day. She didn't really have any "hot" clothes, and she didn't have a bikini at the moment either. She would probably have to cut up one of her shirts. The question was, which shirt of her limited wardrobe could she do without?

Grabbing the paperwork off the printer, Eldalyn scurried out the door. It was late, and she had an outfit to design.

The next morning Eldalyn slipped into the shirt she had cut up so that it was a crop top and tied in the back. She paired it with a pair of her shortest frayed shorts (courtesy of a pair of her most frayed jeans and a pair of scissors), and glanced in the mirror at her thin frame. She drew her hair around to one side of her face and tied it in a low ponytail. Eldalyn considered putting more makeup on than her usual mascara, but didn't have much to go on or the knowledge of what would work best, thus, this would have to do.

She grabbed her backpack and headed towards the door. She had about an hour bus ride to the bar, and she hoped it wouldn't be in vain.

The bus ride seemed much longer as Eldalyn's nerves were on edge. When she finally pulled up in front of the western-themed bar, she let out the breath she had been holding in. *Here goes nothing.*

Eldalyn pushed open the large wooden door. The room inside was dimly lit, but she could see a large bar to her left stretching the length of the building with metal poles going to the ceiling every fifteen or so feet. There were low-top and high-top wooden tables, complete with chairs spread around the large space. In one corner was an open area with a wooden floor which she figured was either a dance floor of sorts or a place for the live bands to set up.

"Well, you must be Cassie's little friend." Eldalyn turned towards the voice to find an attractive man in his thirties emerging from a door marked *Employees Only*. Her eyes were immediately drawn to his jet-black, spiked hair which still looked slightly damp, probably due to all the hair gel he had used.

"Yes, I'm Eldalyn." Eldalyn cleared her throat.

"Mike," the man held out his hand. "I'm the manager here. Cassie tells me you need a job."

Eldalyn shook his hand. "Yes, please. Whatever position you need, I can learn."

"That's the attitude I like to hear." Mike rubbed the stubble on his chin. "Can you take off your jacket please?" Eldalyn did as she was told. "Well you're cute enough. I'm assuming you've never bartended before?"

"No, but I'm willing to try." Eldalyn smiled, trying to come across as confident as she could, even though she knew she came across incredibly shy.

"Well, I require that my girls learn all positions at some point. We will have you start out as a cocktail girl. You'll come to dance lessons two mornings a week. Then you'll be able to take dance shifts as well. After you master that, we will move you up to train for bartending. For right now, I need a cocktail girl Thursday through Sunday. You'll come to dance lessons on Wednesday and Saturday mornings. Pay is minimum wage plus whatever tips you get. Dance lessons are unpaid. Sound good?"

Eldalyn nodded taking everything in.

"Also, those shorts will work, but you need a top that's more western. There's a store down the street that sells flannel. Buy a couple of those and cut off the bottom and tie them like a crop top. And I hate to say it, but you need cowgirl boots or platform heels. Those shoes aren't going to work." He motioned to her well-loved Keds. He pulled a few papers from underneath a wooden podium Eldalyn hadn't noticed before. "Fill these out for your taxes. And think of a new name for your nametag. Eldalyn is not cute enough."

Eldalyn took the papers from his hand and slipped them in her backpack. She planned to go get the shirts at the store he mentioned; she only hoped they weren't too expensive. She would have to stop at the secondhand store for the shoes. There was no way she could afford any new shoes at the moment. Mike shook her hand once more. "So we will see you tonight? Six o'clock?"

Eldalyn felt her eyes widen in surprise that they needed someone that soon, but she knew the Pet Palace would be fine without her. They barely needed her as is. "Of course, six o'clock; I'll be here."

Mike smiled and held open the door for her to exit. "See you then, and be ready with your new name."

Eldalyn heard the door close tightly behind her. She turned to her left heading to the store he mentioned. She recognized the name and knew they were known for their inexpensive clothing. She planned to buy two shirts as long as they weren't more than $20 each. She found them quickly and grabbed two smalls—she hated trying clothes on in the store.

Next, Eldalyn hopped back on the bus and headed back to her side of town. There weren't any secondhand stores in the downtown area by the bar.

The store, Goodwill, was full of shoes, and Eldalyn splurged a little, buying both a pair of slightly worn cowboy boots and a pair of platform heels which looked as if they had barely been worn once. Unless she made some money tonight she wouldn't be eating for the next week. She only hoped she had made a good bet with taking this job.

As she stepped on the bus that would take her close to home, Eldalyn pondered what her new name would be. As much as she loved her name, this was her chance—this was her opportunity to be someone else, to start a new life. And she knew she needed to start it right.

"Emerald, you're sure?" Mike asked a second time before inputting the name into the nametag-engraving machine.

"Yes, I'm sure." Eldalyn nodded and held her head high. She'd thought all day of a new name for herself, and although *Diamond* had come up in her head many times, she knew it was too much of a stripper name for her. After all, she was to be a dancer at most, not a stripper.

"Well, I'm alright with it if you are. I must say, it's a unique choice." Mike brushed off the nametag the machine had just finished engraving. "Now here are the rules. I don't want to hear the word *Eldalyn* in this building or in a twenty-five foot radius. Once you are within twenty-five feet of the property, you are Emerald, okay? It will make this job easier I promise." Mike smiled as she pinned the nametag to her freshly cut-off flannel shirt. "Now, I heard you are friends with Cass— I mean Blondie, and she will be showing you around today and tomorrow." He stood from his chair and opened the office door, beckoning Cassie over. "Do as she says, and you'll do just fine here."

Eldalyn took a step towards Cassie—or Blondie, as she was now to call her. "Hey, thanks so much! You have no idea how badly I needed this."

Blondie smiled. "Don't thank me yet; it's time to show what you're made of."

Over the next three hours, Eldalyn walked more mileage than she probably did working a week at Pet Palace. She'd never waitressed before, but now she knew why Mike apologized before about her shoes; her feet were in pain.

Cassie kept near Eldalyn all night while also giving her space to learn and earn some tips. "Make sure whenever someone orders something that's not a beer, such as a rum and coke, ask if they want a double. It'll make you more money." Cassie breezed by, dropping her such nuggets here and there. Eldalyn nodded furiously; this was all so new to her. She knew some of the liquors and beers thanks to her alcoholic father, but many of the cocktails and their names were foreign to her. The bartender, *Cam*, as her nametag proclaimed, was very helpful all night—being extremely patient as Eldalyn asked questions and rang in impossible drinks that had to later be verified. In fact, all the other employees were very friendly, something that was a nice change from anti-social Trevor and reserved Bernice.

Grabbing the two dollars cash a gentleman in a black cowboy hat had left on the table, Eldalyn sighed. It wasn't turning out to be quite the cash flow Eldalyn had pictured. But around 10 p.m. she'd stopped to count and realized she made almost a hundred dollars without noticing. The one- and two-dollar tips added up.

After ten was when the dancers started to get on the bar, and Eldalyn couldn't believe her eyes. The dancing was the most amazing thing she'd ever seen—she was enthralled. She wanted to dance and to look as amazing as those girls, badly.

For the rest of the shift, every time Eldalyn came to the bar and was waiting for a cocktail to be made, she couldn't help but watch the dancers. Cassie must've noticed because she managed to end up at the bar as the same time as Eldalyn and whispered in her ear "You want to dance, huh? Just ask Mike; he'll let you have a shot."

Eldalyn turned to respond but Cassie was already all the way across the room with a tray of Bud Light bottles. Grabbing her pair of Jack Daniels shots and placing them on her tray, Eldalyn headed to the table that had recently become occupied.

"Be right with you!" Eldalyn used her sweetest voice as she passed the table and heard a wolf whistle in response. Eldalyn blushed, setting the shots down in front of the pair of men at the next table.

"You're a cutie." The man who had whistled gave her a once over, "You're new too. I come in here a lot and never seen you." Eldalyn quickly took in his mountain man appearance, complete with a scruffy beard, broad shoulders, and plaid shirt. The man peered up at her as Eldalyn continued to blush and try to find her words.

"Yeah-uh, uh, first night." Eldalyn mentally smacked herself for stuttering; this was not going to allow her to keep the job. She needed to be more confident.

"Ah, well I'll let you get back to work—" he searched her shirt until he found the nametag on the left side, "—Emerald. Just get me a Macallan twelve, straight up, and you keep them coming till I say stop." He handed Eldalyn a black American Express card, and Eldalyn quickly turned and headed for the bar. Cam saw her coming.

Cam was the head bartender at The Wolf Pack, and even though she was only about five-and-a-half feet tall, you could tell by the way she spoke that she truly ran the joint. With dark brunette hair, small delicate features, and a thin but curvy figure to match, she was also a favorite among the male patrons. She always wore a simple layer of red lipstick and a bandana in her hair, making her look just like Rosie the Riveter. She had the memory of an elephant, which is what had earned her the spot as head bartender, or at least that's what Cassie had told Eldalyn earlier that night.

"Ah, you've met Tyler. He practically lives at that table. Just do as he says and bring him as many of these as he wants." She pushed the already prepared glass of an amber liquid towards Eldalyn. "And he'll tip you twenty percent. Trust me—some nights, that can be a good portion of your money."

Eldalyn thanked Cam for her help and turned back to the hustle and bustle of the evening. Sunday was Girls Drink Free night, which meant that by eleven thirty the room was packed and Eldalyn had over a dozen tabs open.

The pace kept up until about two in the morning, and before she knew it, Eldalyn was closing out her last tab and counting her cash tips for the night. Almost three hundred dollars, she let out a sigh of relief.

As she put her hard earned cash in her purse, Eldalyn looked up to see Mike coming her way. "Hey Emerald, Blondie told me you did a great job tonight."

Eldalyn couldn't help but blush again as she muttered a quick "Thanks."

"She said you were a little shy, but it worked for you and the customers seemed to like you."

Eldalyn blushed again, "I'm trying to work on being more confident."

Mike nodded his head. "Good idea, but as long as you're efficient and guests like you, you do what works for you. Now Blondie told me you really want to learn how to dance?" Eldalyn nodded furiously. "Well let me tell you, I'm a lot more picky about my dancers than my cocktail waitresses. But if you work hard in class and can get a solid dance down, I'll give you a shot. Then we can discuss more dancing shifts from there." Mike smiled.

"Thanks!" Eldalyn couldn't believe her ears; he would let her try it out! "I really appreciate it!" Eldalyn slung her bag over her shoulder. "Am I okay to leave?" She couldn't lie—she was exhausted.

"Yes, see you tomorrow. Thanks again for the good work!" Mike gave Eldalyn a quick pat on the shoulder then turned and headed for his office. When he opened the door to go inside, Eldalyn saw Cassie sitting on his chair smiling. She gave Eldalyn a quick wave before the door closed and the room was encased in almost complete darkness except the backlight from the bar. Eldalyn quickly realized all the other staff had left and she was the only one still here. After one more glance around to be sure she had all her things, Eldalyn slipped on her jacket and zipped it up to her chin, walking out into the cool dark night. Even though she was tired beyond belief, Eldalyn knew this job was exactly what she needed. And she couldn't wait to learn how to dance.

By Thursday night, Eldalyn was even more exhausted than she ever thought possible. She'd spent the week not only learning to dance, but also learning all the different types of alcohol and what went together to make the different drinks on the menu. Her body sore in a hundred different places, and her mind ached with all the new information as well. Her schedule was supposed to be Thursday through Sunday but Eldalyn had discovered very quickly that the other girls were always willing to give up shifts.

As she slid on her jacket over her cut-off shirt, Eldalyn counted the cash in her hand: two hundred and twenty-eight dollars—more money than she made in a week at the dog-walking place. And this had been the slowest night she worked so far. On the weekends she'd brought in over three hundred as a cocktail waitress, and that was with tipping the bartender heavily.

Eldalyn had never held so much cash in her life, and frankly, it made her nervous—so nervous that after dance lessons the day before, she had opened a bank account. But that didn't change the fact she was about to walk home with over two hundred dollars in cash on her. The bus stopped running at midnight every night, and so far, Eldalyn had been done no earlier than two in the morning.

Although both parks were well lit thanks to city-funded street lights, to be cautious, Eldalyn planned to walk around the second park on her way home. Even though she was tired, it was better to be safe than sorry. Eldalyn had seen Terrance every night since she started this job. Most nights he just said a quick "hello" and headed on his way; however, tonight Terrance was nowhere in sight.

As Eldalyn entered the first park she glanced around carefully. At now almost three in the morning the park was empty. Letting out a sigh of relief, Eldalyn let her guard down a tiny bit, still keeping her pace brisk—so brisk, she barely noticed the form lounging on one of the benches until she was almost past.

"Hey."

The masculine voice startled Eldalyn and she spun quickly, almost losing her balance but catching herself on the corner of the bench. Her eyes quickly met those of a young man about her age. She gauged him quickly; he didn't seem threatening. He was about six foot tall and had brown hair and green eyes. He was thin, but in an attractive and sort of handsome way.

"Sorry, I didn't mean to startle you; just surprised to see someone out at this hour." He held out his hand to help her. Eldalyn righted herself without touching his hand. This could still be a trap. She backed up a step.

"It's okay. I'm not used to seeing other people at this hour either." The sound of her own voice coming out without a stutter surprised her. In high school she had been quiet and reserved. This newfound confidence must've come along with the new job.

"I'm Joshua." He held out his hand to her a second time. She glanced at it for a moment then took it hesitantly. For an instant, her mind escaped her as she placed her small, pale hand in his large masculine one.

"I'm El— I mean Emerald. My name is Emerald." She didn't know why she gave her fake name; she was definitely more than twenty-five feet away from work. Something inside her told her it would be safer to keep her real name anonymous even if this stranger turned out to be friendly.

He smiled warmly, seeming not to notice her blunder. "Emerald, that's an interesting name."

Her heart fell a little. What a callous thing to say. "Um, thanks? I guess?"

Joshua immediately noticed his mistake. "Sorry, I meant it in a good way. I just … well, I don't get out much." He quickly realized they were still touching hands and pulled his back to his side.

Eldalyn felt a new wave of confidence come over her once more. "Me neither, but how are you out here so late if you don't go out much?"

He smiled sheepishly. "I guess I set myself up for that one. I'm mad at my parents. I guess you could say this is my attempt at running away from home."

"And why would you be running away from home? Aren't you a little old for that anyways?" Eldalyn raised an eyebrow inquisitively.

Joshua sighed again and ran his hand through his hair. He wondered just how much he should reveal to this stranger. She was unassuming, and seemed easy to talk to. "Well, my parents have a lot of other kids—I mean, I have a lot of siblings, and they just told me they're about to have another. And well, I just kind of flipped."

Eldalyn realized she was awkwardly standing and sat on the bench next to him. "Over your mom having another kid? Shouldn't you be excited?" Eldalyn had never had siblings, and was thus unaccustomed to the thought of how she would have reacted had her parents told her they were having another child. She'd always assumed had her parents had another, regardless of gender, they would've been best friends to conquer the world together.

"Well, my parents are workaholics. They pretty much work nonstop. So I … well, I guess you can say I raise the kids." Joshua closed his eyes and pinched the bridge of his nose. "So I see her having another kid as more work for me."

"I didn't think of it from that angle." Eldalyn tried to imagine what that was like, but in her mind she couldn't even picture her mother anymore. Her father was barely a shadow in some of her teen memories.

"Sorry. I didn't mean to gripe and dump all this on you, especially when you don't even know me. I guess I should feel lucky for the life I have."

"No, it's fine. Sometimes just telling someone who can be objective about the situation helps. I'm pretty sure that's why they invented bars in the first place." Eldalyn smiled and rose to her feet. "Is your plan just to stay here for the night?" She glanced around taking note he had no belongings in the vicinity.

"My stuff is in my car," he said, sensing her unspoken question. "I'll probably sleep there tonight. I didn't really have anywhere else to go." He motioned to his black BMW in the lot about twenty feet to his left.

Eldalyn was torn. She wanted to be nice, but she didn't know this guy. "I have to get going, but I pass by here a lot, so I can bring you food, if you're still going to be here tomorrow?" Eldalyn compromised. She had no idea why she was offering this stranger food, she just felt compelled to be nice—if she could even trust his story in the first place. Suddenly she remembered she was talking to a total stranger and stood up abruptly, taking a step back from the bench.

Joshua smiled at her generosity, watching her movement with an inquisitive look in his eyes. "I'll be here." He smiled. He hadn't noticed this right away, but the girl had a very subtle beauty. However, the clothes she was wearing were very odd, and old. It was chilly, but she was wearing shorts that he could tell she had cut off herself. And the boots she was wearing had definitely been around quite a few years. And rather than a coat, she only wore a hoodie zipped up to her throat. It was an interesting thing to see here on this side of town. He wondered where she lived, and thought for a second about asking, but realized that would probably scare her. He could tell she was a little nervous as it was.

Eldalyn smiled. "See you around five tomorrow then?"

Joshua decided he might as well flirt a little: "It's a date." And with that he stood, smiled, and headed towards his car.

Eldalyn watched him walk a few steps, then turned and resumed her quick walk home. Now it was even later than before. She picked up her pace to a slow run.

Joshua didn't want to seem creepy, but as he walked away he glanced back over his shoulder to check on the small girl. However, she had already slipped into the night beyond his field of vision.

Eldalyn reached home about an hour later. Luckily, no one bothered her on her walk. As she fell into her bed that squeaked under her weight, she thought about the man she met today. There was something about him that made her feel safe, though she couldn't quite put her finger on it. She felt bad that she had given him her fake name, but she reminded herself he was still a stranger to her. She began to plan what she would cook the next day to bring to Joshua. For the first time in years, she drifted off to sleep with a smile on her face.

JOSHUA

OCTOBER 2012

Joshua leaned back the driver's seat in his car as far it would go with his stuff piled in the back. When he left, he couldn't think; he just grabbed all of his clothes, his laptop, and his books and threw them in the car. After he'd driven around aimlessly for about an hour, he'd gone to the bank and had his parents taken off his account. He'd saved almost eighteen grand over the years from his allowance and yard work jobs in the summer in his neighborhood. He'd pulled out all the money but left the account open just in case. It made him nervous to have eighteen thousand dollars cash stashed in his car, but he didn't want to leave an easy paper trail. He should have gone to a hotel for the night, but for some reason he had headed to the park instead. And now that it was almost three in the morning, it hardly seemed worth spending the money for a few measly hours in a hotel.

Tomorrow, he would find a job—something downtown, as far from his parents as he could manage. He didn't want to risk running into them, well, ever. In fact, he was done with college. His parents paid for it, and he knew they wouldn't continue to do so when they realized he wasn't coming back. He didn't want to study pre-med anyway.

Joshua pulled out his phone and pulled up Craigslist to look at jobs. That reminded him that tomorrow he needed to head to the phone company and get his own plan. He had turned off the tracking device on his phone long ago, but he was sure his parents could get a cell company to do their bidding if they wanted to. Most importantly, they were currently paying the bill, and his mom was a lawyer and could be very scary when she wanted something—especially information. By the time his phone beeped to let him know the battery was running low, he had saved four jobs that looked promising. As he put his phone away and tried to get comfortable, his mind drifted to his siblings. He felt guilty leaving them, but he just couldn't take it anymore. He was tired of being a slave. It was time to get paid for his work.

The next morning, Joshua woke early. He had slept little in the seventy-degree angle his seat had been stuck in, not to mention that his long legs barely fit under the dash.

He pulled out his phone, and seeing that the battery was hovering just above death, started his car in order for it to charge. The screen was filled with a variety of text messages, missed calls, and voicemails from both his mother and father. Joshua deleted all of them without reading. Instead, he headed straight to his email. He realized it was a bit too soon to have received email responses, but three of the four places he'd found last night were open now. So Joshua figured he might as well get started.

As he backed his BMW out of the lot and headed for the FedEx store to make copies of his resume, he remembered the girl from last night. She'd said she would bring food around five. Perfect—he could scope out a few jobs and be back by then. But he couldn't get an apartment until he had something to put in the *Employment* section of the application. And day one of sleeping in his car had not gone well.

Considering that the girl had been walking home in the wee hours of the morning, he reasoned she must work a night shift somewhere. Therefore, she was probably home in her comfortable bed right now, and would probably be on the later side of "around five" rather than being early.

Joshua suddenly realized he didn't know if she was home in bed, or if that's where she was heading, or if she was coming from work, or much else other than her name. She'd barely talked about herself last night—he had done all the talking. He did a mental face palm. Although he didn't currently have a girlfriend, he had dated many girls in the past and knew how annoying it was to hang out with someone who only talked about themself. In fact, he had dumped his last, and only, college girlfriend a few months ago because of how self-centered she was.

He resolved to let Emerald do most of the talking when he saw her again today. He also decided by tomorrow he would have a job, and then he could tour apartments this weekend. Maybe he was being a little optimistic, but he knew he could put down a cash deposit on an apartment if anyone asked. He would prefer to use cash anyway; that way his bank account wouldn't show where he was.

As he pulled into the FedEx parking lot, his phone chimed with the tune he had specifically assigned to their home number. He picked up his phone to silence it but then realized his mother and father would currently be at work. With a sigh, he answered: "Hello?"

"Joshy?" Although his voice was high enough to sound like Miki's, Joshua could tell it was Marc.

"Hey buddy." Joshua felt an immediate rush of regret at what he had done, but he knew he couldn't go back now. The freedom of the last day had already been enough for him to want more.

"When are you coming home?" Joshua could tell that even though he was only nine, Marc knew something wasn't right.

"Not for a little while Marc. I'm sorry buddy."

"But why?" Marc was on the verge of tears.

"I have some stuff I need to do, okay?" Joshua could feel his heart breaking for the little brother that looked up to him as if he were a god.

"How much stuff? Like two days of stuff?"

"More than that Marc."

"How much more?"

Joshua sighed; it was hard to explain this type of thing to someone so young. "A lot more, okay? I'll let you know when I'm almost done—sound good?" This promise did very little to lessen the guilt he felt creeping in.

"Okay. But Joshy?"

"Yes Marc?"

"Please hurry and do your stuff fast okay? I don't want to stay with the nanny all the time." He sniffled slightly, but Joshua still heard.

45

"I will Marc." With that he said his goodbyes and hung up the phone, feeling worse than before. As Joshua stepped out of the car with all his paperwork, he resolved to not answer any more calls. And he needed a new number, and fast, before his resolve weakened.

It's not that he hated his parents; he just couldn't do it anymore. And he knew if he spoke to any of his siblings again, he would get roped back in. He had just escaped hell—no way would he return of his own free will.

ELDALYN

OCTOBER 2012

Eldalyn awoke early to put her plan into action. By eight a.m. she had already visited the twenty-four-hour supermarket in her neighborhood, purchased supplies, and returned home to begin cooking. She didn't know why she felt compelled to make her best meal for this stranger. Maybe the loneliness was finally getting to her. She mentally slapped herself at that thought. She and Cassie had been getting along great at work. They had even hung out once outside of work, and it was fun—but much different than it had been when they were younger.

It was kind of neat to reconnect with the woman she had known as a girl. She'd remembered before that Cassie had been the only middle school girl who had understood her pain as she watched her mother die. All the other girls had been more concerned with boys or makeup—that's why they'd become friends in the first place. And Eldalyn was glad their friendship rekindled all these years later.

Cassie had changed though. She was no longer a down-to-earth girl with an ill mother. Sometime over the years she had morphed to become more materialistic and image driven. She'd also formulated an acute interest in the male gender. Eldalyn had approached Cassie during their outing regarding her relationship with Mike. Cassie had denied any involvement, instead stating she was interested in someone else. When Eldalyn tried to probe further, Cassie had quickly changed the subject.

As much as Cassie and Eldalyn discussed their current lives, Eldalyn had quickly realized that Cassie wasn't the person to disclose what had happened in her life over the past seven years. And her omission was a wall, preventing the complete reformation of their friendship.

By midmorning, Eldalyn had the homemade tomato sauce simmering on the stove and was tossing the hand-rolled meatballs inside of it. She set the box of pasta on the counter and headed to her room to prepare for work.

Eldalyn slid on her cut-off shorts, resolving to buy some actual ones the next day. Mike had said they would work, but Eldalyn had quickly noticed how nice the other girls' clothing was. The first day she had wondered how they afforded it; now she knew. Next, she pulled on the push up bra Cassie had insisted she buy earlier in the week. Eldalyn had never been lacking in the breast department, but she certainly wasn't well endowed. Cassie had sworn her tips would increase if she wore it, and so far, Eldalyn had been unable to prove her wrong.

She pulled out the makeup bag she had also purchased earlier that week. It had been on her second day that Cassie insisted they go shopping. Eldalyn hated blowing her entire first night's pay on a bra and makeup but Cassie wouldn't take "no" for an answer. Eldalyn had never worn makeup before. Her mother had passed away before she'd been able to pass on any makeup tips or tricks. Cassie had been helping her the past few nights, but Eldalyn knew sooner or later she would have to master doing it on her own.

Giving it her best attempt, she began to brush the gold eye shadow across her eyelids, wincing when she smudged the eyeliner she had just spent almost three minutes perfecting. Eldalyn looked in the mirror; her face was nowhere near as well put together as Cassie's, but she didn't look horrible either.

Now it was almost three and she would have to leave soon if she wanted time to talk to Joshua in the park. Hurriedly, she pulled on her cut-off shirt, tied it beneath her breasts, and pulled on her favorite worn hoodie, zipping it to her chin.

Eldalyn quickly packed up a hefty portion of the food she had made, leaving a small container in her fridge for herself tomorrow. Glancing at the clock, she headed out the door.

When she reached the park, Eldalyn headed straight for the bench where she had met Joshua the night before. However, he wasn't there. She figured she shouldn't be surprised; it was a big park, and he did have legs after all.

After twenty minutes of walking around, Eldalyn realized just how large the park was. He could be walking around looking for her too, and they would completely miss each other. Realizing she should have planned this better, she sat down on a partial brick wall that served to separate the playground from the rest of the park with a huff, setting the container beside her.

"This for me?"

Eldalyn turned towards the voice, a smile unconsciously breaking out on her face. Her eyes met the green eyes of Joshua from last night. "There you are. I was wondering where you were."

Joshua smiled. "Yeah, I realize I probably should've hung out at that bench from last night, but I get really antsy when I sit for too long so I had to take a loop of the park."

Eldalyn couldn't tell if he was being honest or sarcastic, but she chuckled a little anyways. Joshua picked up the container and peeled open a corner.

"It's spaghetti and meatballs, I made the sauce and meatballs from scratch."

"Wow, this is great! I haven't had anything but microwaved food in so long." Eldalyn realized too late she hadn't bothered to bring him silverware. If Joshua noticed, he didn't say anything.

He did notice that Eldalyn was wearing the same clothes from last night. "Where are you headed anyways?"

Eldalyn gritted her teeth for a moment and made a split-second decision. "Work? I, uh, work with animals. It's pretty dirty." Eldalyn hated lying, at least by omission, but figured the "I'm a scantily clad cocktail waitress" conversation was too embarrassing to share with this man even if he was nice.

"Wow, that's awesome. I love animals. I just got a job this morning working at a psychiatrist's office. Not glamorous or anything, but it's something I know a little about and I'm interested in pursuing. Do you go to college?" Joshua realized he was speaking a little fast, but Eldalyn didn't seem bothered.

"No. I just work." Eldalyn had considered college before. But they don't tend to like it when people who haven't finished high school apply— not that she'd ever tried. If she got accepted into one, she wouldn't have the money to finish anyways. "Do you go to college?"

"I did—until yesterday." Joshua laughed. "I decided to go my own direction."

"That's admirable." Eldalyn looked over at Joshua and smiled shyly. "I've been doing my own thing for a while now. It's tough, but I think someday it'll pay off."

Joshua scoffed, "I sure hope so, otherwise I just ruined my life. I may regret it later, but for now, I'm glad I walked away." Joshua looked over at Eldalyn, and she couldn't help but blush. "You know, you're pretty cute when you blush."

This only made Eldalyn's face even warmer, but she managed to squeak out a shy "Thanks."

"So, do you like to eat food?" Joshua must've run out of things to say.

"Who doesn't?" Eldalyn laughed, and then realized it wasn't much of an answer. "What I mean to say is yes, I enjoy food."

"Any particular kind?"

"Well, my parents were always meat-and-potatoes type of people, but I guess you can say I'm pretty partial to anything and everything." Eldalyn twirled a strand of hair around her finger nervously. Then realizing she was doing it, she quickly let it go. This guy seemed genuinely nice.

"Meat and potatoes type of people? So you like steak then?"

"Why? Is that your specialty or something?" Eldalyn knew she was being a bit sarcastic, but for some reason, she couldn't help but be herself around this man.

"As a matter of fact, I'm pretty mean when it comes to grilling. But I also know this great steak place, if you would do me the honor of joining me?" He smiled, anticipating her answer.

"Like a date?" Eldalyn bit her lip, nervous again. Her emotions were a roller coaster, first nervous, then comfortable, and now nervous again. And something inside was nagging her.

"Yes, I suppose like a date. I could pick you up at your house? I mean, I'm just assuming you don't have a car. I hope that's not rude of me," he rambled.

Eldalyn's unease grew. This man wanted to pick her up at her house? What would he think? He'd probably think she was some sort of street rat. He obviously came from money, considering he drove a BMW and had been in college. He probably wouldn't even talk to her knowing the side of town she came from. She realized he was waiting for her answer. She had to say something. "Uh, I guess that's, uh, okay." Eldalyn cringed on the inside at how stupid she sounded.

"Perfect." Joshua's face brightened. "Let me just get your number and we can coordinate a day."

Eldalyn's mind flashed to the serviceless phone she knew was sitting at home in her top dresser drawer. When her father had left, Eldalyn simply hadn't found the money to continue paying for it. Not that she'd had a reason to anyways. Now Joshua was going to know what a loser she really was. She needed to change the subject, and fast. Reaching into her pocket for the only personal effect it contained, Eldalyn brushed her small key ring in a way she hoped wasn't obvious. The key ring fell to the grass

"Oh shoot, I'm always dropping these things!" She laughed as she stooped to pick up the keys. She searched around in the grass for a moment, knowing full well exactly where they had fallen. Joshua deftly leaned down and swept up the keys.

"I was about to say if these were a snake, they would have bit ya, but then I realized that made me sound like some sort of senior citizen." He chuckled at his own joke.

The conversation lulled for a brief moment. It was enough to make Eldalyn feel uncomfortable as her old shy self reared her head; she decided it was time to make her exit, before Joshua could once again ask for the phone number she couldn't provide. "I, uh, better head to work." Eldalyn stood up and began to step away but paused for just a moment, realizing she didn't know how she would get back her food container, one of very few in her cupboard. In the same moment, she decided it would be okay if she didn't.

Joshua smiled, "Alright, well thanks for the food, and have fun at work. And even if you don't want to give me your number," he gave her a sly grin, "don't forget you promised me a date. We can just decide on the day when you come by tomorrow?"

Eldalyn let out a silent sigh of relief that the phone issue was avoided. For a second, she wanted to continue their banter. "So you live on this wall now?" She couldn't help but smirk at her own sarcasm.

Joshua broke into a wide grin. "Yep, this portion of the wall we are sitting on right now is my living room; that part—" Joshua motioned to a portion further down the wall "—is my kitchen. And maybe if you're lucky, you'll get to see the bedroom."

Immediately, Eldalyn felt very uncomfortable again, and shy. "Sure, uh, see you later." Eldalyn forced a smile and started walking away, consciously trying to keep her pace down so it didn't seem like she was running away. But she knew she couldn't see Joshua again. Her world wasn't for him, and she knew there was no way she could ever fit in his. Plus, she'd already lied to him too much as it was. There was no coming back from this.

Without so much as a look back, Eldalyn rushed to work, resolving to take a different path home that night. She couldn't let her hopes get away from her. Not again.

JOSHUA

OCTOBER 2012

Joshua watched Emerald walk away and couldn't help but give her a once over; after all, he was a man. She was thin, but had curves in the right places—not ones that were in your face, but soft, delicate curves that were perfectly proportionate to her body size. Shaking his head quickly to clear his thoughts, he picked up the food and turned to head to his car. He had hoped to get her number today, but she was obviously nervous so he had decided not to push it. Beyond everything, she had just agreed to a date. and he didn't want to scare her off before it even happened. Putting his key in the ignition, Joshua started his car and backed out of the parking space. It was time to apartment hunt.

If he was going to live in this city without running into his parents, Joshua knew he had to get out of the suburbs and head downtown. He needed to sell his car, and the sooner the better. It was the only thing left his parents could track. He'd separated himself from their phone plan just before he'd reached the park that afternoon. In fact, he had sold his phone at a pawn shop and then bought a new plan with a different carrier. That would keep them busy if they decided to come looking for him. The car was in his name, but he knew his parents had the plates and could use their connections to have people report back to them. Besides, he could use a different, less-flashy, less-expensive car anyways.

He figured at this point his parents knew he was going to be gone awhile. However, also knew they would be expecting him to turn up at home broke one day, and he resolved not to give them the satisfaction.

Heading downtown, Joshua stopped at each high-rise apartment he saw. The first one didn't have anything available until next month, the second was a little more expensive than he wanted, and the third—well, it was perfect.

They'd shown him three units, but the one he ultimately decided on was a one bedroom with a large kitchen that opened to an equally sizeable living room, and wall-to-wall wood floors. There were one-and-a-half bathrooms, and an in-unit laundry—two of his only requirements. The apartment was high enough up that he could have a decent view without paying the high prices of the higher floors.

The apartment was completely furnished, with a masculine black leather couch taking up most of the living room. The couch faced a nice sized flat screen TV that was conveniently mounted on the wall. Joshua wasn't much of a TV person, but it was still nice to have. Behind the couch there was a small glass-top table with four leather chairs. The rest of the room was dominated by an island with handsome granite countertops, complete with a breakfast bar and bar stools. The bedroom was fairly basic, but had a king-sized bed. There wasn't a comforter, but he figured if he had to buy something, at least a comforter would be easy.

The place would cost him sixteen hundred dollars a month—a little more than he wanted, but it included utilities as well. The ease of having only one payment would be a relief.

After signing the papers and handing over almost five thousand dollars (first and last months' rent plus security deposit), he was handed the key and quickly began unloading his stuff from the car. It didn't take long to put his clothes in the closet and his box of books on the living room floor. He added buying a bookshelf to his mental list of things to purchase.

On his last trip up from the car, he grabbed his container of spaghetti and meatballs, thankful that Emerald had actually come through with food. In this day and age, so few people did as they promised, and Joshua liked that she had done so even though she barely knew him.

He put the container in his new microwave and dug a fork out of one of the drawers. Leaning against the black granite counter, Joshua looked around his new home.

His new job didn't quite pay well enough to afford this place and his other expenses—like food and gas—but he had his savings to get him started. Further, since he was planning to sell his car and buy something a bit older and less expensive, that would help too.

The microwave dinged, and Joshua sat on one of the black barstools and began eating. It was delicious. As he ate, Joshua began thinking of other ways he could save some extra money, looking up online forums for suggestions. He did not close his computer until he finally glanced at the clock on his stainless steel oven: *3:30 AM.*

He tossed the now empty spaghetti container into the sink and headed to bed. He would take a much-needed shower in the morning.

ELDALYN

FEBRUARY 2010

Looking in her long, full-length mirror, Eldalyn slipped on the pink dress and gave a little spin. The Valentine's Day Dance was only a week away and this year, she had a date.

It was her senior year, and all through high school Eldalyn had been mostly invisible—until this year, until Jeffery.

Jeffery was tall, lean, and with a chiseled jaw that made him seem much older than his seventeen years. He was easily the most attractive guy in the school. He was over six foot tall, well built with broad shoulders; he had blonde hair and what were known to be the most amazing blue eyes. He wasn't a jock; in fact, he didn't play any sports other than street hockey after school. This fact only made him even more attractive, as most of the football players tended to be jerks and follow the social preconceived notion that they should only notice and date cheerleaders.

He'd noticed Eldalyn one day in study hall. Study hall was usually Eldalyn's favorite class, because it didn't involve any participation and it let her get most of her homework done so she had more free time at home. On the day in question, Jeffery had occupied the usually vacant seat in front of her.

When he sat down, he didn't even look in her direction; rather, he continued to joke with his friend Brian, who, finding his usual desk occupied, had taken the one right next to Eldalyn. Eldalyn was surprised as she always sat in the desk in the corner of the room near the study hall monitor's desk. Most popular kids avoided this corner like the plague.

As their conversation came to a close, Jeffery was about to turn around to his desk when his gaze caught on Eldalyn. He seemed to give her a once over, his eyes coming to rest on her lip, where there was currently an angry red gash.

"Who'd you fight?" Eldalyn couldn't believe the most popular guy in school was talking to her; no one ever noticed her. She was in such shock it took her a few seconds to realize he had indeed asked her a question and was waiting for an answer. When she didn't answer right away and continued to stare, Jeffery reached to move a piece of hair that had fallen in front of Eldalyn's face.

No guy had ever touched her like that before; Eldalyn blushed and tried but couldn't get her tongue to move. Great, now he would think she was stupid. She opened her mouth then quickly closed it again, only to force the words meekly out of her throat: "No one."

If he noticed her momentary inability to speak, he politely said nothing. "Well must be a great story then." He noticed her cell phone sticking out of her purse and quickly grabbed it. Eldalyn tried to protest, but again her dry mouth wouldn't cooperate. Jeffery began typing on the phone. When he turned it to face her, she saw a ten-digit number staring her in the face. "My number. Text me anytime." Then he flashed her a spotless white smile. Eldalyn could practically see his teeth sparkle.

Slightly shaking, Eldalyn took the phone. Jeffery maintained eye contact the entire time, and Eldalyn found herself unable to look away and couldn't help but notice how icy blue his eyes were. She didn't know what to say, not that she could get her mouth to move anyways. She resolved just to nod instead, then lowered her head back to the calculus assignment in front of her, finally breaking whatever spell that had been holding her in place. Jeffery, sensing their dialogue had ended, turned back around in his seat, resuming his conversation with Brian.

After a moment of squinting at the derivative question and trying to process it, Eldalyn set her pencil down quietly and touched the cut on the left side of her lip Jeffery had been referring to.

Her dad hadn't been doing well lately. He'd just lost his job. He'd been an alcoholic for years, but suddenly he'd been drinking even more. The cut had been an accident. Eldalyn had walked into the kitchen at the wrong time when her father had been tossing empty liquor bottles around looking for anything that was left. A broken one had caught her in the lip. Her father had seemed, or pretended, not to realize it. But in his defense, Eldalyn didn't say anything either. She'd simply turned and left the room, grabbing some paper towels to compress the bleeding on her way out. She wasn't mad; she couldn't be—he was her father.

The day after Jeffery gave her his number, Eldalyn finally found the nerve to send him a text. And she found talking to him via text was much easier and less uncomfortable than their first encounter had been; she could speak to him freely without stammering or freezing up. When he'd responded that first time, Eldalyn was so excited she did a little dance around her room and texted her best friend Rosalee. She didn't tell her about the awkward first meeting, just that he had given her his number. The two of them gushed all night as Eldalyn replayed their conversation word-for-word for Rosalee.

The texting relationship continued over the next two weeks, even though they barely saw each other at school. Jeffery had started taking an extracurricular during study hall and so was only there one day a week. Eldalyn didn't mind; she found her confidence came through much stronger over text than she could ever do in person. And then he had done the inevitable—he called her. Eldalyn had stared at the phone for the first four rings, unsure what to do, only picking up on the fifth and final ring, in the nick of time with a meek "Hello?"

"Hey Eldalyn, it's Jeffery." Eldalyn felt a smile spread across her face, and took a rushed breath to try and prepare a non-embarrassing response.

"Oh, hey." Eldalyn slapped herself on the forehead. Could she have sounded any more like an idiot?

"How are you?" Jeffery was only creating polite conversation, but to Eldalyn this entire exchange was like hiking Mount Everest. She'd only said two words to him, yet she was already out of breath.

"I'm, uh, good. An—and you?" Eldalyn winced as her stammering started up again. This was not going well.

"Great actually." He paused for a moment, and Eldalyn was suddenly scared she would have to think of something else to say. But fortunately he spoke next. "Listen, I was wondering if you wanted to go to the Valentine's Day dance with me?"

Eldalyn nearly dropped the phone in shock. She'd never been to a school dance before; no one had ever asked her. And now, not only would she attend, but with the hottest guy in the school. Suddenly, Eldalyn realized once again he was waiting for her response, and there was an awkward silence in its place. "Yes, I would love to." Eldalyn managed to squeak out, suddenly remembering her manners.

"Great! I'll text you the details, but let's plan to get dinner somewhere downtown first. My treat. See you later." And with that the line went dead.

Eldalyn couldn't believe it! She jumped up out of her chair and spun around her room, excitedly texting her friend Rosalee. She was going to the school dance—with *Jeffery*.

Eldalyn had then taken some of the precious cash she earned at her weekend job and had gone and purchased the pink dress she was wearing now. It was pale pink chiffon, gathered at the waist with a high halter neckline. It wouldn't have been Eldalyn's first choice, but it was one of the few things on the sale rack she could afford with the fifty dollars she'd allowed herself. Regardless, it fit her perfectly.

Only a week to go, and she couldn't wait. She didn't know a whole lot about dating, but she was thinking that perhaps the dance would be the night Jeffery asked her to be his girlfriend. But if he didn't, that was all right; they could take it slow. With one last glance in the mirror, Eldalyn slipped out of the dress and hung it back on the plastic hangar.

Only one week to go.

JOSHUA

OCTOBER 2012

Joshua awoke to the sun shining in his eyes, and with a glance at the clock he realized he needed to figure out how to work the blinds, and quick. It was seven in the morning, and he'd only been asleep for less than four hours.

As he fumbled around for the remote to close the blinds and shielded his eyes, Joshua had a brief thought that this would be his last Friday without having to go to work. But somehow, the thought did not daunt him; he was more than ready to enter the workforce.

Joshua finally found the correct remote on the side table and began pushing the button that looked like a down arrow. The black-out shades rolled down with a whirring sound, encasing the room in darkness, and Joshua quickly rolled over to his side. As he drifted back off to sleep, he thought of his siblings for a quick moment. He missed them, but he knew they would be okay. They just had to be.

It was almost noon when Joshua awoke again. As he slowly came to consciousness, he heard the distant beeping of his phone. Out of habit he quickly threw his feet over the edge of the bed and began dashing for the phone. As he passed the bathroom in the hall that preceded the kitchen, he realized no one important had his new number—he hadn't even memorized it yet—and he slowed down. He finally came to a stop and lifted his phone from its face-down position on the counter, only to see it was only some sort of sales call.

Joshua silenced the call without answering and opened his laptop to begin wading through the ocean of sales emails that assaulted him every day as a college student. Halfway through, he began seeing emails thanking him for his applications to their various jobs. Ah well, he already had a job anyways.

Joshua rubbed his eyes and began searching the web for the sites his new boss, Dr. Dave, had asked him to become familiar with. Joshua was to serve as his assistant with checking in patients, as well as an assistant to help the secretary with maintaining patient files and transcriptions. The practice currently had more patients than they could handle, and Dr. Dave was looking to hire another doctor as soon as he could. When that happened, Joshua would be an assistant to them both. It wasn't necessarily his dream job, but it seemed like a step in the right direction.

Most of the websites were various medical services that Dr. Dave would be recommending to patients—everything from hypnotism to water therapy. Although Joshua had been pre-med for almost two years, he found many of these practices to be completely foreign to him. After looking through a few more websites, Joshua minimized the window and closed his laptop.

Grabbing his keys from where he had tossed them on the floor the night before, Joshua made an impulsive decision. He grabbed his laptop as well as his phone and was heading out the door right when he remembered he had yet to shower as he had promised himself he would. With a sigh, he turned around, tossing his keys on the floor by the door, and begrudgingly headed to the bathroom. His list of things to do only seemed to grow.

By eight that evening, Joshua was spent. He'd successfully traded in his black 2004 BMW for a trusty, barely used, silver 2011 Toyota Prius. In addition to cutting back on costs, he also felt good about taking care of the environment. The Prius had been pricier than he had originally planned on, but with trading in his BMW, he had broken even. He considered himself very lucky to not have a car payment as most young adults do when they are starting out. Then he'd gone to a department store to purchase a bedspread. It wasn't anything fancy—just a black silk comforter. But he'd picked out some silvery/gray sheets in his novice attempt at interior design. Maybe someday he could hire someone to help decorate his apartment, but for now, this would do just fine.

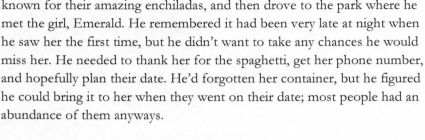

Joshua grabbed a quick dinner at a local Mexican place that was well known for their amazing enchiladas, and then drove to the park where he met the girl, Emerald. He remembered it had been very late at night when he saw her the first time, but he didn't want to take any chances he would miss her. He needed to thank her for the spaghetti, get her phone number, and hopefully plan their date. He'd forgotten her container, but he figured he could bring it to her when they went on their date; most people had an abundance of them anyways.

Joshua pulled out his laptop and prepared to wait.

Joshua waited.

And waited.

And waited.

Finally, at almost four in the morning, he called it quits. She wasn't coming. Dejected, Joshua started his car and headed back to his apartment. There would always be another night.

But there wasn't. For the next month Joshua waited every night he could in the park. He found it harder to wait for her on the days he worked, but he tried nonetheless. He even turned to scouring facebook and other social media sites, messaging anyone who went by the name Emerald.

It was futile. And after the fourth week of waiting various nights for varying lengths of time, Joshua finally gave up. He figured his chance encounter with the beautiful girl named Emerald had been just that—a chance encounter. It was now Thanksgiving with Christmas only weeks away, and Joshua was preparing for his first one completely alone. It was tough, but he knew he would survive. He was ready. And he no longer had time to wait on a beautiful young stranger in a park. If it weren't for the container that had been on his passenger seat the last month, he would've thought she was completely imaginary. Then again, he could've just gone crazy.

With a sigh, Joshua tossed the container in the back of his cupboard and headed for bed. Tomorrow was a new day, and it was time for him to become the person he knew he was always meant to be.

ELDALYN

FEBRUARY 14, 2010

Eldalyn sat on the porch, her bare feet resting on the bottom step. It was almost six p.m. and Jeffery hadn't texted her yet. He said he would text her the day of with the plans, but the dance was in two hours and nothing yet.

Eldalyn's phone had been oddly silent all week besides the occasional text from Jeffery.

Rosalee and Eldalyn had a falling out after the night Jeffery had called her. The two girls had made plans to attend the dance together, and Eldalyn had mistakenly assumed her friend would understand that this was *Jeffery* they were talking about—but Rosalee hadn't wanted to hear it. She'd gotten angry and accused Eldalyn of being a horrible friend; they hadn't spoken since. Eldalyn missed her best—and somewhat only—friend, but she wasn't going to let her come between her and Jeffery. Plus, Rosalee had no idea what she was talking about. Eldalyn knew Jeffery was the one for her and she couldn't pass up an opportunity to go to a dance with him.

It was chilly, and Eldalyn thought about going back in to grab a sweater, but the thought of covering her dress with one of the ratty old sweaters residing in her closet made her cringe. So, she wrapped her arms around her shoulders and leaned down to huddle her knees as best she could while keeping her dignity. She would give him a few more minutes then head back inside. Her dad was already passed out on the couch after a waltz with a bottle of Hennessey he had found on the top shelf in the pantry.

Just then, Eldalyn's phone played the signature tune it played when she received a text. In excitement, Eldalyn flipped open her phone and in her excitement could barely push the buttons. The text was from Jeffery. He wanted her to meet him downtown in thirty minutes.

Downtown was at least a forty-minute bus ride from where she was, but Eldalyn didn't care—she would run if she had to. Slipping on her simple silver strappy heels which were waiting by the bottom step of the porch and gabbing her small cross body purse, Eldalyn took off without a second thought, texting Jeffery back to say she was on her way.

Eldalyn was so eager that the bus ride seemed like an eternity. This was her first date with pretty much her first real boyfriend. They'd been talking nearly a month; he had to like her to keep talking to her like he was, Eldalyn reasoned.

As she stepped off the bus in front of a burger restaurant, Eldalyn glanced at her phone again to look up the name of the restaurant where he wanted to meet. Eldalyn glanced to her right and saw the sign up ahead for the fancy Italian place. She'd never been anywhere this nice in her life, even when her mom was alive.

Arriving at the restaurant, Eldalyn looked around, and when she didn't see Jeffery, she took a seat on one of the benches outside. He would show up soon she was sure.

It was almost eight p.m. by the time Eldalyn saw Jeffery walking up. He'd said half an hour in his original text; what had taken him so long? But he looked so handsome in his purple collared shirt and black slacks, Eldalyn decided not to ask. It was better not to ruin the perfect night.

"Eldalyn!" Jeffery shouted, quickening his pace. As he neared Eldalyn, he stopped and leaned down to give her a peck on the cheek. Eldalyn blushed. "Come on, this place is great!" He smiled his signature smile as he took Eldalyn's hand and they walked hand in hand to the host stand.

As the hostess led them to their seat, Eldalyn couldn't stop smiling. She'd never had a boy hold her hand like this before. And as they sat down, Jeffery continued to hold her hand on the table. It was so romantic, Eldalyn nearly swooned. She could barely read the menu she was so excited. She'd only seen dates like these in the movies; never had she imagined *she* would be on one!

When the server came around to ask for their order, it was all Eldalyn could do to order the fettuccine alfredo without stuttering. Jeffery ordered the lasagna.

They chatted while they waited for their food, mostly about school, and a little about their different friend groups. Eldalyn was surprised at how relaxed she was. Unlike all their previous encounters, Eldalyn was able to speak somewhat clearly without stuttering. There were still hesitations and times Eldalyn mixed up her words, but if he noticed, Jeffery didn't say anything. He asked a couple times about Rosalee, and Eldalyn told him all about their friendship and how Rosalee was really the only friend she had. Eldalyn decided to leave out the fight they'd had earlier that week. Beyond everything, Eldalyn still hoped to mend her one and only friendship. Most of the kids didn't want to hang out with a girl from Eldalyn's side of town.

When their food arrived, there was a break in the conversation. Eldalyn considered asking Jeffery why he was late, but was too afraid he wouldn't like her if she asked too many questions. Instead, she brought the topic back to school and they discussed what teachers they liked best.

They finished dinner, and the check came. While Jeffery counted out bills from his wallet, Eldalyn glanced at her phone. It was nine-thirty, and the dance ended at eleven. How were they even going to make it in time?

As if reading her mind, Jeffery grabbed her hand. "Let's not keep everyone waiting any longer, shall we?" Eldalyn smiled and stood up. Jeffery must've driven his car here. It was no secret that Jeffery drove the newest car in the school lot. With rich parents, he'd been the only kid she knew of to receive a brand new car as a gift on his sixteenth birthday. Not only was it a brand new car, it was a Dodge Charger, upgraded with all sorts of features Eldalyn had heard of but could only imagine what they meant. She still remembered the day he had received it, and the crowd that had gathered in the school parking lot as he had shown off the massive sub-woofers in the trunk. The show had finally come to an end only when a teacher had ventured out to herd the students back inside.

As they walked down the empty street, Eldalyn couldn't help but wrap her hands around her shoulders; it sure was chilly this time of year. Jeffery did not seem to notice, as he just started talking about how his after-school hockey game had gone the night before.

They walked for about ten minutes, yet they still hadn't reached his car yet. They stopped in front of an OfficeMax store not far from the station where the bus had dropped Eldalyn off.

"I think I parked this way—come on." Jeffery gently pulled her hand and Eldalyn turned just in time to see they were headed into an alley.

Eldalyn felt uneasy, and was about to turn to tell Jeffery they shouldn't head this way when she felt a push, and her head cracked against the wall. Stars danced in front of her eyes. When she was able to focus again, she saw Jeffery hovering in front of her, a smug smile on his face.

"Jeffery?" Eldalyn could barely hear her own voice. He said nothing as he roughly pulled aside her dress and began fondling her breast. "What—" Eldalyn trailed off as she saw his smile widen.

"Shhh…" he hissed as leaned in to kiss her, covering her mouth with his own.

Eldalyn couldn't look anymore and closed her eyes. She began pushing him off by the shoulders, but her small five foot three inch frame was nothing against his six foot muscular one.

As she felt his hand move down to her underwear, she began to feel water rush down her cheeks. She didn't remember thinking she was about to cry; she just knew there were suddenly tears on her cheeks. Eldalyn felt numb.

He touched her for what seemed like an eternity as she struggled. Then he let go of Eldalyn with one hand and reached down to undo his pants. Eldalyn saw her chance. She knocked his arm away and began to run back the way she thought they'd come.

It wasn't enough. With a grunt, Jeffery tackled Eldalyn and flipped her over, dragging her back across the rough ground. "I wasn't done yet," he huffed and got on top of her. Eldalyn turned her head away and felt the tears come again. This time they were accompanied by sobs. Eldalyn barely recognized the sounds coming from her chest. They must've been loud, because Eldalyn felt a sudden flash of pain hit her cheek, then the blackness crept in.

When she came to, it was still dark. Eldalyn was on her back, and she laid there and looked at the night sky for what seemed like a very long time. Finally, she found the strength to sit up. As she did, her back screamed in pain. She could feel the cold night air making its way into the scrapes there. Her dress must be torn.

With a wobble, she got to her feet. She looked around. Her shoes— her only pair of heels—were gone. Her purse was on the ground ten feet away. She picked it up halfheartedly.

Everything hurt. But she couldn't take the bus; she didn't want to see anyone.

She felt the tears on her face again and began to furiously wipe them away as she limped back to the sidewalk and in the direction that was her home. She could feel shards of glass poking her feet. She didn't care.

It was sunrise when Eldalyn turned onto her street, and almost seven when she unlocked the door to her house and passed her dad, asleep on the couch. She stepped in the shower and let the water scald her back until she was sure there wasn't an inch of skin left. It was eight when she crawled into bed.

It was two days later when she finally got out of bed.

But Eldalyn never went to school again.

Part Two

JOSHUA

JULY 10, 2014

"911, what is your emergency?"

"Hello, yes, my uh, my keys are locked in my car."

Joshua sighed and rubbed his forehead. The number of these calls that they received were maddening. "Sir, is there any person or animal in the vehicle?"

"No."

"Sir, please hang up and call a locksmith." Joshua began typing notes about the call, indicating, for the record, that it wasn't an emergency.

"But they're gonna charge me! I don't have money," the caller tried again.

Joshua rolled his eyes; the ignorance of society was starting to get to him. "Sir, we are going to charge you as well, and trust me, it'll be much more expensive. If you call a locksmith, it'll be about sixty dollars. If I dispatch someone to your location, it will be almost three hundred dollars." Joshua finished his notes, but waited for the guy's response before hitting the submit button.

"Oh. Okay." And with that the line went dead.

Joshua had been a 911 dispatcher for almost a year now, and he couldn't deny that although there were slow days, and some even pretty rough, overall he loved his job. He liked talking to people, being the voice of reason in a crisis. In fact, he liked it so much he couldn't understand why he ever wanted to be a psychiatrist in the first place.

He'd worked under Dr. Dave for about a year when he'd seen the job opening for a 911 dispatcher. The pay was even better than the $20 an hour he was making as an office manager for Dr. Dave. Honestly, it sounded like more of a career path that suited him, rather than working in a private practice he had begun to detest.

Clicking *submit* on his report, Joshua adjusted his headset and leaned back in his chair, waiting for the next call.

The past two years had been kind to Joshua. He'd severed all ties with his family and changed his life for the better. He was now living his life for himself, which is all he wanted in the first place.

He'd hired an interior decorator to fix up his apartment, and they'd ended up dating for just over a year. Her name was Leslie, a bombshell blonde with an exciting personality to match. She wasn't an engineer, but she kept him on his toes with all her random science knowledge.

They'd gotten along great at first. She was a lot of fun and had an innate sexuality he'd never seen in another woman, but as the year went on he began to notice things. She never seemed to want to work, but she was very concerned about money—especially his money. And he never seemed to be making enough to keep her happy. She wanted him to buy her things—not just a gift on her birthday, but all the time. And when Joshua tried to tell her he wasn't going to do that, she got upset and would give him the silent treatment. After the third or fourth occurrence, Joshua was fed up with the childishness and broke up with her.

He was back on the dating scene now, when his job permitted. He worked the night shift at present; all new hires had to until they reached enough seniority to hold day shifts, and for Joshua, that would be at least a few more years.

He liked the night shift though. Getting to and from work was easy with very little traffic. And, he only worked three, twelve-hour shifts, leaving four nights a week to live his life, or go on dates as he pleased.

He had continued his friendship with Liam and some of the other guys he'd met playing soccer. And they tried to go out for drinks once a week as often as possible.

That was about to change though—Liam was getting married. Joshua shook his head at the thought. Liam said they would continue to hang out after he got married, but Joshua knew what happened after marriage—there would soon be bills, kids, and even in-laws to care for.

He felt a tap on his shoulder and looked up to see his daytime relief, Bobby, over his shoulder. Joshua glanced at the computer to make sure there were no imminent calls then stood up. Bobby sat down in the chair and Joshua passed him the headset. Bobby smiled and slipped it on. "Have a good day man." He smiled at Joshua before turning his full attention to the computer.

"You too." He gave Bobby a quick slap on the shoulder and went to grab his empty lunch bag out of the fridge. Digging his keys out of his pocket, Joshua headed to his car, unlocking the door and tossing his things on the passenger seat. It was seven in the morning, time for him to get some sleep.

Joshua pulled into his apartments' parking garage just as the bulk of people seemed to be leaving for work. Pulling into his assigned spot on the third floor, he grabbed his things and headed up in the elevator to floor fifteen.

Just as he got off the elevator, his phone beeped indicating he had a message. He glanced at the screen to see it was from Liam, seeing if he could go out that night. He replied quickly that he couldn't, and asked if Monday would work. Liam agreed. Joshua placed his phone on the counter and stumbled to his bed. He couldn't keep his eyes open a minute longer.

Joshua jolted awake from a deep, dreamless sleep to the sound of his alarm which had been set for four p.m. He sighed and reached over to shut it off; he had to be at work in three hours.

Picking up his phone and scrolling through his emails, he found a few from the dating website he had signed up for. He skimmed each email before deleting it. There were so many women who messaged him daily, he had decided long ago that he needed to weed through the candidates. So he'd listed on his profile three questions anyone who wanted him to respond needed to answer. And none of the messages he'd just received mentioned any of the questions. The women hadn't even read his profile. He sighed, tossed the phone aside, and headed for the shower. He was only trying to save their time as well as his own.

After he finished with the shower, Joshua headed to the kitchen, turning on the stove to make himself a quick stir-fry while also packing a salad for lunch. He enjoyed eating out when he could, but on the three days he worked, it usually wasn't an option. All the 911 operators received an hour break at some point during their twelve-hour shift, as well as two fifteen-minute breaks. Some of them went out to eat, but Joshua had quickly found that during the night shift all that was open was fast food places, and he really wasn't fond of fast food.

So now he packed his lunch every day. He usually packed a salad, sandwich, or occasionally a soup if he woke up before his alarm, which seemed to only occur on his first workday of the week.

Joshua headed down to the parking garage, climbing into his Toyota Prius which, much to his joy, had yet to have a single problem. As he exited the garage, he waved at the evening-shift security guard of his apartment building. Joshua had no idea what the guy's name was, but he was always friendly and waved back.

The soft chords of guitar music filled the car as Joshua's car connected to his phone via Bluetooth. He liked all music, but as he'd gotten older, he noticed his tastes had changed from heavier rock to softer classical music or techno music. He found listening to someone sing words was occasionally exhausting and too distracting; it took away from the relaxation music provided.

With a sigh, he pulled into his parking lot at work. While he loved his job, the third shift of the week was always the toughest, as he was always tired and never seemed to get enough sleep during the day.

"Hey Joshua!" Nadine, the woman who usually sat next to him, waved as she exited her car across the parking lot. Joshua waved back politely, grabbing his salad out of the passenger seat. Nadine was pretty, in a subtle, exhausted sort of way. She looked much younger than her thirty-two years, and her small figure made it difficult for Joshua to believe her when she mentioned her three children.

"Hey Nadine. How are the kids?" Joshua wasn't usually one for small talk, but every now and then he indulged Nadine.

"Great! My youngest is starting to fight taking baths and having her hair brushed though. I'm not sure what to do besides let her run around the house looking like a Neanderthal!"

Joshua laughed and felt a small pang in his heart. He wondered how Marc, Miki, and Juni were doing, as well as the new baby which would be over a year old right now. He was surprised his parents had never been successful at contacting him, assuming they had tried. But if they had, they had been unsuccessful. He figured his parents by now thought that he had left town, making it easier for him to hide right under their noses.

"How's your girlfriend?" Nadine had caught up to Joshua, even though her legs were considerably shorter, and fell into step next to him as they swiped their badges to get into the building.

"Ex-girlfriend, you mean, and I assume she's fine." Joshua didn't mean for it to sound as snarky as it did when he said it, and cringed as he heard himself.

"Oh, I'm sorry." Nadine placed her thin hand on his shoulder. He brushed it off gently.

"Don't be. I barely even miss her, which tells me she wasn't for me in the first place." Joshua quickly placed his salad in the office fridge and turned towards his desk.

"You know, I never pictured you with a blonde." Nadine shook her head as they relieved the day workers at their spots. Bobby gave him a thumbs up as Joshua slid into his chair and slipped on his headset.

He shrugged as Nadine slid on her headset and focused her attention on the screen. It was Saturday night, which meant it was going to be a long one. On Saturday nights there were always more domestic violence calls, bar brawls, and various other alcohol-related calls to take. And there was always a chance there wouldn't be a happy ending.

It was almost two in the morning when the call came in.

"911, what's your emergency?"

"Yes, uh, something happened at my neighbor's house."

"What happened ma'am?"

"I'm not sure. I heard screaming and glass breaking, and so I rushed over here and there's a girl. She's lying on the floor. There's blood, and glass, and blood..."

Joshua quickly pushed the button to track the call and began clicking to alert both cops and EMTs. "What's the address ma'am?"

"I don't know the house number, but it's Clearview Street. My house number is six-one-four-three. It's the house to the left of mine."

Joshua had already dispatched the cops and EMTs and sent them the updated location as the cellphone signal triangulated.

"Help is on the way. Can you tell me if the girl is breathing?" He held his breath. He hated when these calls ended badly.

"Yes, her chest is moving. But there's a lot of blood and I can't tell where it's coming from."

"How old is she?" He needed to keep her talking while getting all the information he could.

"I don't know. Maybe in her twenties? I'm no doctor, just the neighbor—oh my god, there's blood everywhere, on the walls—"

Joshua suddenly became concerned for the caller's safety. "Is there anyone else in the house?"

"No. I don't think so. But there must've been. I don't think she could've done this to herself. There's blood all over the walls and the carpet..." The caller trailed off as Joshua transcribed their entire call for the record. Joshua heard the sirens in the background from the call.

"Can I get your name ma'am?"

"Brianna Walker. Oh, I just noticed the woman is wearing a name tag, I think I can see through the blood—." He held his breath, his fingers paused as the woman tried to read what she could off the nametag. "I can't be sure because there's so much blood, but I think it says, *Emerald?*"

And just like that, Joshua's world came to a screeching halt.

He couldn't move. He couldn't breathe. He couldn't respond.

Was this the girl? The girl from years ago? The one from the park?

Suddenly he realized he was still at work and snapped out of his reverie just as the woman confirmed his fears. "Yes, it definitely says *Emerald*. Oh the EMTs are here!" The woman began describing her story for someone off the phone, and he figured it was time to hang up.

"Alright, thank you Brianna. Please listen to the EMTs and police officers when they arrive." Joshua was barely breathing. He waited for her response, but there wasn't one and the line went dead. At least she received the message.

For another minute he was paralyzed, as he looked at the "Victim Name" blank in his report. He slowly and shakily typed in *Emerald* but didn't push *Submit*. If he did, he would be open for another call. Instead he watched as the GPS on the ambulance updated its location. It was headed to the hospital.

Joshua mentally noted the hospital name and location, wincing as he recognized it and forced himself to click the *Submit* button. He then sat and stared at the screen for what felt like an eternity.

The rest of his shift passed in a fog. He was sure he answered other calls, but couldn't remember any details. All that consumed his mind is the fact that the girl who'd been so kind and generous to him, the one he had never forgotten, had been hurt, possibly killed.

When Bobby turned up to relieve him, he grabbed his empty lunch container without so much as a word to anyone, rushed out the door, and sprinted to his car. He had to get to the hospital.

Twenty minutes later, Joshua pulled up in the parking lot of Briar Medical Center. He quickly parked his car, grabbed his phone from the center console, and rushed inside.

As he approached the woman at the desk, it suddenly hit him that he had no idea was Emerald's last name was. Regardless, he was going to try his best—he had to see her.

"Hello, how can I help you today young man?" The woman at the desk was a petite woman of Hispanic descent. Although friendly, Joshua could see she was swamped with paperwork, and the phone was continuously ringing.

"Yes, I'm here to see a woman who was brought in earlier this evening. About two in the morning. Her name is Emerald." He crossed his fingers below the desk. This had to work.

The woman shuffled some of the papers in a pile to her left. "I'm sorry, I don't see an *Emerald* in here. Do you have a last name?"

Joshua gritted his teeth. This was it. "Unfortunately she neglected to tell me. We went on a date earlier this evening,"—(lie)—"and it ended abruptly, but I was concerned and really wanted to know if she was okay. She's a smaller girl, about five foot three, with brown hair."

The woman shook her head. "I'm sorry, but if the woman didn't give you her real name, there's nothing I can do. Are you sure she was brought here?"

Joshua realized he was stuck. If he told her how he knew for sure, he would be fired. "No, I guess I'm not sure. Sorry for bothering you." He turned away from the desk to leave, but then suddenly remembered the wild card he hadn't played.

"I'm sorry to bother you again—" The woman looked up. "—but is there a Dr. Williams on the floor tonight?" It wasn't what he wanted to do, but desperate times called for desperate measures.

The woman looked at a list on the wall out of Joshua's view. "Yes, but unfortunately he is busy. Can I give him your name?"

Joshua thought for a very long second. This was the fork in the road. "No. Just tell him his son was here, and I'll be back later."

And with that he turned and walked out of the hospital.

"So, what happened to her?" Joshua sat next to the woman he had previously only known as Emerald, holding her unmoving hand.

"I'm not sure. It looks as if she took quite a beating. I only wish she could tell us so they could put the son of a bitch away." Joshua's father leaned on the door jam, flipping through the girl's chart.

Eldalyn Wren—Joshua had finally found out her name. And even as beaten and bloody as she looked lying there helpless on the bed, he couldn't deny he still felt an instant attraction. He was drawn to the woman for reasons he couldn't fathom. And she had somehow become more beautiful over the past two years, if that was even possible. The planes of her face had become harder, more defined. And her arms had filled out a bit; she was no longer as thin and waiflike as before. But she still had a delicacy about her that triggered Joshua's primal instincts and need to protect her.

Joshua knew the questions were about to start, but decided to ask a few of his own while he could. "Will she recover?" He couldn't hide the quiver in his voice.

"Yes, however there may be some permanent damage. It's hard to tell how hard she was hit, not to mention what she was hit with." His father took a deep breath. The room was thick with tension. "Did you two really go on a date last night?"

Joshua smiled sadly. "No. We met a couple years ago but lost touch. I tried to find her but then—" He paused wondering how much information to give his dad, "—life got in the way. Until today."

"You really hurt your mother, you know."

Joshua had known this was coming. "No Dad, that's not true and you know it. Losing her job would hurt her. My leaving was simply an inconvenience."

His father looked as if he was going to argue, but then slowly shook his head. "I wish you would come back. We all miss you. Especially Marc, you know, he really needs his—"

Hearing his brother's name sent the familiar, but not as brutal, pang to his heart. Joshua cut his father off before he could once again waiver his resolve, "Not going to happen."

His father seemed a bit taken back by the harshness of Joshua's words, but he was quiet and didn't press the subject.

Joshua squeezed Eldalyn's hand, wishing she would wake up, but he knew he couldn't stay here much longer without paying the price. At least he knew her name now, so he could come back. Joshua stood with one last look at Eldalyn and headed for the door. "Thanks Dad, but I have to get going."

"Where are you staying?" his dad hedged.

Joshua shook his head once more. "I have to live my life now, not yours." He realized his words sounded harsh once again, but he couldn't get sucked back into the world of family life again. He wouldn't. "Bye Dad." Joshua walked down the halls towards the elevator, feeling his father's eyes on him the whole time.

Joshua had to admit that he missed his father some days. Of his parents, his father had always been the understanding one when Joshua had wanted to grow up and have his own life. His mother—well, not so much.

In the back of his mind, he wondered about Marc; he would be eleven now, old enough to live in the basement, probably in the room Joshua had once inhabited. Miki would be nine, and Juni—well, she would be about to start kindergarten. Joshua let go of the breath he didn't know he had been holding in as he walked to the car. Living his own life had come at a cost, but he wasn't sure it was worth the price anymore.

ELDALYN

JULY 15, 2014

Beep.

Beep.

Beep.

Eldalyn reached her arm up to shut off her alarm, but her arm felt weird, heavy.

Beep.

Beep.

She tried again, teaching for where her cell phone should be, beeping that it was time to get up for work.

Beep.

Her hand encountered something that definitely wasn't her phone. She tried to open her eyes, but they felt crusty, like she'd been asleep for years.

Beep.

Beep.

Eldalyn pried her eyes open to encounter what looked like a hospital room. Her muddled brain tried to process why she was here. She looked down at her legs. Well they were there. She lifted both of her arms, clenching and unclenching her hands. One arm was wrapped in a bandage, but not the type they put on a broken arm—more the type they put on cuts or burns. One of her fingers was in a splint, and the tip she could see looked purple. Well, that was broken.

Eldalyn lifted the sheet that covered her body; she was horrified by what she saw. There were bruises occupying every inch of her stomach, with a path of spots leading down each of her legs. There was a large bandage under the left side of her ribs, and she could see the edge of what looked like stiches peeking out.

But her head—well her head hurt the worst of all. Eldalyn pinched the bridge of her nose and closed her eyes, realizing her arm was hooked by a number of wires to the machine that was beeping.

Eldalyn suddenly realized her throat was very dry. She opened her eyes again, searching for what she knew would be there. When she found the little red button, she pushed it without hesitation, closing her eyes against the headache once more.

Within moments, the door opened and a nurse in purple scrubs and a round, matching cap walked in. "Miss Wren?"

Eldalyn opened her eyes again, opening her mouth to say "water," but instead a squeak came out.

The nurse rushed over and began taking vital signs while using the black device in her pocket to page someone. "I can't believe you're awake! You've been out for so long, we weren't sure if you were going to make it." The nurse attached a blood pressure cuff to the least bruised portion of Eldalyn's arm she could find.

Eldalyn found it was hard to swallow, and closing her eyes helped her headache. "How long?" she managed hoarsely.

"Almost four days." The nurse pulled out a light and peered into Eldalyn's eyes.

The light made her head hurt even worse, and Eldalyn once again muttered for water. This time the nurse obliged and placed a straw between Eldalyn's lips. She wasn't sure where it came from, but she was grateful.

"Slowly," the nurse reminded Eldalyn as she sipped on the water. It was room temperature but soothed her parched throat.

Once her immediate need for water was sated, Eldalyn began trying to think of how and why she was in the hospital. But her mind was blank.

The nurse noticed her strained expression. "What's the last thing you remember?" she asked in a smooth voice just as an older man in a white doctor's coat entered the room. He seemed to notice they were in the middle of something, so he quietly took a seat next to the nurse. She passed him the chart.

Eldalyn scrunched her forehead trying to remember. But her mind seemed so blank. "I'm really not sure."

The doctor set the chart down and moved his chair closer to Eldalyn. "Do you know who you are?"

Eldalyn nodded. "My name is Eldalyn Wren."

The doctor smiled "Well, that's something. Can you tell me how old you are?"

Eldalyn nodded. "Twenty-two." That she was sure of.

"Good. What else do you know?" The doctor prodded. Eldalyn noticed that the nurse was writing things on her chart.

"I know I live alone. My mom died. My dad left." Eldalyn felt oddly separated from her memories. It was as if they were there, buried in her mind, but closed off from her—behind a curtain that she could barely see through. All she got was snippets of information.

"Alright. Anything recent? Do you remember who attacked you?"

Eldalyn shook her head. "The memories are there, but it's like I can't access them." Eldalyn put a hand on her forehead and closed her eyes. She still had a massive headache.

"Okay Eldalyn, don't strain yourself. We can try again after your brain feels a little less muddled. You have a bad concussion." The doctor stood, looking into Eldalyn's eyes again.

"What else?" Eldalyn closed her eyes and leaned back.

"Mostly bruising. However, one of the blows ruptured your spleen, so we did have to remove that. You do have a couple broken ribs on your left side. Other than that, you were extremely lucky." The doctor pressed a few buttons on the machine, and the nurse covered Eldalyn with the sheet again.

Eldalyn wasn't asleep, but could feel herself drifting that way. Her brain was just so fuzzy; maybe she would feel a little better after some sleep. And with that, Eldalyn slipped back into the black abyss she had just emerged from.

"Do you ever think about your mom?" Eldalyn looked to her left to find a brunette sitting beside her. She looked down and saw there was green. It was grass.

"Sometimes." Eldalyn was surprised to hear herself answer. It was as if she was both observing and part of the scene in front of her eyes.

"Do you miss her?" the brunette asked, turning to look at her. Eldalyn took in her delicate and symmetrical features. She recognized this woman, but she wasn't sure from where.

"Not anymore," Eldalyn heard herself say.

The brunette stood, turning to look at her. "Come on, let's get something to drink."

Eldalyn looked around at the meadow around them, wondering where they were going to get a drink here. As she focused, the meadow faded away to a city scene. And when Eldalyn looked back for the brunette, she found a blond-haired man in his place. He opened his mouth. She felt a sudden surge of panic.

"You're mine now, Eldalyn."

It was when a nurse was switching out her IV bag that Eldalyn jolted awake from the dream. Her mind was still fuzzy, and she was barely able to get out a muffled moan before the nurse called the doctor in.

He started trying to ask Eldalyn the same questions as he had before.

But every time she tried to reach the dream she had just experienced, or her memories, she only fell short and felt physically exhausted. After a few minutes of trying to no avail, the doctor made a note in her chart and left the room.

Eldalyn leaned back against the scratchy hospital pillow and closed her eyes ready to drift into dreamland once more, when she heard the squeak of shoes against the floor.

Figuring the doctor had returned, Eldalyn inched open her eyes, only to find a young man standing in the room. It took a moment for her to scan his features before her brain came up with the answer: "Joshua?"

The young man's face quickly registered surprise, both that the young lady had opened her eyes and that she had said his name. "You remember me?"

"Barely," Eldalyn mumbled as she closed her eyes; she was just so tired. The blackness behind her eyelids became a parade of images of the man in front of her. The images were disconnected and meant nothing, but there were quite a few.

"I waited for you. The next night, and every night after that for a month. You never came back." There was a note of hurt in his voice.

Eldalyn searched her mind for a memory that once again she couldn't find. "I'm sorry, I don't really remember. Things are so…fuzzy right now." Eldalyn trailed off as she yawned, her mind starting to drift to dreamland. If she could just get a little more sleep…

"You know you're better than him." There was a young man sitting next to Eldalyn. She was close enough she could see the deep acne scars that marred his complexion. Eldalyn knew this man had a name, but she just couldn't come up with it.

"Who?" she heard herself ask, but again she was both an observer and partial participant in this dream.

"You know who I'm talking about. We've been friends long enough for me to

know, Eldalyn." The man reached over and grabbed Eldalyn's hand. She tried to focus on his face, but the more she did, the more his image seemed to fade. She reached up a hand to touch his face, but when she did, she saw the blood.

Looking down she saw that she was covered in it. But she didn't feel hurt.

Eldalyn desperately tried to make some sense of what was going on. But the harder she tried, the more the dream faded, until she was left standing in the middle of a field of grass. But this time, she was alone.

JOSHUA

JULY 15, 2014

Joshua sat by Eldalyn's beside for a couple more hours before his father returned.

"Ah, Joshua." His father grabbed Eldalyn's chart and flipped it to the page he needed in one smooth, languid motion. "You came back."

Joshua knew what his father was hinting at and quickly corrected him, "For her."

His father barely looked up from her chart, not seeming to care at the obvious insult his son had just muttered. "She was awake earlier."

"I know." Joshua reached over and touched the woman's wrist softly. The swelling on her face had decreased immensely, and she looked much more like the young woman he had encountered two years previously. "I spoke to her. She remembers me."

Joshua's father cocked an eyebrow in disbelief. "Is that so? This girl, who barely remembers her entire life, remembers you?"

"I know, I know, it's strange, but she saw me and called me by name. She doesn't remember how we met though, or the details of how we parted." Joshua ran a hand through his hair then rested his chin on the palm of his hand.

"How did it end?" His father had set her chart completely aside now and was listening as a father as opposed to a doctor. These moments were rare, but they were the ones Joshua missed the most.

"Well, that's the complicated part. We met a couple times, but didn't really exchange numbers or make concrete future plans." Joshua thought back to that afternoon in the park all that while ago. "I guess I assumed we would just see each other again the next day, and for whatever reason, she never showed. And she doesn't remember why that is.'"

Joshua's father studied him for a moment, then ran a hand through his hair just as his son had done moments before. "Well, I don't know this young lady well—besides what she has told me, that is. But something tells me she doesn't have many people in this world."

Joshua nodded. He didn't know why he was here. After all, it was two years ago, and she obviously hadn't wanted to see him again; otherwise, she would've been there one of those nights that he waited. Joshua couldn't explain it, but he felt inexplicably drawn to this woman. And though he knew deep down he was stood up, he couldn't help but hope it was some other life event that had kept her away all those years before. And he hoped she didn't turn him away again.

"Well, I've got to get back to my rounds." Joshua's father stood up, giving his son one last look before leaving the room. At least this time he didn't try to argue about him coming home.

Joshua spent the rest of the afternoon with Eldalyn, watching her breathe and listening to the bustle of the hospital right outside the door. Every now and then he would feel himself drifting into the sluggishness that comes right before sleep and allow himself to doze for a few minutes before a foreign sound would wake him. Working at night was really damaging his sleep schedule, but he didn't want to leave in case Eldalyn awoke once more.

At five, Eldalyn still hadn't opened her eyes again, so Joshua had to head to work or risk being in trouble with his boss. But he resolved to return as soon as he got off in the morning, even if he was dead tired.

It was nearly eight in the morning when Joshua stumbled his way back into Eldalyn's hospital room, only to find she was awake, alert, and watching him curiously.

"How did you find me?"

Joshua smiled, "Well 'good morning' to you as well." Joshua noticed she seemed to be eating some sort of oatmeal that was placed on the tray in front of her. So she was eating solid food, which was a good sign. Joshua opened his mouth to answer her question, but she cut him off before he had a chance.

"I'm just saying, it's a little weird how the guy I met two years ago is suddenly in my hospital room when I wake up." Eldalyn shrugged her shoulders than looked down at her oatmeal. "I mean, not that I'm saying you need to leave or anything, it's just, odd."

Joshua sank slowly into the chair he'd been occupying the afternoon before at Eldalyn's bedside. He debated for a moment on whether to lie or tell her the truth, but he knew with one look at her inquisitive eyes that he had to do the latter. "I never forgot about you, as creepy as that sounds. These past two years...well, I wondered what had happened to you." Joshua felt intimidated by Eldalyn's eyes boring directly into his and had to glance down quickly before continuing. "I'm a 911 dispatcher now. Your neighbor called 911, and saw your name was Emerald on your nametag, and well, I thought I'd hit the lottery."

Eldalyn seemed to weigh a few things on her mind in the silence that followed his confession. "And they just let you in the hospital on the basis that you knew the name on my work nametag?"

Joshua was a bit taken aback. Hadn't this girl just had a concussion? Well apparently her common sense hadn't suffered any. He chuckled, "No, of course not. Your doctor, well, he's my somewhat estranged father."

She smiled at this. "Pulled all the strings, didn't you?"

Joshua smiled back. "I couldn't take the chance that it was you and not find out what happened two years ago. I guess you could say curiosity killed the cat."

Eldalyn continued looking at Joshua with her piercing brown eyes. "And what if I told you it was because I decided I hated you last time I saw you?"

He could sense the humor in her voice. "Then I guess I'll leave." He stood, trying to hide his smile; he knew she was joking.

"No, sit down. I was being sarcastic." Joshua's smile widened. "I still don't remember why I never showed. The memories, well, they're MIA still." Eldalyn's smiled faded and a confused look stole over her features.

"It's okay, don't put pressure on yourself. I'll be here as long as you want me here, and if you remember that you really did hate me, well, then I'll leave and we can call it."

She smiled. "You've got yourself a deal. So you're a 911 dispatcher now? I don't remember what you were before, but I am pretty sure it wasn't that."

"Your memory is correct. I was pursuing work in a psychiatrist's office before. But then I decided the medical field wasn't for me." Joshua moved towards her bedside and sat on the edge of her bed. It wasn't much of an upgrade from the hard pleather chair, but it was closer to her.

"Ahh, and why is that?"

"I'm not really sure. I guess I had all these ideas of what the job was supposed to be, and well, it turned out I was more of a paperwork Mongol than anything."

"Wow, that sounds degrading." She took another bite of the oatmeal on her tray.

"Yeah, well, I never went to medical school, so I suppose that's the best they could offer considering the circumstances." He glanced down at the bowl Eldalyn was eating out of, and from this view the oatmeal looked extremely lumpy and unappetizing. "How is breakfast?" he asked.

Eldalyn made a face. "Any way I can get you to smuggle me in some French toast? This oatmeal tastes like dirt."

He smiled, "Oh, so you've been eating dirt?"

She laughed, "No, but if I did, I assume this is what it would taste like."

"Well as an avid dirt eater during my childhood, I must say I disagree—dirt was pretty tasty."

"Your mom let you eat dirt?" Eldalyn asked incredulously, setting her spoon down on the tray.

"Nah, but she said every time she turned her back I did it anyways," Joshua smiled. "Now about that French toast, I'm barely in my dad's good graces as is, but after they release you from this prison, I will take you to get some of the best French toast in town."

She raised an eyebrow. "That sounds like a bribe for a date."

"And if it is?"

"Consider me bribed." She smiled and pushed her hospital tray to the side.

Joshua yawned and quickly realized that if he was going to be able to drive home safely, he needed to leave, and soon. "I hate to leave you, but I work nights, and well, I need to get some sleep before my next shift this evening." Joshua pulled the lunch menu from the tray next to Eldalyn and used the pen from the chart to write down his phone number. "I want to do things the right way this time. Here is my number; you can text or call whenever. And if they release you today and you need a ride, please let me at least see you home."

Eldalyn smiled and took the menu from his hand. "I will of course...I just... I'm not sure what happened to my phone. I really can't remember when or where I had it last. The few days before whatever happened to put me here are completely black." She frowned slightly.

"It's alright. Call me from the hospital phone while you're here and I'll see what I can do about finding out if it was on you when you were admitted." He touched her hand lightly, and to his surprise, she didn't pull away.

"Thanks so much. I really appreciate it."

Joshua yawned again, "No problem, now I've really got to go but you have a good day, alright?"

She smiled, "I will, and you too."

And with that Joshua left Eldalyn's room and headed for his car, thankful that he didn't run into his dad anywhere in the halls. He would have liked to ask his father to alert him before Eldalyn was discharged, but that would require giving his father his father his number. He would just have to cross his fingers and hope she would call him; he could try and help her figure out what happened to her phone, or what happened to her period.

When he got back to his apartment, Joshua went straight to bed, barely bothering to remove his clothes. He set his alarm for three in the afternoon, which was only six hours away, but he planned to go back to the hospital before work and ask about Eldalyn's belongings. And with that he drifted off into a dreamless sleep.

Joshua signed for the bag of bloodied clothing at the nurse's station, thanked his father on the other side of the counter, and began walking back to Eldalyn's room. On the way there, he began to rummage gently through the bag until his hand encountered what it was looking for.

Pulling out the thin touchscreen phone, Joshua inspected the charging port just as he turned the corner into Eldalyn's room. She was lying flat on the bed with her eyes closed. He assumed she was asleep and took his backpack off his back and pulled out the mass of tangled chargers he had brought with him. He was only on his second one when he heard the rustle of the bed sheets moving.

Joshua turned to see Eldalyn sitting with her legs hanging over the bed. "Planning your great escape?" He tried the third chord, to find that it fit perfectly in the charging port.

"Nah, I'm still on a leash." Eldalyn raised her left arm where Joshua could tell the IV had been removed from the back of her hand, but there was still a port to receive medication and a wire which he assumed monitored her vitals. "I just like to pretend I'm going somewhere."

Joshua smiled and held up the phone. "Found your phone, and luckily I had a charger to match at my place." He began to look around the room for an unused outlet, finding one below the TV near the floor. He plugged in the phone, watching the little empty battery appear on the screen.

"Are those my clothes?" she asked, motioning towards the bag. He nodded. "Can I see them?"

"Are you sure you want to?"

"I need to try and remember what happened. The police are going to come by to talk to me, and as of now, I have nothing to give them." Eldalyn sighed in resignation. Joshua hesitantly handed her the bag, sitting on the edge of the bed next to her as she pulled out the first piece. It was a short jean vest that would come down to just below her breasts. Joshua could see the nametag, and the smudges from where the neighbor had wiped away the blood to see the name. Joshua wanted to ask, but he didn't—not yet.

The next piece was a lacy pink bra, cut in the middle by the paramedics during rescue work. Eldalyn turned the bra over in her hands a couple of times before setting it aside. Then she pulled out a pair of short, frayed, jean shorts with some bedazzling on the behind. She barely glanced at these, but instead immediately felt in the back pockets, looking confused when they were empty.

The last item in the bag was a maroon hoodie. It looked very worn compared to the other items but was equally as bloody. Eldalyn again checked the pockets.

"Missing something?"

She smiled sadly. "Yeah, I'm a bartender—or was, I should say. I always make cash tips. I can't say for sure without going to my house and looking for my wallet, but it seems my last night of pay is missing."

Joshua had noticed the lack of shirt in the bag. "Bartender, eh?"

She giggled nervously. "Yeah, at The Wolf Pack downtown. I used to be embarrassed to tell anyone, but not anymore. It's a job; it's not who I am." Eldalyn ran her hand over her still swollen face, gingerly touching the stitches that ran along her scalp line. "I don't know what I'm going to do now. They've definitely already fired me for not showing up, and they won't rehire me looking like this."

Joshua took her hand, removing it gently from her face and returning it to her side. "Let's not worry about that yet, okay? You have some healing to do first."

A pained look passed over her face for a moment. But she didn't say anything more. "Are you hungry?" Joshua tried changing the subject.

"Always these days it seems." Eldalyn reached behind her for the hospital menu. "And nothing on here looks appealing."

He glanced at his phone, noting it was time for him to head to work. "I have to go, so I can't really help in the dinner department, but how about I bring you breakfast on my way home?" Joshua had spoken to his dad earlier while grabbing her clothes, and he had informed Joshua they wouldn't be releasing Eldalyn for at least another day.

"That sounds amazing." She smiled wider than Joshua had ever seen. "Thanks."

Joshua picked up the phone on his way out, checking the battery; it was at almost half charge. He unplugged it and handed the chord and phone to Eldalyn. "Text me your breakfast order by seven in the morning, alright? If I don't hear from you, you're gonna get the Joshua special."

"And just what is the Joshua special?" Eldalyn smiled and powered her phone on.

"A surprise until seven a.m." With that Joshua smiled and left the room, closing her door quietly behind him. As he turned to head down the hall, Joshua's eyes caught on the chart which had been relocated to outside her room now that she wasn't in critical condition. He glanced both ways down the hallway, making sure his dad—and no other medical staff—were anywhere in sight before he picked it up. He knew what he was about to do was definitely against hospital rules and probably illegal, but he couldn't help himself.

The front page of the chart was a lot of legal jargon and scribbles that Joshua didn't bother reading. He was only interested in one thing: the emergency contact.

It was blank.

ELDALYN

JULY 16, 2014

Eldalyn picked up her phone and scrolled through the contacts. There were only about twenty-five names, and although she could picture some of them, she really couldn't place any of them as being someone who could tell her what had happened to her. Eldalyn quickly entered Joshua's number from the menu on her table. She liked Joshua—*really* liked him. And she had a feeling that could be why she hadn't shown up before.

Eldalyn's thoughts were interrupted by her stomach rumbling, loudly.

As unappetizing as it sounded, she was having a reprise of the soggy turkey sandwich she'd had the night before. The nurse who came to check on her every few hours had told her it was about the only edible thing on the menu. The meatloaf was capable of putting someone in the hospital according to said nurse.

Eldalyn heard the door to her room opening, anticipating her food tray, but it was the doctor, and he wasn't alone.

"Hello Eldalyn, these are Officers Gutierrez and Cathey. They'd like to speak with you if you're up to it." Dr. Williams smiled hesitantly, as if he was scared she was going to get up and run. But she had nothing to hide.

"That's fine. I am waiting on dinner, but I guess other than that, I can clear my schedule." Eldalyn noticed how no one laughed; her jokes were always lost on the serious crowd.

"Hello Eldalyn, I'm Officer Gutierrez." The man was about six feet tall and had a large, muscular frame, and a mustache to match his profession. He sat quickly in the seat Joshua had recently vacated. The other officer, Cathey, pulled out a pencil and paper as well as what appeared to be a company issue cell phone. He was tall as well, but dark skinned with a thinner face and jaw than his partner. He looked as if he could have some muscle hidden beneath his clothing, and he kept himself clean-shaven. He stepped past Officer Gutierrez and placed the phone on Eldalyn's side table, pressing a red button that she could only assume meant to start recording.

"Interviewing Eldalyn Wren on the events that occurred on the evening of July eleventh two thousand and fourteen." And with that the second man ran a hand through his black, curly hair and leaned back against the wall next to the chair.

Eldalyn glanced toward the door to see it was closed, but Dr. Williams had remained in the room—probably to make sure they didn't grill her too hard. She had seen the cop shows; she knew how this was about to go.

"Alright Eldalyn, tell us what you remember of the night you were attacked." Gutierrez leaned forward as if she was incapable of speaking loudly.

"That's easy: nothing." Eldalyn knew they wouldn't be satisfied with that answer.

Officer Cathey spoke up. "Eldalyn, if you're protecting someone, or afraid of them coming back, we can protect you."

"I'm not scared. I just honestly don't remember anything. I actually remember very little of my life before. I remember some people, names, places, but I can't recall specific events to save my life." Eldalyn took a deep breath and smoothed out the hospital sheet covering her legs. "It's like my memories have been replaced with only snapshots. So I can see the people, but the movie portion is missing." She debated whether or not she should mention the dreams, but figured she'd better keep them to herself until she could remember them better and had names to go with the faces.

The officers obviously didn't trust this answer and turned to Dr. Williams for confirmation. "It's true gentleman. She suffered a nasty concussion and hasn't been able to tell me much about her life at all." Dr. Williams flashed Eldalyn a concerned smile.

Officer Gutierrez still wasn't satisfied. "Well if you remember names, you must remember if you were dating someone."

Eldalyn pinched the bridge of her nose and closed her eyes, but the answer wasn't there. She pictured the man in her dream with the acne scars. He had referred to himself only as a *friend*. "I don't know for sure, but I have a feeling if I was dating someone I would know, so put that down as a no."

Cathey scribbled notes in his pad. "Do you know of anyone who would want to hurt you?"

She shook her head, "My father and I had some issues in high school, but most of the injuries that resulted were small and accidental. Plus, I haven't seen him in years and I doubt he would have a reason to come back."

This piqued Officer Cathey's interest. "Why, and when did he leave?"

"He was an alcoholic. Why he left, I don't know. But he left when I was nineteen, years ago."

Cathey nodded and flipped the page on his notebook. Gutierrez spoke up next, "Eldalyn, were you working anywhere?"

Eldalyn nodded. "The Wolf Pack." The officers raised their eyebrows. "I know how it sounds—I was a bartender, and I have been for a couple years. I don't remember if I met anyone there the night in question. And before you ask, no, I know I would never take a customer home with me. I wasn't that type of girl." Eldalyn shook her head, "I'm *not* that type of girl."

Gutierrez stood up and grabbed the recorder, shutting it off. "I'm sorry you don't remember more Eldalyn, I was hoping this would be a cut and dry arrest."

"I'm sorry too." She hung her head slightly, feeling an itch start at the base of her neck. She reached up to scratch it gently in case it was a scab.

Cathey closed his notebook and both officers headed for the door, but not before placing a card on the table beside her. "If you remember anything, call us. We're going to head to The Wolf Pack and see if anyone there saw anything. Is it okay if we come see you again?" Eldalyn nodded and looked at Dr. Williams for confirmation.

"Eldalyn is showing amazing progress besides the memory function. We will most likely release her tomorrow as long as there is someone who can keep an eye on her." And with that he showed both the officers out the door.

Panic began to seize Eldalyn. She didn't know anyone—she didn't have family; the only numbers in her phone were those of coworkers, and something in her subconscious told her she wasn't necessarily close to any of them. Not only that, but how was she going to pay this massive hospital bill once she was released? She couldn't go back to The Wolf Pack as long as her face and body looked like a bruised fruit, and by the time she could, she would have long since been replaced by a "Candi" or "Diamond." And although her memory failed her, something told her she didn't have many other marketable skills.

Without realizing it, Eldalyn had begun to cry. She felt the hot tears sliding down her cheeks and looked to the table for tissue. There were none. She stood on shaky legs and headed to the small bathroom attached to her room.

She used a tissue, then splashed water on her face to cool herself down. She looked in the mirror only to notice her arms were shaking. She covered her face with her hands as more tears came. She could feel the swelling of her eye sockets underneath her fingers.

Wiping the tears off once more, Eldalyn shut off the light and lay in her bed. She didn't care what time it was, and she no longer had an appetite for the sandwich she had ordered. She cried herself into a dreamless sleep.

When she awoke later, the room was dark and a blue light seeped under the door which was closed as before. But someone must have opened it at some point because a wilted, untouched sandwich and bottle of water sat on the stand by Eldalyn's bed, along with the form for her breakfast selection.

She opted to only take a sip of the water then rolled onto her other side, only to remember that Joshua was bringing breakfast. She rolled back over to check the time on her phone to find it was almost four in the morning. She still had time to tell him her order.

After a long moment of debating between an omelette or French toast, Eldalyn remembered she wasn't working at The Wolf Pack anymore and chose French toast; a few carbs wouldn't hurt her.

Keying in the passcode on her phone, she was momentarily blinded by the blue light the phone emitted. Her eyes adjusted quickly and she selected Joshua's number out of the contacts. She texted him her name and the words *French toast*. Within moments a text came back that read nothing more than *roger*. Eldalyn smiled and set her phone back down, rolling over once again.

This time when she drifted off to sleep, she had a dream—a dream of a blond-haired man she couldn't name. And for some reason, she felt afraid.

"Eldalyn, my girl." The blond-haired man touched her cheek. She was facing him as they stood in some sort of mist. "Come with me."

She felt unsure at this demand and looked around. A brunette woman stood in the mist behind her. Eldalyn waved as she began to fade. When she turned back around to face the blond-haired man, she found herself looking directly into his eyes. "Come with me," he whispered again.

She felt her knees go weak. He began to lead her forward. And up ahead, there was a beautiful blonde woman shaking her head no. The name bubbled to her lips before she could stop it. "Cassie!" Eldalyn shouted.

The blond-haired man turned back to look at Eldalyn, anger in his eyes. She tried to pull her hand from his, but he only tightened his grip.

After a momentary struggle, Eldalyn was loose, and running, but so was he. The mist was thick; she couldn't see her way. She could hear him. She needed to run faster.

Suddenly, his hands were around her waist and she was being dragged back. She opened her mouth to scream but no sound came out.

Then her vision went black.

OFFICER MARCUS GUTIERREZ

JULY 16, 2014

Officer Gutierrez sat at his desk tapping his pen lightly against the wood. He had been with the police force for nearly twelve years now, choosing this path straight out of high school. Sometimes he wondered if he had made the correct choice—he had been a stellar student and could have gone on to do most anything. His partner of four years sat across from him staring blankly at the notepad resting on his lap.

"Do you think she's lying?"

Officer Cathey's head snapped up. "Do you?" This case was one of the most interesting ones that had come across his desk in a long time. Although the city was a big one, the area he covered was often only riddled with petty crimes such as theft and public intoxication. This was the first serious assault case they had been assigned in almost a year.

"I'm not so sure. I wanted to gauge your opinion first." He set his pen down, instead opting to rest his elbows on the desk. Dennis Cathey was almost six years his junior, but they were nearly perfect complements to each other. Where Cathey excelled was often where Gutierrez lacked, and vice versa.

"I mean, she seemed very sincere, but that doesn't mean she isn't protecting someone." Cathey flipped through his notes, obviously looking for an answer that wasn't there.

"I think she was holding something back," Gutierrez said, leaning back in his swivel chair and picking up the documents he had printed out before going to see Eldalyn. "Let me clarify: I believe she doesn't remember the attack, but I think she remembers more than she let on."

Cathey nodded in obvious agreement. "Her record came back squeaky clean though, I doubt she has anything serious to hide."

Gutierrez and Cathey sat in silence for a few moments. Gutierrez picked up the scan of the girl's driver's license and inspected it, squinting. Nothing jumped out at him.

"We just have so little to go off of. How does someone live in society today and leave no paper trail?" Cathey shook his head, pulling out his phone as it vibrated in his pocket.

"That the wife?" Gutierrez asked playfully.

"Told you I'm not married."

"Might as well be, the way she keeps tabs on you." Cathey cracked a smile at whatever he was reading then slipped his phone back in his pocket. Gutierrez was glad to see his partner kept a healthy personal life but was able to keep focused on the job. Often with others on the police force, it seemed like it was an either/or situation.

"Back to the case… what did you find out about The Wolf Pack?"

"They open at six. The manager was the one who answered the phone and said we could come by any time. He's there all day."

Cathey stood up. "I say we better get going then."

Gutierrez smiled at his partner and grabbed his keys from where he stashed them in the top desk drawer. He hoped this little visit would speed up their investigation.

The two officers pulled up outside The Wolf Pack almost an hour later, thanks to a detour Cathey had suggested due to his hungry stomach. Gutierrez hadn't been big on the diner style restaurant Cathey had chosen, but the food had been edible.

"Can't believe I've been in town this long and have never been in this little gem." Gutierrez gave the building a once over. It was in what seemed to be a partially degraded state, either by happenstance or design—he couldn't tell. There were no windows and only a single wooden door, which he couldn't believe still functioned as the thing looked like it came from some medieval castle.

Cathey knocked on the door since technically the bar wasn't open yet, but not surprisingly, no one answered. Gutierrez knocked once more while pulling on the iron handle of the door. It swung open easily.

"Hello?" he called out.

"One second!" The muffled voice came from the back room. Gutierrez looked at his partner and they shared a moment of silent communication. Cathey peeled off and began to go poke around what looked like a performance stage saddled up next to a giant dance floor. The other half of the room was a bar, with various tables and chairs haphazardly stacked to one side. Obviously there had been some cleaning going on.

Steps began to echo through the empty building as Gutierrez turned to watch the man—who he assumed was the manager—approach him from down the hall. Gutierrez had his hand out and waiting. "Officer Richard Gutierrez."

"Mike Palomino. Welcome to The Wolf Pack." Mike wasn't an idiot, and his eyes began to scan the room looking for the partner he knew a cop wouldn't travel without.

Gutierrez saw his glance and smiled. "My partner, Cathey, went to find the bathroom." Whether this was true or not he didn't care; he just hoped if there was any evidence to be found here, it hadn't been hidden.

"Ah, very well then. What can I do for you gentlemen today?" Mike wasn't particularly tall, but Gutierrez could tell he was used to commanding a room with his presence. He had a charismatic attitude, and his tone of voice was smooth to the point of almost being mesmerizing.

Gutierrez pulled the picture from his wallet. "We are trying to find out information on this girl, Eldalyn Wren. She is an employee here?"

Mike nodded in affirmation, "Was. She was a great employee actually, till she stopped showing up a couple days ago. I'm guessing your visit has something to do with why she didn't show? I thought maybe she had just gotten strung out on drugs or moved on. You wouldn't believe how flaky the girls are these days."

Gutierrez wanted to make a comment about how sleazy joints attract sleazy employees, but he kept his focus on the work questions only. "What day was it that Ms. Wren first didn't show up?" Gutierrez pulled out his phone to make a few notes.

"I don't know off the top of my head. Maybe last night, or the night before?"

"That's it?" Gutierrez typed the note in but something didn't add up.

"Well, I can't be sure. We don't really keep very good records here. I could check her time card, but employees are free to trade or give shifts to whoever. And depending on the employee, I may not even notice their absence."

"What do you mean you wouldn't notice?" He was starting to get a real odd vibe from Palomino, and he wasn't sure why.

Mike must've felt Gutierrez's suspicion because he suddenly began to adjust the collar on his pale blue shirt as if the room had risen in temperature. "I have a lot of girls working here. And most nights I schedule seven or eight cocktail waitresses and four to five dancers. And most of the girls can do either job, so sometimes if someone is missing, the girls don't tell me and they pick up the extra slack so they can make extra money."

This sounded plausible. "So how did you even know Eldalyn was gone?"

"That's just it, the only specialized job we really have is bartending, and even then most of the cocktail girls can do it if needed. I only noticed because she's head bartender a couple times a week, and one of the girls came to me at the end of the night unsure who to check out with because she couldn't find Eldalyn." Mike moved across the room to the pile of furniture and selected a table and two chairs. He motioned for Gutierrez to sit.

"I'm fine thanks." He added the new information to his list. "And

104

what bartender was this?"

Mike reached up to touch his spikey hair, "Oh man, they all run together sometimes, too much estrogen, but maybe it was LeeAnn?"

"You're not sure?"

"No, sorry, I'm not."

Gutierrez seriously wondered how a man could run a bar with so little knowledge of the comings and goings of his staff. Either way, he needed to move on to a different subject. "Did Eldalyn have any friends here?"

Mike sat for a second, pressed his lips together as if something had made him angry, then he finally spoke. "No... well yes, she did. This girl Cassie Lane is the one who referred her for the job. They were pretty tight until Cassie up and quit. Left me hanging for weeks."

"So in a bar where you claim the girls are completely interchangeable, you are saying one girl quitting left you hanging for weeks?"

Mike must have suddenly realized he had revealed more than he wanted to because his voice suddenly wasn't so smooth. "No, I mean yes, I mean..." He took a deep breath. "Cassie quit mid shift. There were tables that went unserved and customer complaints to deal with. That I notice. Various girls picking up extra tables for extra cash, that goes under my radar."

He had to hand it to this guy—he had an answer for everything. "So after Cassie left, did Eldalyn make new friends?"

"Not that I know of." There was a noise behind them as Cathey made his presence known. Gutierrez made eye contact with him and a small moment of unspoken communication passed between them once more. Cathey hadn't found anything. He came to stand next to the table where they were sitting, and Mike quickly got up to untangle a third chair.

Gutierrez stopped him. "We're almost done here. I just need to know if any patrons, or staff, or anyone really, seemed to take an unnatural interest in Eldalyn?"

Mike laughed. "This is a bar with barely clothed women, and Eldalyn was popular."

"I figured that, but did anyone ever try to take her home, maybe? Or approach her in a way that she felt uncomfortable?"

Mike shook his head. "If she did, she didn't come to me. We have security guys who are supposed to report anything major back to me, but I've never heard anything regarding Eldalyn. She takes care of herself pretty well to my understanding."

He nodded and looked to Cathey to see if he had any input. His partner shook his head, but then something came to mind. "Would you consider yourself to be on good terms with Eldalyn?"

Mike didn't seem taken aback by their question at all but answered with a somewhat suspiciously straight face: "Eldalyn and I have always been on great terms."

Fifteen minutes later Gutierrez and Cathey were back at the office combining their findings of the club.

"Anything interesting come up during your self-guided tour?"

Cathey cracked a smiled at their inside joke as he pulled out his phone and flipped through some pictures. "Nothing out of the ordinary—basically the usual stuff you would expect to find at a bar such as that. As far as I could see, the employees don't have lockers or anything, and I didn't see any personal effects of any sort." He handed his phone over to Gutierrez who flipped through the various pictures of the bathroom, back room, and beer cooler. Nothing jumped out at him either. "What did you think of the manager?"

"Well besides being Rico Suave, I get the impression he lets the bar run him instead of the other way around." Gutierrez pulled open his notes section on his own phone. "Doesn't know when employees aren't there, doesn't know who's friends with who—I mean what twenty-something girl doesn't have a work friend or two? I find that unbelievable."

Cathey nodded in agreement. "I mean I wasn't there for long, but something was up. Usually when you ask if someone is on good terms with you, your face shows the answer. People on bad terms make a sour face, and people on good terms usually smile."

"I agree. That straight face was strange, and probably forced or faked to hide his true feelings." Gutierrez began to absent mindedly rub the back of his neck as he mentally lined up all the facts they'd uncovered in the case so far.

"So, maybe something went down between Mike and Eldalyn, but the question is whether or not it's even related to this investigation. Maybe she has rejected his advances? Or maybe they hooked up at some point?" Cathey leaned over the desk to look at the notes on Gutierrez's phone. "And who's this Cassie person?"

Gutierrez sat up straight and turned his attention to the files that had recently been downloaded to his computer. The beautiful blonde in the driver's license picture looked almost identical to the picture Cassie's mother had provided for the missing persons' report on file, even though they were taken almost a year apart. "Cassie was an employee at The Wolf Pack just as Mike said. However, it seems she hasn't been seen since a few days after she 'quit.' Nothing. No activity on credit cards, bank accounts, or her phone. Her mother insisted on keeping the phone line active and pays for it on her family plan. She's convinced Cassie will just pick up the phone and call one day. However, that has yet to prove true, except for some calls from Eldalyn the day prior to her attack, her phone record reads empty for the past year and half. It's like she vanished into thin air."

"So it's 2014 and Eldalyn didn't think to text her friend?"

Gutierrez shook his head. "Apparently not. Only the calls, none of which were answered. And there were no voicemails either."

"Now that's interesting. Our victim's only supposed 'friend' simply vanishes?" Cathey shook his head. "We all know that vanishing usually doesn't mean anything good has transpired. Did Eldalyn call Cassie anytime prior to the day of her attack?"

"No … well at least not as back as the records we got." Gutierrez eyed his partner. "Do you have a best friend, Cathey?"

"You bet."

"And do you call him or her frequently?"

"It's a 'he,' smartass. And yeah, we check in on each other at least once a month by way of a night at the bar." Cathey's mind was obviously on the same track. "So, it's far more than *weird* that Eldalyn wouldn't call her so-called best friend in a year and a half, and then call her thirteen times in two days."

"I agree. Think Eldalyn's attack had something to do with Cassie's disappearance?" Gutierrez turned back to his partner who had stood up and was leaning over the desk, peering at the computer screen. If only pictures could talk, it would make his job so much easier.

"I can't say for sure, but I'd be willing to bet a year's salary that it does."

JOSHUA

JULY 17, 2014

Joshua stared at the clock on his computer, willing it to count the minutes faster. It read *6:45 AM*—only minutes to go. Joshua reached discreetly into his pocket, making sure he had no missed notifications on his phone. They weren't supposed to have their phones on them at all, but Joshua was afraid Eldalyn would need something and call.

Joshua couldn't be sure about what happened two years ago, but it really seemed as if Eldalyn was alone. He assumed she must have one family member, or a friend or two, but if she did, where were they now? Why had none come to visit her? Joshua wished he could press Eldalyn for answers, but he knew she probably didn't know much more than he did. She said she remembered names but not events; that is, if he trusted that she wasn't lying. He shook his head at the thought. She had nothing to gain from lying to him, even if she did need a friend. Whether he liked it or not he trusted this girl, cared about her, and ultimately, worried about her. He'd only known of her for two years, spoken to her a handful of times, but somehow he felt an attachment to her. And that scared him.

Even with his girlfriends in the past, he had never felt this nurturing feeling that had taken over him now. In fact, after leaving the parent role he had resided in for so long, Joshua was surprised he didn't feel at all repulsed by the feelings. But he also knew that Eldalyn didn't want to be taken care of the way most girls wanted. She was different.

Glancing at the clock, Joshua realized just how quickly his last fifteen minutes had passed. And before he even finished that thought, Bobby was tapping on his shoulder to relieve him. He jumped up, grabbed his lunch box—which he had pre-emptively stored underneath his desk—and headed quickly to the door. He had a breakfast to order.

Arriving at Eldalyn's door with his arms full of food, Joshua found it to be closed and the curtain by the side window to be drawn. He was unsure what to do now that Eldalyn was up and around. What if she wanted her privacy? Joshua finished weighing the chances of intruding before he knocked lightly twice, pausing when there was no response from within. After another moment he turned the knob and inched the door open slowly so he could peek in.

It was dark, with a small amount of light filtering through the blinds. Eldalyn was laying on her side with her knees slightly bent, facing the door, and the blanket pulled up to her neck. Joshua didn't turn on the light but noticed she opened her eyes a crack before shifting on to her back.

"Ughm, morning already?" she murmured, closing her eyes once more. He noticed an uneaten sandwich lying on her table, which worried him. He was no expert, but the sandwich definitely did not look fresh.

"Yes, and I brought food, which, by the looks of that sandwich, you need."

Eldalyn rolled her neck to the side, opening her eyes to glance at the sandwich before moving them to his face. "Yeah, uh, I don't really know what happened."

Joshua shrugged, "It's not important. What *is* important is that I have French toast." And with that Joshua pressed the closure on the Styrofoam container causing it to pop open, revealing a double order of French toast with cream and berries.

Eldalyn's mouth fell open briefly before she quickly sat up, raised the back of the hospital bed, and moved the tray in front of her. She handed him the sandwich as he handed her the French toast. Not even waiting for silverware or syrup, she picked up the first piece and took a huge bite.

Joshua quickly stepped to turn on the lights, momentarily blinding himself and Eldalyn. That didn't stop her from taking a second, and an immediate third bite of the French toast.

"Whoa there Nellie, here's a fork." Joshua barely finished speaking before she grabbed the fork, flashed him a smile, and re-dug into the

French toast.

He pulled out his egg, bacon, and hash brown breakfast, and the two of them ate in silence for a few minutes. But it wasn't awkward or uncomfortable at all. In fact, it was oddly calming.

They were still both eating, with an occasional glance at each other, when they heard a throat clear.

"I didn't know we were ordering breakfast."

Joshua stood up quickly coming eye-to-eye with his father. "Hey Dad." He grabbed the one bag left on the floor. "I didn't know what you would want, but I got some pastries for you and the nurses."

Dr. Williams had been joking but cracked a genuine smile at his son's forethought. "Thanks Josh."

"Joshua."

"Right, Joshua." His father winked as he picked out a cherry Danish from the bag. "It's a good thing you're here. We're going to discharge Eldalyn today, and she's going to need a ride I assume."

Joshua glanced at Eldalyn and noticed her face cloud over with what appeared to be worry. Was she afraid to go home? "Already? I mean she still has memory loss—"

His father cut him off. "I can't hold someone simply for memory loss, Joshua. Also her insurance won't cover her staying any longer. In fact, they may not cover last night as is. She will have outpatient rehab once a week. But for now, her vitals are normal, and the swelling in her brain has receded enough for her concussion to be treated on an outpatient basis."

"Are you sure…" Eldalyn's meek and shaky voice broke into their conversation about her "… that I have insurance?"

Dr. Williams looked past Joshua at Eldalyn. "Yes, I don't know if it's through your job or parents, but when we put your Social Security number in the system, you were insured." He looked down at her chart in his hands one more time. "And even if you were not, I would never discharge a patient prematurely. I'm sure you're ready. Your scan yesterday came back with minor swelling comparable to a minor concussion. Again, you will need to complete outpatient therapy, but spending more time in the hospital won't help with that." Dr. Williams signed a paper towards the rear of the chart and placed it on the stand. "Finish your breakfast, then I'll have a nurse come in to get you packed up."

Eldalyn looked around, "I don't have much. But, uh, I can't wear the clothes I came here in." She bit her lip. Joshua felt she might be about to cry. Her love of the French toast had been long forgotten.

Before giving any thought to what he was doing, Joshua spoke up: "I'll run and get you some clothes real quick. What size?"

His dad smiled, turned, and walked out the door as Eldalyn rattled off her most basic sizes. She blushed a little, but requested that he buy her thong style underwear. He gently touched her cheek, grabbed the trash from his breakfast, and headed out the door.

Joshua kept his back turned as Eldalyn slipped on the clothes he had purchased. He hadn't been sure enough of himself to try and buy her a pair of jeans, so he had chosen black yoga pants, a t-shirt, and the most basic bra and underwear they had in her size.

"I don't know how I can ever thank you for this," Eldalyn sighed.

"That's easy—just go on that date you promised me." Joshua cracked a smile.

Eldalyn smiled sheepishly but avoided Joshua's obvious attempts at flirting. "Are you sure you don't mind driving me home?" Joshua jumped as he felt Eldalyn's hand on his bicep. He spun around to find her completely dressed, but her hair was still a mess.

Eldalyn noticed the direction of his gaze. "I'm going to brush it as soon as we get to my house."

Joshua nodded, and against his better judgment leaned in to place a kiss on Eldalyn's forehead. She looked surprised for a moment and unsure what to say. Joshua took Eldalyn's hand putting it in the crook of his arm. "Shall we?"

Eldalyn smiled, and Joshua led her to the nurse's station to check out. There really was no reason to wait for a nurse to come wheel her out in a wheelchair; Eldalyn was walking fine on her own.

They stopped at the desk and the nurse handed Eldalyn a large packet of paperwork as well as her driver's license and Social Security card, which were clipped to the packet. She stopped short. "I have a driver's license? I mean, I guess I don't know why I wouldn't, but I just don't recall ever driving a car. I remember taking the bus everywhere."

The nurse nodded. "These were found in your jacket pocket when you came in by ambulance. You'll have to double check with the cops to make sure they didn't take anything as evidence, but I don't think you had a wallet on you."

Eldalyn nodded, "Thanks." And she looked at Joshua with a look that he knew meant she was ready to go.

When they reached the car, she handed him her driver's license. "Here's my address if you need it. Hopefully I'm one of those people who keeps my license up to date."

Joshua laughed, took the ID, and put the address in the GPS in his phone. He helped Eldalyn into the passenger side of his car, then headed to the driver's side.

The ride to her house was relatively uneventful, both of them engaging in small talk mostly involving their favorite foods.

Eldalyn's positive mood fell the minute they pulled up in front of her house.

There was crime scene tape crossing the front door and fluttering in the wind. Her mouth fell open. But she took a deep breath, reached for the door handle, and got out of the car.

Joshua rushed around to help her up the steps, tearing down the police tape as Eldalyn tried the knob. It was unlocked.

The door swung open and she gasped. He too looked on in horror.

The entire house was destroyed. The walls were gutted, as if someone had smashed them with an ax. Wiring and insulation stuck out from every which direction. The floor was littered with glass, wood, plaster, and papers of every sort. Furniture was overturned and pulled apart. There was fingerprint dust on every surface imaginable.

"Did—Did the police do this?"

Joshua looked around and shook his head, "No, I mean, yes, I mean—" He took a deep breath. "No, the police wouldn't ax the walls or break things, but yes, they obviously have dusted for prints."

Eldalyn ran her hand down an exposed beam in what used to be the living room. "Who did this?"

"I can't help you there," Joshua shrugged sadly. He wished he could solve all her problems and just make them disappear.

"There's one thing I know."

"Yes?" he asked, his tone hopeful. Maybe she had remembered something vital.

"I don't know what, but they were looking for something." Eldalyn held her head in determination and began to head to what Joshua assumed used to be her bedroom. He followed.

The bedroom was in just as bad of shape. There were clothes and papers strewn about everywhere, with a fine layer of plaster dust covering everything like a film. Eldalyn's mattress had been hacked. Whoever had done this was indeed looking for something—if only she could remember what.

"You can't stay here," Joshua declared.

Eldalyn shook her head. "I have nowhere else to go."

"Did you look through your phone contacts?" Joshua reached out to rub her arm reassuringly. She was looking so pale that he was starting to worry that she might pass out.

"Yeah, but none of the names stood out. I can't remember if I had any friends." Eldalyn must've realized how bad that sounded, because she continued: "I mean, I know I had friends. But my vivid memories are all from high school or before. The last two years are practically blank."

Joshua thought for a moment, but knew what he had to do. "Then you'll stay with me until we figure this out."

Eldalyn looked at him, mistrust evident in her eyes. "I don't know…" Joshua suddenly realized that she was scared of him. And after what she'd been through, she had no reason not to be.

He came around to stand in front of Eldalyn and face her. "I know you have no reason to trust me, but I promise I'm doing this because I really do like you Eldalyn. I did when we met two years ago, but I never got the chance to tell you." Joshua took a deep breath. "I'll let you have my room. The door locks, and I'll take the couch. Okay? I'll even give you my dad's number if it makes you feel any better."

Eldalyn seemed to think for a moment. She glanced around the room and realized she had no other options. "Alright."

He smiled, and she smiled back hesitantly. She was obviously still nervous.

Eldalyn began to gather what clothes seemed to be salvageable, placing them into a canvas bag that had survived the damage, but there wasn't much. Then she headed back to the living room and began digging through the rubble there.

"Careful, there's glass in there," Joshua reached down to stop her.

"I really need to find my wallet."

Joshua nodded. "I know—let me look. You go to the bathroom and get what you need from there." Eldalyn nodded and headed for the bathroom.

It took a few minutes of carefully sifting through the glass, paper, and couch stuffing, but Joshua finally found a dusty dark purple wallet. Inside was a navy-blue debit card with a matching credit card for a local bank, but nothing else.

"Found it!" Joshua called towards the bathroom.

Eldalyn quickly reappeared carrying a hairbrush, toothbrush, and what looked like some sort of makeup bag. "This will do for now. I'll have to come back at some point." Eldalyn looked at the wallet in his hand with a hopeful look in her eyes. "Anything?"

"Just a debit and credit card."

Eldalyn shrugged, "Better than nothing."

As they turned to head out the door, Eldalyn grabbed her spare key from where it was by the door, locking the door as she closed it behind them. "There's one thing that baffles me."

"What's that?" Joshua took the items from Eldalyn's arms and placed them in the back of the car. He would vacuum the seat later.

"All that glass. I mean, I know my memory is faulty, but no windows or doors were broken. I remember being a clean person, and I remember not having much. So where did all that glass come from?"

Joshua helped Eldalyn into the passenger seat and walked around to the driver's side once more and got in. "I don't know, but I do know one thing—you need to tell that to the police."

Eldalyn nodded. "I have their card and number, but please can we head back to your place first? I need a shower."

Joshua smiled. "Of course."

"Are you sure this is okay?" Eldalyn asked through the crack of the bedroom door.

"Yeah, I love this couch, super comfy." Joshua mimicked fluffing the pillows and flopping down on them dramatically. Eldalyn giggled.

"Okay, but I promise I'll find a place, and fast. I don't want to abuse your generosity."

"It's okay, really," he promised. For some reason he felt better knowing Eldalyn was here safe instead of in that dinky little house she was living in. "Take all the time you need."

"Thanks again, you've been so nice to me and such a help I can't imagine how I'm ever going to repay—"

"No repayment needed. Unless, of course, you're gonna stand here thanking me instead of letting me get some sleep—then I'd have to charge you double." Joshua laid down, closed his eyes, and feigned sleep.

Eldalyn giggled again. "Goodnight."

"And don't think I've forgotten that you owe me a date!" Joshua shouted from the couch.

"All right, all right, we can plan a date," Eldalyn relinquished. Even with his eyes closed Joshua could hear the smile in her voice.

He did a fist pump in the air like Judd Nelson in the Breakfast Club. Finally he had gotten her to agree once again.

"Goodnight Joshua."

"Goodnight Eldalyn." He watched through a crack in his eyelids as Eldalyn closed the door, and then he heard the lock turn. Even though he was a bit disappointed, he expected nothing less. The girl had just been brutally attacked after all. Luckily, he had the next couple days off to hopefully get her to trust him.

He wasn't sure why he wanted this woman to trust him so badly. He'd never had a problem getting a girl before, so why go for the one who clearly didn't trust him?

Joshua had all this in mind as he drifted off to sleep.

ELDALYN

JULY 18, 2014

Eldalyn jolted awake panting for breath.

Pinching her eyes closed she tried to recall the dream she had just had. Grimacing, she felt it drifting from her mind.

Glancing around the room quickly, Eldalyn located a pen on the desk in the corner. She edged out of bed and grabbed it while quickly asking for forgiveness for what she was about to do. She really wasn't normally a snoop, but she needed a piece paper, and bad.

Opening the top drawer, she scanned its contents, only finding various staples, paperclips, and rubber bands. Eldalyn took a deep breath and opened the second drawer. This time she was in luck; there was a notepad. Bingo.

She quickly scribbled down everything she could remember about the dream. She was dancing, in an outfit very similar to the one she had been taken to the hospital in. And there was the blond-haired man there. He was talking to her. Eldalyn couldn't hear what he was saying, so she leaned in closer to him, and that's when he grabbed her neck and began to choke her. And then Eldalyn had jolted awake.

Satisfied she had written the majority of the dream down, Eldalyn turned to lay back down and return to sleep. Then she remembered something else that had been bothering her.

So far, her short-term memory had proved to be functioning correctly, but Eldalyn didn't want to take a chance. She wrote *insurance?* underneath the dream recount. She needed to figure out where this insurance came from, and how she was going to pay what it didn't cover.

Then Eldalyn remembered the cards in her wallet. She added *bank?* to the list. Maybe she had some money put away. She would assume so.

Unless that's what the person had raided her house for. She had a feeling though that the amount of devastation indicated they had not, in fact, found what they were looking for.

Tapping the pen on her chin, Eldalyn pondered all the mysteries surrounding her life right now. The list could go on forever. Deciding to put the most important things first, Eldalyn added *glass?* to the list, then impulsively, below that, she put *Cassie?* Eldalyn hadn't wanted to tell Joshua, but she remembered Cassie as being her friend. She remembered Cassie getting her a job at The Wolf Pack, but for some reason, something in her subconscious nagged her. Something told her that Cassie wouldn't have been willing or able to help her. Eldalyn wasn't sure why, but she felt she needed to pursue that thought further.

With a yawn, Eldalyn placed the pencil down and returned to bed to try to sleep once more. It turned out Eldalyn didn't have to try hard at all; within moments her eyes were heavy and sleep crept in at the edges of her mind. Eldalyn was quickly returned to sleep where her subconscious ran rampant and she began to dream once more.

"Like this." The blonde placed her hands on Eldalyn's hips. "Now try."

The dream version of herself began trying a complicated dance move. She must've done it right because the blonde started clapping. A name squeezed its way through Eldalyn's mind. Cassie. She looked at her and smiled.

Eldalyn felt her dream-self open her mouth to start talking. "When can I meet him?"

"Oh, not yet. We are keeping it a secret for now." Cassie smiled and looked down at something out of Eldalyn's view.

She tried to follow with her line of vision but found that her vision became fuzzy as she looked down. When she looked back up, she came into contact with the blond-haired man once more.,

And the smile on his face was pure evil.

When Eldalyn awoke once again, light was streaming in the room from the glass windows at every angle. Joshua had told her that she could lower the shades, but she had forgotten in her exhaustion.

Glancing at the clock on the bedside table, Eldalyn noticed it was just past eight. Holding her breath for just a moment, she listened for any sound from the apartment. She heard nothing—Joshua must still be asleep.

Tiptoeing over to the desk, Eldalyn grabbed the pad she had jotted her dream down on as well as the packet of papers from the hospital, adding her new dream to the list. She returned quietly to the bed and began to spread out the hospital paperwork around her.

First, there were the check-in papers that contained most of the information Eldalyn already knew about herself: her name, age, weight, height, and the injuries she was admitted with. After that came an insurance page, which was blank, and another page to put her current doctor's information, which was also blank. Eldalyn turned to the fourth page to find a copy of her ID and wrist band she had been wearing during her stay in the hospital. Turning to the fifth page, Eldalyn finally found what she had been looking for.

It was a fax coversheet, and in the description it only had two words: *insurance card*. Eldalyn flipped the page over to find a scan of a card that had her name on it. Looking at the company logo, she pulled out her phone and googled the company. Once she found a customer service number, she pushed talk and held the phone to her ear.

It wasn't until someone answered that Eldalyn realized she had been holding her breath. "Hello, customer service, how can I help you?"

She took a deep breath. "Um, yes, my name is Eldalyn Wren, and my member number is three nine six seven zero five. I was just curious as to what account it is being paid from." Eldalyn figured if she came straight out and asked how she had insurance, the lady would think she was nuts.

"Let me have a look here." It was a female with a distinct southern accent. "Aha, found it." She paused for a moment, then came back hesitantly. "Uh Miss Wren, it looks like this account is under another name."

"What do you mean?"

"This plan is paid for by a man."

"Oh." Eldalyn wasn't sure how to proceed without spilling the truth.

"You'll have to speak to the gentleman paying for the plan for more information. I'm sorry."

Eldalyn sighed in frustration. "Is there anything you can tell me?"

The woman seemed to have sympathy when she responded. "Unfortunately, ma'am, I've already given you as much information as I am able to provide."

"I understand. Thank you." Eldalyn hung up the phone. Well that was a dead end.

Climbing out of bed, she headed for the adjoining bathroom to prepare for the day. As she was putting her hair up in a ponytail, Eldalyn cringed as she noticed the stiches protruding from her hairline. She'd hoped a ponytail would cover it, but it looks as if she'd misjudged her hair. With a sigh, Eldalyn lowered her hair and began experimenting with the part to see what she could do. She was startled when she heard a knock at the door of the bedroom.

"Eldalyn, are you awake?"

She laughed at herself for being so jumpy. Of course it was just Joshua checking on her.

She walked over and opened the door. "Good morning." Eldalyn smiled as she took in Joshua's rumpled appearance. Obviously he had just woken up.

"Good morning to you as well," he grinned. "Can I come grab some clothes out of the closet real quick?"

Eldalyn smiled sheepishly in return. She felt really bad about kicking him out of his room, but she didn't see another solution. She needed to figure out what was going on with her life, and fast. "Of course." Eldalyn stepped aside and let him pass.

As he did, Eldalyn couldn't help but notice how attractive he was. She found herself wanting to reach up and run a hand along his broad shoulder. But she refrained, and mentally reprimanded herself for having such inappropriate thoughts.

Joshua grabbed a t-shirt from the closet and headed to his dresser on the far side of the room, digging in the second drawer from the top for some jeans. Eldalyn didn't realize she was staring until he looked up and caught her eye, smiling once more.

"So, what's on the agenda today?"

"Well, I guess we better head to the police station, and then maybe we can find out some information about my bank accounts?" Eldalyn decided not to tell Joshua about the dreams she had, at least not until she knew more.

"Sounds good to me." Joshua stepped out of the room and headed for the bathroom in the hallway, leaving the one in the bedroom solely for Eldalyn's use.

As he turned on the light and began to close the door, Eldalyn thanked him again. "Really," she said, "I don't know what I would do without you."

Joshua smiled as the door began to impede her view. "You're welcome, really, it's no bother."

"And if it's any consolation, I don't think I was avoiding you two years ago. I think something happened."

He smiled, closing the door to start getting ready. Eldalyn followed suit and closed the bedroom door and began to do the same.

After they both finished getting ready and Joshua fried them each an egg, they got back in his car, and this time headed for the police station.

"Here's the deal," Officer Cathey pulled a tape recorder out and set it on the table next to the legal pad right in front of him. "You're going to tell me everything you know about the last few years of your life. Then we will tell you what we have found out and see what fits." He looked at Joshua. "He can stay or leave—your call. But if he stays, I don't want any input influencing your memories, okay?"

"He stays." Eldalyn reached over and placed a hand on top of Joshua's, who jumped slightly at her contact. Eldalyn quickly withdrew her hand, but Joshua stopped her and placed his hand atop hers.

"Alright, start when you're ready." He pressed the tape recorder and a green light flashed on.

"Well after my dad left, I was living on my own and I remember I was struggling, moneywise. The exact details escape me, but I can remember not having enough money."

"Were you working a job?" Officer Gutierrez cut in.

"Yes, I was a dog walker at Pet Palace."

"Why did you leave?" Cathey was scribbling notes on the legal pad.

"I can't tell you exactly. But I don't think it was in bad blood. I think I found the job at The Wolf Pack and I made more money there." Eldalyn rubbed her forehead; her brain was already feeling strained. Joshua began to calmly rub circles on the back of her shoulder. "I think it had something to do with Cassie. She really stands out in my mind. I almost called her from the hospital but something about her had been nagging me, so I didn't."

Cathey's eyebrows shot up and both cops glanced at each other. Eldalyn wondered what was going on, but neither cop said anything. Instead they both looked at her to continue. "I remember I was a bartender. But it was a promotion. I'm not sure when or how it happened, but when I think of it, I feel hapy and proud of myself in a way that I know it was a big deal." Eldalyn took another deep breath. "I remember I worked with Cam. Her number is in my phone as well, but she doesn't stand out like Cassie does, so I didn't call her either."

The officers nodded and jotted down more notes. Eldalyn continued, "The only other people I remember from The Wolf Pack are my manager Mike, and this guy who came in every night named Tyler. Neither names are in my phone."

"We will want to look through your phone."

"I figured." Eldalyn slid the phone over to their side of the table. "I really haven't had a chance to dig deep myself, but the text messages are deleted and the call log is empty." Officer Gutierrez raised his eyebrows and Eldalyn understood his question. "I think maybe I deleted them myself. I'm real big on clearing out clutter."

Officer Cathey nodded. "What else?"

Eldalyn shrugged, "Honestly, that's about it. I'm sure if you ask questions things will pop up. But the movie in my mind is very foggy; just the people stand out. And occasional views of my life, but it's like I'm watching through a curtain." Eldalyn didn't realize she was pinching her nose until Joshua touched her hand and put it gently on the table with his hand on top.

"Alright, well let's start with a few easier questions." Officer Gutierrez pulled out a stack of papers from beneath his notepad. "We ran a background check on you and it came back clean, so you've never committed a crime, or even been accused of such. Your work places check out—meaning you only have the two. But it also says there was an attendance issue in high school. A truancy officer was sent to your house after two weeks of absences without a parent phone call, but no one answered so it was assumed you moved."

Eldalyn closed her eyes and leaned back in the chair, the alley forming in front of her eyes. This, she did remember.

When she opened her eyes again, a tear slid down her cheek and both officers were looking at her expectantly, Joshua looked alarmed.

Eldalyn debated for a moment what to say, then decided it was time to talk about it. After all, it had been years.

"I, uh, I—I was attacked." Eldalyn didn't realize she was shaking until Joshua began to rub her shoulder again. "By another student. It's fuzzy, like everything else, but less fuzzy than the rest."

"Trauma can do that." Officer Cathey handed Eldalyn a tissue; her tears were flowing freely now.

"Then why can't I remember who did *this* to me?" Eldalyn motioned to the stitches on her head.

"The memory is a funny thing. Now tell us what you do remember about the attack in high school."

Eldalyn looked over at Joshua. How much could she really say in front of him? Eldalyn swallowed, "It—It was more of a sexual assault re—really." Eldalyn felt more tears fall down her face. She was wrong—she wasn't ready for this. "I—I—that's it."

Officer Gutierrez raised his eyebrows, but Officer Cathey seemed to understand. "It's alright Eldalyn. We can discuss it in more detail later. Do you at least remember the classmate's name?"

Eldalyn nodded, the tears blurring her vision. She motioned for the pad and pen in Officer Cathey's hand, and he slid it over to her. She wrote the name quickly, and slid it back before Joshua could see.

Officer Cathey read the name, then quickly turned the page. "We will look into it just to make sure it wasn't a repeat offense." Eldalyn nodded.

"So, can you go into more detail about Cassie for me, Eldalyn?" Officer Gutierrez was impatient to get back on subject.

"She was really pretty. We had known each other for a long time. Since we were kids. As for exact details, I think she was dating Mike, but I'm not sure. She was dating someone, but it was a big secret for some reason." Eldalyn thought back to all the dreams she had about Cassie recently. She'd given them about everything she'd deduced. "That's about it."

"Well Eldalyn, we went to The Wolf Pack to talk to Cassie, and she hasn't been there in a long time."

Eldalyn gasped. "Oh my god, is she okay?"

Officer Cathey shook his head, "We don't know. We believe she may be on the run from something."

"No, no, no. That's not right. Cassie wouldn't hurt a fly." Eldalyn shook her head then rested it on her hands on the table. Her brain was strained and even her current thoughts were beginning to muddle.

Officer Cathey pulled out another piece of paper and placed it in front of Eldalyn. It was a bunch of numbers, a call log, and a certain number was highlighted over and over again. "Really? Because no one had seen her in months. They say she said she was going to visit her mother. But we called her mother and she never showed. Her mom filed a missing persons' report about a month ago. Said this long of an absence was odd, even for a free spirit like Cassie. We went to her place, and there was no sign of foul play."

Eldalyn's mouth was agape. "But, maybe she just moved or something?"

"Without telling anyone?" Gutierrez burst her bubble. "Now you need to be absolutely honest with us. If you know where she is, you have to tell us."

"Why do you think I would know? If she's a missing person, wouldn't that mean you investigated this all before?" Eldalyn was very confused as to what was going on. And her jumbled mind wasn't helping any.

"You called her three times the day you were attacked. And she didn't answer a single call." He pulled out another paper with the same layout. "In fact, you called her ten times in the day prior and she didn't answer. You also texted her multiple times. So, you can see why we would think you possibly might know where she was hiding."

Officer Cathey cut in, "It's also possible you could've known too much and she, and possibly an accomplice, are the ones who attacked you."

Eldalyn was in shock. Could her friend really have done this to her? Is that why she didn't feel like calling her was a good idea? But could Eldalyn really consider the gentle Cassie she had known as a child as a violent criminal? No… Eldalyn shook the image away. All of this just didn't add up. Looking back down at the paper, Eldalyn noticed another number that popped up multiple times. "Whose number is this?"

Cathey's face was grim, "We were hoping you could tell us. That is a prepaid cell phone, paid for in cash. We have no name attached to it."

Eldalyn quickly grabbed her phone from the officers' side of the table and typed in the number; nothing came up. Eldalyn sighed and passed the phone back.

"That's about as far as we got Eldalyn. We were hoping you could give us more to go off of today to help jump start the investigation." Officer Gutierrez gathered up all his papers and stacked them on his notepad.

"There is one thing," Eldalyn blurted out. Officer Cathey's finger froze mid-air as he reached to turn off the recorder. "All the glass in my house—I don't know where it came from. The doors and windows weren't broken, and I think I would remember having items that would cause that much glass to be there." Eldalyn rubbed her chin lightly, "And how was it everywhere? Like an equal amount was broken in every room."

Officer Cathey scribbled down a few notes. "I'll have the crime lab go get a few pieces and test it, and then we will call you back in. Alright?" Eldalyn nodded. She was exhausted even though she'd only been awake for a few hours.

They exchanged pleasantries, promising to call Eldalyn when they had more information, as well as making her promise to call if she remembered anything else. As soon as she was out of the door, Eldalyn began to cry again.

"Shhh," Joshua hugged Eldalyn tightly, running a hand down her hair. He didn't say anything else and Eldalyn was glad. She couldn't take anymore talking.

Joshua let her cry for as long as she needed. Eldalyn couldn't really gauge the time, but when the tears finally slowed, Joshua leaned in and gently gave Eldalyn a peck on the lips. Eldalyn was surprised and froze, unsure of what to do, but Joshua didn't hesitate and grabbed Eldalyn's arm and led her to the car, "Let's go home."

She shook her head. "No, I'm okay. I really want to go to the bank today."

He helped Eldalyn in the car, "Alright, but let's get some lunch first. You going to be okay?"

Eldalyn smiled sadly and turned towards the window, "I have to be."

Hours later they were finally headed back to the apartment. They were both silent for a while as Eldalyn shuffled through the massive pile of papers on her lap. Joshua finally asked, "So?"

She smiled, "I have money." Then she realized it sounded stupid and rephrased it, "I mean, I have enough money saved up that I can hopefully cover the uninsured hospital bills and probably afford to get a small apartment." She continued to flip through the two years of statements that the banker had provided her with. She'd intended to create a map in her head of where she'd been, but found it was harder than she'd anticipated. Purchases at Target and the Kroger didn't exactly nail down her whereabouts and activities.

Joshua's smile faded a little bit, but then his eyebrows scrunched together as if he had heard something confusing, "Will you?" he finally asked.

Eldalyn looked out the window. "I don't know. I honestly don't know what I'm going to do. But either way I need to pitch in for your apartment while I'm staying there."

"Out of the question."

"Why?"

"I don't want to take your money from you; who knows when you'll work again." The words came out harsher than he intended, and he appeared to have hit a nerve. Eldalyn didn't respond. Instead she stopped shuffling the bank documents and looked out the window to her right. "I mean, I don't need the money, it's not like you being there is costing me hardly anything." That didn't sound much nicer.

Eldalyn was quiet for a moment, then she decided there was something else she needed to say. "Listen, about what happened at the police station—"

Joshua cut her off, "We don't have to talk about it if you don't want to."

Eldalyn shook her head. "I need to tell you this." She took a deep breath, "What happened to me, it... I was a wreck." Her voice waivered in a way she hadn't heard in a long time. "Especially two years ago. When you met me, I couldn't trust anyone. I don't know what happened for that to change, but back then, well—"

"That's probably why you didn't come back," he finished for her.

She nodded. "But now, I've grown, I mean, I'm not that scared little girl anymore. And as much as I hate what happened, I wouldn't change it for the world. It made me who I am. It made me strong, resilient. I probably wouldn't have survived this long if it hadn't been for that."

Joshua didn't say anything. Instead, he reached over the center console and placed his hand on hers. That was all the answer she needed.

The rest of the ride home was silent. Eldalyn was glad she had found out her bank account had money in it. Plenty of it, actually. Though she had struggled while working at the Pet Palace, she obviously hadn't been struggling the past couple of years. In fact, Eldalyn sensed she had been saving the money for something special. What, she didn't know. Hopefully it would come back to her. She also wished she had been less of a cash user. She knew she had gotten paid in cash, and although she had some various charges on her credit card, they seemed more like occasional charges than habitual ones. She would have to go over them further when she had a notepad and highlighters to indicate the repeating ones. Right now, they were a jumble of words and numbers.

Eldalyn looked over to Joshua, noticing how the hard planes of his cheeks reflected the sun, making him almost look like a beacon to her. She couldn't deny she was attracted to him, and she sensed he was, and always had been, attracted to her. What step would she take next?

She had always been a bit shy, never one to make the first move. Though she knew her confidence had increased over the years, she still thought that she wasn't very outgoing when it came to men. At least she didn't think she was.

They pulled into Joshua's assigned parking spot, but neither made a move to get out of the car. When Joshua shut off the engine, Eldalyn glanced over to find he was leaning towards her.

Without consciously thinking, Eldalyn began to lean towards him until their faces were only an inch away. And then, their lips touched.

It took a moment for Eldalyn to adjust to the feeling of his lips on hers before she began to kiss him back, reaching behind him to run her fingers through his hair.

They kissed for what seemed like forever, and Eldalyn felt her body responding in the only way it knew how. And she wanted to go further.

But just as she was about to take initiative and deepen the kiss, Joshua pulled away, a giant grin occupying his face. "Let's go inside, shall we?"

Eldalyn grinned sheepishly and followed Joshua inside. Foolishly, Eldalyn assumed they would resume kissing the moment they stepped in the door, but instead Joshua headed to the kitchen and began pulling out pans to cook something. Eldalyn wondered if she was a bad kisser. Why hadn't he tried to kiss her again upstairs? With a million thoughts running through her mind like a hormonal teenager, Eldalyn quickly mumbled something about taking a shower and headed to the bathroom.

All through dinner Joshua made small talk, asking Eldalyn about varying facts of her life, helping her gauge even further what she could remember. The bank documents sat next to her on the table, and occasionally she would leaf through and ask him what he thought a certain charge was. Eldalyn kept thinking he would bring up the kiss, but he never did. Instead he told her bits and pieces about his brief childhood.

She thought for sure he would bring it up after dinner, or at least kiss her again, while they sat in close proximity on the couch watching an evening TV show. When neither occurred, Eldalyn's panic once again returned. What if Joshua had decided he didn't like her anymore? Maybe he didn't feel the same connection she did. She slid over closer to him, closing the few inch gap that was in between them. She set her hand on his leg, and Joshua rested his large warm hand over hers. She waited; he still didn't make a move. Eldalyn was so nervous that she was doing something wrong that it must've begun to show, because next thing she knew Joshua was asking her what was wrong.

"Oh nothing, just tired."

"Well you're welcome to head to bed. Don't stay up on account of me. We do have a full day tomorrow."

"We do?" Eldalyn didn't remember planning anything.

"Yeah, you have a checkup remember? Then I figured we could head back to your house and see if it brings back any additional memories."

"But we've already been there." Eldalyn's shoulders were tense at the thought of returning to her house.

"Yes, but we were in a hurry and weren't really prepared to shift through the glass. This time we will be."

Eldalyn nodded and rose from the couch. Joshua rose too, bringing Eldalyn to his chest and kissing her chastely on the lips. Eldalyn was disappointed but said nothing. Quietly, she headed into the room and brushed her teeth then crawled into bed.

She could still hear the TV on in the main room and Joshua wasn't in her line of sight. With a sigh, she rolled over to go to sleep, leaving the door wide open. If he needed a hint, she hoped that was enough.

JOSHUA

JULY 19, 2014

Joshua awoke to the sunlight trying to burn holes through his eyelids. With a groan he reached for the remote to shut the blinds, only to realize he was on the couch and there was no remote for the blinds out here.

With a grumble, he rolled over to his left side and placed his arm over his eyes; he was still wearing the same clothes from the previous night. Jolting up on the couch, Joshua noted the TV had timed off, but he had never made it to the bathroom to change or brush his teeth before bed. Well, better late than never.

He walked into the bathroom and brushed his teeth, stripping off his clothes out of habit before he stopped dead in his tracks.

He had just walked into the master bathroom.

Had Eldalyn forgotten to lock the door?

He tried to remember if he had opened his door on the way in. His brain was too muddled to be sure.

That's when Joshua also realized he had forgotten to bring a change of clothes with him in the bathroom as well. But of course, usually that wasn't necessary—he could walk around stark naked and no one but the birds on his balcony would know.

Mentally kicking himself, Joshua reached down to put the dirty clothes back on, even though it was one of his biggest pet peeves, when he suddenly had an idea.

Peeking around the corner of the bathroom into the bedroom, Joshua noticed Eldalyn was sleeping soundly. Her back was to Joshua, but he could see the soft rise and fall of her breathing. He could do this.

Quietly, he tiptoed over to his dresser, easing open the drawer as silently as possible. It was to no avail.

"Good morning," Eldalyn mumbled from the bed. Joshua glanced over to see that she had rolled over. Her eyes were only open a crack, and there didn't seem to be a trace of anger in her face that he had barged in on her.

"Shh, it's too early… go back to sleep." Joshua eased the drawer shut and began to head for back into the bathroom.

"Please stay."

Joshua stopped dead in his tracks. Had he really heard that? He spun around. "You sure?"

She smiled and patted the bed next to her.

He needed no further invitation and sat on the covers next to Eldalyn but still a respectable distance away, as he was wearing nothing but his boxers. But before he knew it, Eldalyn had closed the gap between them and had begun kissing his neck.

"Eldalyn—"

"I knew it. You don't want me." Eldalyn began to pull away.

Joshua stopped her with his arms. "No, it's not that. I just want to make sure you want this. I don't want you to feel any pressure because you're staying with me." She seemed confused. "I want you to be with me because you want to, not because you feel you're in debt to me."

Eldalyn shook her head. "I would never be with a guy just because I felt like I owed him something."

"Are you sure about that?"

Wrong move—his comment only served to anger Eldalyn who pushed him away. She huffed and rolled back over to her other side.

"I'm sorry," he tried to apologize.

"I wish you would trust what I'm saying to you."

"I do trust you; I just really don't want to take advantage of you."

Joshua ran a hand through his hair. He debated reaching for Eldalyn but decided now wasn't the time.

"How noble of you, my *knight in shining armor*."

"You don't have to be so sarcastic."

"Are you sure about that?"

Joshua laughed and pulled the covers up over Eldalyn's shoulder before grabbing his clothes and heading back into the bathroom. After grabbing a quick—but slightly colder than usual—shower, he slipped on the new clothes he had selected from his dresser and ran a hand through his hair. He dug through his bathroom drawers looking for one of the nicer colognes he knew he had stashed in there. After spraying himself lightly, he closed the bedroom door and headed back to the couch.

He awoke hours later to the sound of his alarm reminding them it was time for Eldalyn's appointment. Joshua groaned as he pulled himself off the couch to shut his alarm off.

Heading back into the bedroom he had vacated only a few hours earlier, he found Eldalyn sleeping peacefully on her back, her nose wrinkled in her sleep. She must be dreaming.

Joshua leaned down and kissed her lightly on her forehead. She didn't stir. He kissed her again on the cheek, followed by another kiss on the lips. Eldalyn sighed and peeked out through one cracked eyelid. "Well, if it isn't my knight in shining armor becoming prince charming."

"Alright, 'Princess Sarcastic' needs to get out of bed."

She laughed, "And if I don't? Do I get, I mean, *have* to go to the dungeon?"

It was Joshua's turn to start laughing, "No, but you might miss your royal appointment."

Eldalyn pulled the pillow over her face and then said something muffled that Joshua subsequently couldn't hear. He could only assume it was some excuse for her not going. Joshua responded by inching the pillow off her face slowly, after prying her fingers off of one end.

"Alright, alright—I'm up!"

Joshua smiled and headed for the kitchen. "Eggs for the princess?"

"Anything is fine!" Eldalyn shouted back as she headed into the bathroom. Joshua grabbed the eggs out of the fridge and cracked a few into the pan sitting on the stove. He would need to learn to cook more breakfast foods soon before she grew tired of eggs.

The sound of the shower turning on reached his ears and Joshua walked quickly back to the bathroom door. "Careful of those bandages on your ribs!"

"I'm just washing my hair!" Eldalyn shouted back, and he chuckled, turning back to the kitchen to go flip the eggs he had started frying on the stove. He couldn't believe he had turned down such a beautiful girl this morning, but he knew he would never forgive himself if ever felt like he had taken advantage of her while she was injured. He just hoped he hadn't offended her too badly; but most importantly, she had joked with him right after.

He heard the bathroom door open and Eldalyn waltzed into the kitchen wearing a purple V-neck t-shirt and a pair of leggings. On anyone else it would've looked plain, but for some reason the color of the shirt made her skin look radiant. Joshua smiled and leaned over, placing a peck on her lips. "You look absolutely adorable this morning."

Eldalyn blushed and mumbled a "thank you" as Joshua placed an egg on the plate in front of her on the breakfast bar.

"Eat up—we've got a long day ahead."

The glass crunched delicately beneath their feet as they entered the war zone that used to be Eldalyn's house. This time they were armed with gloves and wearing the proper shoes. Eldalyn walked ahead, exploring what was left of her room. She walked delicately, and he wondered if she was hurting. She had not allowed him in the room during her appointment. He understood that she trusted him, but still needed some privacy of her own.

Plus, it had only been about a week since they reunited; Joshua had to keep reminding himself of that little fact, for fear of going too fast and scaring her off. He couldn't help himself though. Eldalyn was cute, witty, and sharp minded—everything he wanted in a girl, even if her memories were partially missing.

Joshua leaned down to pick up one of the pieces of glass, holding it up to the light, watching the colors as they refracted through. He picked up another piece, and then a few more, holding them all in the palm of his gloved hand. They didn't look as if they fit together, but it was hard to tell with the pieces being so small. He wondered how it was possible that glass could even break this small. It must have been something very delicate, or it had to have been smashed on stone and brought here.

"Something's wrong."

His head snapped up to find Eldalyn standing in the doorway to the bedroom. "What's going on?" He dropped the pieces of glass and headed towards her, brushing off the gloves on the way over as he stepped through even more debris.

"This stuff… it's all old."

"Well you hadn't bought new things in a while, presumably?"

"No, that's just it. Yesterday when we went to the bank and I looked at my statements, I had purchased things: clothes, shoes, jewelry. There were several hundred dollars in purchases for the past four months." She paused and looked around. "And nothing here was purchased within the last two years. The clothes—they're mine, but they're old. And the makeup bag I grabbed the first time we were here? Well, the makeup is all dried up. And I know I wasn't in the hospital long enough for that to happen."

"What are you saying?" Joshua couldn't read the look on her face.

"I don't think I lived here."

"But—"

Eldalyn interrupted, "I know I was here the night of the attack, but I think I had been living somewhere else and came here as an escape."

Joshua sighed and surveyed the room as well. "Well then where?"

"That's the weird thing; when I looked at my statements, there were no payments that appeared to be rent. Or a mortgage payment of any sort. The utilities for this place were on automatic payment being deducted from my account every month. And get this—there was a car payment." Joshua could feel his eyes widen.

"Why didn't you tell me all this last night?"

She shrugged and offered him an apologetic smile. "I meant to. I was just letting it soak in first. And I only put the car payment thing together this morning when I looked up the finance company it's being paid to; they only finance cars, and it is the same amount every month. It doesn't say what type of car or anything really useful."

He walked to the front window and pulled the curtain. "So where is this car?"

"That's my question exactly."

Without another thought, Joshua pulled out his phone and called Officer Cathey's direct line, explaining to him about what they found in the bank statements and about the possible car loan. He handed the phone to Eldalyn to let her explain why she felt she hadn't lived there. After she was finished, she put the phone on speaker so they could both hear the officer on the other end of the line.

"So here's what we are going to do. A lab tech came and got a few pieces of glass last night, and we should have the analysis back within a day or two. I'm going to contact the DMV and see if they can find a car registered in your name. Also, I need one of you to fax over the bank records if that's okay with you Eldalyn?" He paused for her to respond.

139

"Yes sir, I can do that."

"Thanks, that saves us the trouble of getting a warrant. And Eldalyn, I know there isn't much you can do, but please try to think real hard about where you might have been living. We will let you know if we ever locate your friend Cassie."

Eldalyn seemed to think for a minute, then she spoke, "Could I have been living with Cassie maybe?"

Crickets seemed to chirp in the silence that followed, and she chuckled a bit as she realized how absurd it was to ask them whom she might have been living with.

At that moment, Joshua's phone vibrated letting him know he had a call on the other line. "Hey, sorry Officer but I have another call coming in. Are we finished?"

"Yes. I'll call when I have more info. Just fax those sheets please; the number is on my card."

"Will do." He hung up and switched lines. "Hello?"

It was Liam. He wanted Joshua to meet him and his fiancée Rita for dinner tonight.

"Sure, but can you make the reservation for four?" He smiled at Eldalyn who was standing in the same spot as before, an inquisitive look in her eyes.

"Of course Buddy! See you at seven?" Joshua agreed and they hung up. Eldalyn waited.

"How do you feel about meeting a couple of my friends tonight?"

"Sounds lovely." She flashed him one of her thousand-watt smiles, looking around the room one last time. "I think we're done here. I don't know what else I can find out by being here."

"No memories have returned?"

"None. But I have a feeling I wasn't here the last two years. Wherever I was, that's where the memories will be. At least that's my theory." Eldalyn walked out to the porch and sank down as gracefully as she could onto the step. He had noticed her balance was getting better, but her movements were strained at times—usually ones that involved movement around her ribs. The doctor had changed the bandage this morning and said the stiches should dissolve in a couple of days. She had been ecstatic at the time she had told him. Now she just seemed tired.

He sat down next to her. "We will figure this out, I promise."

"How did I get so lucky?" She grabbed his hand and held it delicately to her cheek before leaning in for a kiss.

"I should be the one asking that. It's only by chance I found you again." He smiled down at her as Eldalyn leaned against his shoulder. They sat there contentedly for a few minutes before Joshua finally gently lifted Eldalyn's chin and rose to his feet. "Let's go get ready for this double date tonight, shall we?"

"We shall." Eldalyn took his hand and they walked to the car.

"After you my lady," Joshua joked as he opened the door of the restaurant, allowing Eldalyn to step past. She was a vision in the outfit she was wearing, even if she didn't think so.

They had returned home earlier only for Eldalyn to realize she didn't have anything nice enough to wear on a double date. He had reassured her that the place they were going was business casual and his friends wouldn't care what she was wearing, but that had done nothing but get him shut out of the bedroom while she tried to figure out what to do.

She had ended up choosing a V-neck shirt that she had tucked in to the only skirt she had purchased when they had gone to the store after leaving the hospital. Joshua had told her how beautiful she looked when she emerged from the bedroom, but it again hadn't seemed to help much.

Now Eldalyn was all smiles as they approached the host stand and were led to the table where his friend Liam and his fiancé Rita were seated. Rita was a gorgeous woman of mixed Hispanic and Native American descent. Her skin was the tone all women envied, and her black hair always looked sleek and shiny. Joshua couldn't deny that he had been a little jealous when Liam had been the one to steal her heart.

"Joshua my man!" He clapped hands with Joshua then turned to Eldalyn, "And this must be your lady! You should have warned me she was a looker." Eldalyn looked surprised as Liam embraced her gently. He had forgotten to warn her that Liam was usually a hands-on sort of guy.

If Rita was jealous of her fiancé commenting on another woman's looks, she hid it well, instead standing up and embracing Eldalyn in similar hug-like embrace. "I'm so happy to meet you. Joshua has told us a lot about you." Rita was an abnormally tall woman, reaching almost six feet. Her hug made Eldalyn look smaller than ever.

"He did?" Her eyebrows rose and she turned to look at Joshua.

"Well yes and no; he told us about this amazing girl he met and then never found, but he's been too busy to catch us up on the now." She winked and sat back down, pulling out the oversized menu. Eldalyn smiled and followed suit.

Rita's words spurred Liam on, "Our buddy Joshua here went looking everywhere for you! I mean *everywhere*! Well okay, not *every*where, just all the places that had jobs where people worked with animals." Liam realized he probably shouldn't have said this and smiled at Joshua sheepishly.

"Thanks man," Joshua rolled his eyes and picked up the menu. "You're gonna make her think I'm some sort of stalker."

Eldalyn smiled and put her hand on Joshua's leg under the table. "Trust me, my mind already went down that path when I woke up and you were in my hospital room. I don't think it's creepy. It makes me feel special." The two of them shared a silent moment as he gazed into her brown eyes. "It makes me feel like you're actually into me if you went through all that trouble looking for me."

"Well Liam exaggerates. I did look for you, but *only* on the side of town we met, and the places there that involved animals, pet stores, and such."

"What are we eating for dinner?" Apparently Liam had realized the topic was making Joshua a little too uncomfortable and decided and it was time to return to his favorite subject: food.

Rita laughed and turned toward Eldalyn to explain. "This restaurant is family style. They say the dishes serve two to four people, but with the way this guy eats," she said, patting Liam on the shoulder, "we need to order two dishes and probably a side."

"How about a steak for one of the entrees?" Joshua suggested, looking over at Eldalyn as if they shared a private joke. If Eldalyn remembered, she showed no sign of recognition.

Liam nodded, "And I vote we get the herb chicken for the other one. How about two sides? Sweet potatoes and..."

"Maybe a salad?" Eldalyn interjected.

"Sounds perfect," Rita responded just as the server came over to take their order.

Eldalyn looked at the server, and visibly froze. Joshua squeezed her hand and waited for her to glance his way. She continued to stare straight at the server. Joshua leaned over and whispered in her ear, "Everything okay?"

She seemed to snap out of it. "Yeah, I just... something came back to me just now," she whispered to Joshua.

"What?" he whispered in response as the server finished taking their order and turned from the table to walk away.

"Nothing important really. Just that I had a really good friend."

"What friend?"

Eldalyn scrunched her eyebrows in obvious frustration. Joshua was beginning to become accustomed to this look on Eldalyn's face. "I don't know her name, but we were having some sort of movie night, she and I, and we were eating popcorn." She pinched her eyes closed as if she were willing something else to materialize. "Ugh, that's it, it's already fading."

"Is anything wrong?" Rita asked as both she and Liam looked cautiously at Eldalyn as if she were about to explode.

"No," Joshua said, "Eldalyn was just telling me, uh, that she has a slight headache, but once we get some food, that will help."

"Oh, well, speaking of headaches, remember the time we were playing soccer and you kicked a ball straight into my head while my back was turned?" Just like that the mood at the table became light once again. Liam was always good at turning things around.

Joshua rolled his eyes and was about to respond when Eldalyn turned to him. "You played soccer?"

"Yeah, in college, I thought I told—I mean, never mind." He smiled and leaned over placing a kiss on Eldalyn's forehead.

"You guys are so cute it makes me sick." Liam pretended to gag but ended up coughing instead, which then led to him laughing.

Joshua started laughing along with him. It was so nice to be around friends again. And for the first time since the 911 call a week prior, he felt that his life was returning to normal. And the thought that someone was out to get the beautiful girl by his side was, for once, far from the front of his mind.

ELDALYN

JULY 20, 2014

Eldalyn awoke to the sound of her phone vibrating atop the wooden bedside table.

Opening her eyes, she squinted as they adjusted to the dark at the same time as she realized something heavy was laying across her chest. It was an arm. Eldalyn jumped, but then quickly realized it was Joshua lying next to her; she mentally groaned as the night before came back to her.

As silently as possible she untangled herself from Joshua, wincing as the headache came to her as she stood up. Suppressing a moan as she winced, Eldalyn looked to see if the movement had woken him, but he still seemed to be in a deep sleep. Glancing at her phone, Eldalyn noted it was barely eight. Tiptoeing out of the room and bypassing the wooden board that creaked, Eldalyn made it to the door and slipped into the hallway without a sound.

Heading into the kitchen, Eldalyn pushed the answer button and put the phone to her ear, "Hello?"

"Eldalyn? This is Officer Gutierrez."

"Yes, it's me." Eldalyn grabbed a bottle of water and began searching the cabinets as quietly as possible. Above the sink she found what she was looking for. Swallowing two of the Advil quickly, she then walked towards the door that led to the balcony and stepped outside.

"How are you doing today?" He was being cordial, but Eldalyn sensed that whatever her answer was really wouldn't affect him.

"Fine, and yourself?"

"Great, listen, we finally got some information for you." Eldalyn sat down on one of the wicker chairs that were situated outside. The pale morning sunlight hurt her eyes. "The lab analyzed the glass from your house, and apparently it came from a set of dishes."

"A set?"

"Yes, a very expensive set. The brand is Solaris. Each set is three plates and one bowl—you know, a dinner, appetizer, and salad plate, plus the bowl. The lab techs have no idea how many sets you had, but based on the amount of glass they observed, they think you possibly had enough settings for about fifty people."

"Fifty people?!" Eldalyn wracked her brain trying to think of why she would ever have that many place settings, much less expensive ones.

"Yes, can you think of why you would have so many place settings?"

"I can't even think of why I would have any sort of nice dishes. I remember my parents had some nice china from their wedding, but I'm pretty sure I sold it to pay bills years ago."

"You're *pretty* sure?"

Eldalyn huffed. She was getting tired of them questioning the way she worded things. "Yes, like ninety-nine percent sure. I mean I can't remember where I sold them, but I know I did. Plus, like I said that was china, not clear glass."

Officer Gutierrez must've noticed her annoyance because his tone softened with the next question. "Did your bank statements show any such purchases? The faxes came through late last night; I just haven't had time to comb through them yet."

Eldalyn quickly stepped back inside the patio door, grabbed her bank statements from where she left them on the coffee table, and headed back outside. "I've looked through them a couple times, and I don't see anything. Most of this appears to just be clothes and shoes. Any luck on the car?"

"Not yet, but hopefully by the end of today or early tomorrow at the latest. The DMV was sent the information; they just aren't the quickest with getting back to us. Good news is you don't have any tickets, otherwise we would already have the information." He sighed. "Now back to the dishes. This specific brand is sold at Z Gallerie—spelled with an *ie* at the end. Anything?"

She flipped through the pages on her lap. She'd highlighted all the types of purchases in different colors, and the ones in blue were those she wasn't sure of. "Nope, I have quite a few charges I don't recognize, but nothing with the word *Gallerie*."

"I think you would notice if you had. These sets of dishes are fifty dollars a set and they estimate there were fifty sets there, so..."

"That would be twenty-five hundred dollars."

"Exactly."

"There definitely is not a charge of that amount on either my debit or credit card." That came out a little more defensively than Eldalyn meant for it to.

Officer Gutierrez must've sensed it, because his voice was reassuring when he answered. "I believe you. We've contacted the company to see if they've sold that many clear glass sets to any one customer. We will let you know when we hear back from them."

"Anything else?" Eldalyn crossed her fingers they had found something else out.

"Not yet, although we did track down Jeffery." Eldalyn's breathing stopped for a second. "He's still in town; we sent officers out to interview him this morning. I'll call you if there's anything significant or concerning to report."

She nodded, and then, realizing he couldn't hear a nod, squeaked out an "okay."

"Also, we are looking for your father, but we really have nothing to go off of but his name. Do you know anything that might help us? Does he have a friend who might know his whereabouts? Did he own a car? Have any resources he might have used to leave town?"

"Not that I know of. I was young, so I didn't really understand the finance portion of his life before he left." Eldalyn closed her eyes and tried to picture her father for a moment, and she found the images didn't want to come. His face was more of a shadow than an actual photograph. "I know he had to sell our car after he lost his job. That would have been sometime in two thousand eight, I believe. It was a dark blue truck. I know it was a Ford, possibly an F-150? Maybe he made some money off of that?"

"Alright that's something. I'll call you back either later today or early tomorrow depending on when we get all this information back. Call me if you think of anything else, okay?"

"I will," Eldalyn promised, then ended the call. She placed the phone on the small table between the two chairs on the patio and walked over to the railing. Taking a deep breath, she leaned just slightly over the railing and closed her eyes, willing her mind to come back to her. This limbo she was stuck in—of knowing who she was, but not *really* knowing—was starting to wear on her. She remained there for a few minutes, staring out over the city, and then headed back inside to grab a pen.

Eldalyn made herself comfortable in the chair on the patio once more and picked up the bank statements. On the corner of the first page she began to jot down notes. She decided she needed to retrace her steps from a couple years ago, or at least what she could remember. Pet Palace was at the top of the list, followed by the park she and Joshua met in, and then a place she should have already visited: The Wolf Pack.

A light breeze blew past the patio, rifling through Eldalyn's hair like gentle fingers. Despite her current predicament, she couldn't remember the last time she had felt this free. Maybe she never had. Closing her eyes, she tilted her head back to enjoy the summer air once more.

She must've become completely lost in her thoughts, because she was startled when felt the touch of a warm masculine hand on her shoulder.

Eldalyn opened her eyes to meet his. He didn't say a word; he smiled, kissed her forehead, and sat down in the chair next to Eldalyn, taking her hand. No words were needed.

They sat there until the day grew uncomfortably warm, at which point

Joshua stood and led her inside to the couch. But Eldalyn didn't sit as he intended. Instead, she followed him into the kitchen.

As Joshua began to pull out various pans to cook lunch, Eldalyn placed a hand on his arm, "You've been taking such good care of me. Allow me." He smiled and stepped back, letting her step in front of him. He placed his arms around her waist and kissed her neck. "I don't think I can cook while you're doing that," she said with her eyes closed, a smile on her face.

He laughed, "Alright, alright, I'll let you be. I need to go shower anyways."

Joshua headed back in to the bedroom as Eldalyn pulled out sausage, peppers, and onions from the fridge. Checking the cupboard, she found the rice she needed to make a gumbo and started a pot of water to boil on the stove. Heading back to the fridge, she looked for ingredients to make a salad but came up empty. She wasn't that surprised; after all, this was a bachelor pad—well, until recently.

Eldalyn groaned as she pictured herself as Joshua had seen her last night. She had only had two glasses of wine with dinner, but apparently she was an extreme lightweight and that had been enough to get her tipsy.

She remembered saying goodbye to his friends and Joshua being a gentleman and opening her car door for her. They had then headed back to his apartment where he had tucked her into bed and given her a kiss goodnight. Eldalyn had then proceeded to grab his neck and pull him on top of her. He had tried to protest that she needed more time to heal, but with her alcohol-fueled confidence, she hadn't listened. Eldalyn put her hands over her face, simultaneously grimacing and blushing.

Suddenly Joshua was behind her, pulling her hands from her face and wrapping his arms once again around her middle. He must have seen her flushed cheeks. "Don't be embarrassed about last night. You are so beautiful." This only made Eldalyn blush further. "Plus, I am equally responsible." He kissed her lightly on the cheek.

"How did you know that is what I was thinking? Maybe it's just warm in here." Bringing further attention to it only made the heat rising in her face even worse. If the truth were told, no one had ever been so observant of her moods, her thoughts, her emotions; or if they had been, they hadn't cared.

"Because I do. Now listen to what I'm saying and don't be embarrassed, okay?" She smiled and answered him with a kiss that was intended to be quick, but instead quickly became passionate. When she wrapped her arms around his neck, she felt something and pulled back; it was a lanyard with his work ID badge hanging from the end of it.

"I have to go to work in a couple hours." He kissed her on the cheek once, then walked over to the couch tidying up the pillows and sheets that made up his makeshift bed. "Guess I won't be needing these anymore?" he said as he grinned.

Eldalyn blushed once more as Joshua headed to put the sheets and pillows away.

They ate lunch at his small dining table, which he confessed he had barely used since he moved in. "Most days I end up eating at the counter. I guess when it's just me, it makes no sense to sit at a table with four chairs."

"But you have to have had friends over at some point, right?"

"We always go out. Even when my ex and I were together, she always wanted to eat out." Eldalyn felt a surge of jealousy go through her at the mention of another woman in Joshua's life. She quickly tamped it down, telling herself there was a reason he used the word *ex* and not her name. There were no longer feelings involved.

Eldalyn realized how little she knew about Joshua's past. It was time to change that. "Tell me about your family."

Joshua set down his fork and looked at his plate in silence for a moment. He slowly wiped his mouth with a napkin and raised his eyes to meet Eldalyn's. She kept quiet and waited for him to speak. "Well you met my father." His voice was pained.

"Yes, but what about the rest?"

He shook his head. "I haven't seen them in a long time. My parents and I had a falling out the night I met you. Do you remember?"

Eldalyn searched her mind for a long moment; only snippets of conversation from that night long ago finally filtered through. "Yes, but barely."

He nodded in understanding. "My mom told me she was going to have another baby, and I just couldn't take it."

More and more pieces were coming together. "What are your siblings like?"

Joshua smiled a sad smile. "Well there's Marc, my little brother—always kind of a handful, I haven't seen him since that night, but I assume he's now an unruly pre-teen. He looked just like how I did as a baby, so I'm assuming we will look almost identical someday, even if we are twelve years apart." He chuckled to himself.

"And there's Miki, one of my sisters. She and Marc were always at each other's throats. She was smart though... definitely knew how to get her way. I spent a lot of time trying to outsmart her. Even as young as she was, she was quick as a whip. And Juni, my youngest sister, well, she was the easiest to handle." His smiled faded, and Eldalyn could tell he was no longer in the room with her but off somewhere in his mind. "She couldn't talk, or should I say hadn't learned to talk yet. I suppose by now she could be telling stories by the fire for all I know..."

Joshua trailed off and ran a hand through his disheveled hair. "Even though you would think she would need the most watching, I often found she needed the least. She would quietly play with whatever you put in front of her, even if it was something as simple as a cereal box." The corner of his lip moved up in an almost smile. "She'd eat anything too. That was actually the only thing I really had to deal with—fishing various toys and foliage from her mouth. I really hope she still isn't eating leaves and sticks, but I guess I'm being a little pessimistic. She's five now..." Joshua let his voice trail off again, and a forlorn silence hung between them.

The silence was so heavy Eldalyn almost felt bad for asking, but she knew that she would have had to sooner or later. Joshua's family was obviously a large part of his life growing up, and leaving his siblings had definitely left a hole, even if he hated to admit it. Eldalyn often wished she had been granted a sibling. She especially did now, because maybe then she could better understand what Joshua was feeling.

"So, what are you going to do tonight, Babe?" Joshua had snapped out of his somber thoughts and was obviously trying to lighten the mood.

Eldalyn blushed at the pet name and looked down at her almost finished bowl of gumbo. "I was going to go check out my old work place and see if anyone can give me more information. I think I'm remembering more every day, but there's still some large holes."

He nodded, "That sounds like a good idea." He thought for a moment. "But how are you going to get there? The doctor hasn't okayed you to drive yet."

Eldalyn set her fork down. "Well I was hoping you could drop me off at Pet Palace, and then I could take the bus from there to The Wolf Pack."

He shook his head. "No bus."

"But—" She opened her mouth to protest but Joshua quickly cut her off.

"I'm not saying you can't go, but I don't want you walking to and from the bus stop. It's not safe. Give me your phone—I'm going to download the Uber app you can use to call a car. It'll be hooked up to my account, so don't worry about the cost. And I can't have my phone on me during work, but I'm going to put Liam's number in your phone. If you need anything at all, call him okay?"

Now it was her turn to shake her head. "You can download the app, and put in Liam's phone number, but we are hooking it to my bank account—end of story."

The look on Joshua's face indicated he was about to protest, but instead he decided not to argue and held up his hands in surrender as Eldalyn ran to get her phone.

It was six thirty in the evening when Eldalyn walked in the door of Pet Palace. The bell on the door brought back a sense of *déjà vu*, but no solid memories formed. The desk in the front was empty; Bernice must've gone home early. She could only assume she was waiting for whoever they had hired to replace her to come to the desk.

There was a wall of collars and leashes by the desk that Eldalyn assumed were for sale. She was kneeling down looking at a pink-studded one close to the bottom when someone cleared their throat.

Eldalyn stood and whirled around, so quickly that she almost lost her balance and had to catch herself on the desk. When she looked up she came face-to-face with a baby-faced young man.

She squinted. *Oh my god!* She recognized the man from one of her dreams, yet didn't feel the fear that always came with them. For some reason she didn't quite understand—she felt calm, and this perplexed her. He wasn't the man that was in her scariest dreams; rather he was the one with the acne scars that often sat next to her. She thought for a moment and had to mentally make the hair a little shaggier… "Trevor?"

A smile broke out across the young man's face. "Hey Eldalyn!"

There was something different about him. In her memories Trevor was a shy, withdrawn recluse, but now he seemed to be more outgoing and confident; that's why she hadn't recognized him in her dreams. Eldalyn quickly realized she was being rude as the silence hung between them. "How are you?" At least that hadn't changed: Trevor still wasn't a conversationalist.

"Good. You don't look so great though."

She reached up to touch her eye which was less swollen but still an ugly green color. She knew the stitches on her head looked worse than they were. At least he couldn't see the map of green and brown bruises which still covered the rest of her body.

"Yeah, I've had better days." Eldalyn looked at her feet and realized she would just have to come out with it. "Listen Trevor, I know we were never really close but, can you tell me what you remember about me? I uh, was attacked, and I've lost a large portion of my memory."

He looked startled, then stared at Eldalyn long and hard for a moment. "We were friends. You don't remember?"

Her eyebrows scrunched in confusion. "We were?"

Trevor shook his head and walked around the desk to come stand next to Eldalyn. At least that what she assumed he was doing, but she noticed quickly he was bringing Bernice's stool for her to sit on. "You must've been hit hard."

"I was." She waited patiently for him to explain.

Trevor sighed, "Well I guess I'll start from the beginning."

"Please." Eldalyn sat on the stool and crossed her legs. She really didn't remember Trevor and her being friends, but maybe she didn't remember as much as she had given herself credit for.

"When you first started working here, I had the biggest crush on you. And I was young. But... well, the crush made it hard to talk to you. And you weren't really talkative either, you know? You were shy. Withdrawn. Living in your own little world." Trevor shook his head, leaning on the desk and looking out the window.

When Eldalyn didn't say anything, he continued. "We really didn't get to know each other, you know? I mean we barely spoke. And when we did, it was all I could do to get an answer out in a complete sentence, much less try to impress you."

Eldalyn felt bad now that she barely remembered Trevor. In fact, he was barely a blip in her memory, while Joshua had stood out like a light the minute she had seen him in the emergency room. Maybe things would have been different—.

"Anyways, then you left for that other job. At first I was mad at myself for not making a move, but then I realized I couldn't let that happen next time I met a girl I liked; otherwise, I would never be able to date anyone. So the next time a cute girl with a dog came in, I started talking to her. And we've been dating ever since. So thanks Eldalyn." She smiled. "But, back on topic... after a few months you came back to visit—Bernice I think, I honestly don't think you cared to visit me. You came back with that blonde, Cassie. You two were really chummy."

"Did we say we were living together?" Eldalyn couldn't help but interject.

Trevor shook his head. "We didn't talk much, just surface stuff. You told me about the job, and Cassie bragged about how great of a dancer you were. And well, I was too embarrassed to say much back, that time anyways." Trevor stood and walked to stand by the door. "You came back again, and again, and again. Every month there for awhile. Sometimes you brought cookies. Other times it was coffee. Bernice asked me why you kept coming back, with your new flashy job and all, and she assumed it was because you were sweet on me. I assured her that wasn't the case. I thought you came back because you were lonely."

A familiar feeling Eldalyn couldn't place began to creep in her heart. "I was lonely?"

"Why else would you come back here? Over time you began to come hang out in the back with me when Bernice was busy, and we would talk. Nothing too deep, but things friends would talk about." Eldalyn raised her eyebrows. "Not about your life though. You never wanted to talk about your life. You only wanted to talk about mine, or dogs, or politics. Anything to keep your mind off of whatever was going on, I guess."

She closed her eyes and tried to think, tried to place pictures with the pain that was in her heart. She could feel it—the loneliness; it hurt, and was all consuming. But still the video reel that should have contained her memories continued to elude her.

"But then things seemed to have gotten better. For about six months, you stopped coming in regularly. In fact, I only saw you once during that time. And you seemed really really happy. In fact, you were bouncing off the walls with energy."

"Did I tell you why?"

"No." Trevor released a large breath from his lungs and ran a hand through his hair. "But I figured it out." Eldalyn's ears perked up. "There was a new man in your life."

She felt her eyes go wide. "What? Who?!"

Trevor shook his head. "You never told me. You just told me you had a date one night, and then the last time you came in here…" He trailed off. "What happened to your ring?"

Eldalyn looked at both of her hands. "What ring?"

He lifted her left hand as if she was hiding it from him, releasing it quickly. "Last time you came in here you had a huge diamond on that finger." He pointed to her left ring finger. She was frozen in shock. She had been engaged? "I asked you what man could afford it, and you had told me your fiancé. But you didn't give a name."

The wheels turned, and little pieces began to fall into place. The ring. The plates. She had been planning a wedding. "I said 'fiancé'—you're sure?"

"Yes. You weren't married yet anyways."

"When was that?" Eldalyn tried to do the math in her head.

"April."

Her mouth fell open in shock. She had been engaged in April. But to whom? And where was this fiancé now? Her head spun. Had she sent out invitations? Were people showing up for a wedding somewhere and she wasn't there? And what about Cassie? Wasn't she her best friend in all of this?

She must've been silent for a decent amount of time because Trevor touched her shoulder. "You okay?"

"Yeah, just shocked."

He nodded. "And you're sure he isn't still around? Your fiancé, I mean?"

Eldalyn pinched her eyes closed. Had she been engaged to Joshua? Is that why he was in the hospital room? Was he lying to her to help soften the blow? Did he not want to marry her anymore? Had he been the one to beat her up? Eldalyn's head spun. She felt dizzy. Taking a deep breath, she stood up; she needed to get air.

"Thanks Trevor," she mumbled as she pushed past him and the door to outside. Trevor was right behind her.

Gasping for breath, Eldalyn sat down on the bench in front of Pet Palace and put her head on her knees, breathing deeply to calm herself.

"Are you sure you're okay?"

"Yeah, I'm just overwhelmed. Everything is so confusing. And my mind is like alphabet soup. I have letters, but no words. And every time I almost put things together, it's as if things float further away."

Trevor said nothing, opting to rub her back in a brotherly way. They sat there for a few minutes until Eldalyn's breath returned to normal and the dizziness abated. Finally, Eldalyn stood. It was getting late and she had another stop to make.

"Thanks Trevor. I owe you." He smiled. "And I'm sorry we didn't get to catch up on your life this visit. I promise once I get my life together I'll come back. And I'll bring lunch."

"I'd like that. But there's no hurry. I'm your friend, that's what I'm here for." He embraced her briefly, being cautious of her finger, which was still in a splint.

She smiled. "Thanks. I'm glad we ended up being friends."

"Me too." He returned her smile.

Trevor went back inside to check on the dogs, and Eldalyn summoned a car with the app Joshua had downloaded. The car arrived in less than five minutes.

She hadn't told Joshua, but she planned to visit the parks she used to walk to, especially the one she had met Joshua in. She just had to, especially now that this had happened. She wanted to call Officer Gutierrez, but it was past eight p.m. and she knew that he had gone home for the day. She would have to call first thing in the morning.

As the car pulled up to the first park, Eldalyn thanked the driver and stepped out of the car. She began to walk down the sidewalk, breathing in the warm summer evening air. The playground equipment tucked in one corner was empty, and the swing moved slightly in the soft warm breeze. The half wall separating the child's play area from the rest of the park was also empty. The grass was well maintained, and there wasn't a weed in sight. There were benches along the sidewalk at equal intervals of what Eldalyn guessed was about twenty-five feet. There were a few other people strolling through the park—mostly single adults walking dogs, but also an occasional couple.

She walked from one end of the park to the other and then back.

Nothing.

She knew she had met Joshua here, but nothing came back about their conversation or why she didn't return. She couldn't help but think about the fact that she had been, or maybe was, engaged—perhaps even married. What was she going to tell Joshua?

She still wasn't sure that Joshua wasn't the one who attacked her. But she didn't feel any fear around him. Not like she did about the blond man who appeared in her dreams. That's who she needed to be looking for.

But looking for a blond man in a large city was literally like looking for a needle in a haystack.

Eldalyn left the first park and began to walk to the second. Joshua's words about taking a car rang in her ears. But it was so close, and she didn't want the driver to laugh at her for requesting a car for something that short.

The second park was more crowded than the first, but not nearly as lively. There were a few tents here and there which Eldalyn could only assume the homeless were sleeping in. The grass in this park was worn down, and there were bald spots everywhere. The playground equipment in this park was overrun by the homeless. She could tell the gentleman sleeping with his legs sticking out of the purple connecting tube had resided up there awhile. There was even a curtain to block the sun when it rose. There was no half wall here, and not nearly as many benches. And the benches which did exist were mostly occupied, either by drug users waiting to meet up for their next fix or homeless people who didn't have a tent or rights to access the tube.

Eldalyn tried to look at every homeless person's face that she passed. She had vague memories of a man named Terrance who used to live in this park. His picture in her mind was fuzzy, but there. She remembered that he had always been kind to her over the years, and that he had daughters her age.

She couldn't check the tents, or the purple tube, but out of the people lying on the benches or the grass, Terrance wasn't among them.

Eldalyn hoped this meant he had bettered his life and gotten a job, but she knew that most likely he had finally been picked up by police once again, or succumbed to his drug addiction. The latter thought made her chest hurt, but she pushed it aside and made a mental note to ask the officers on her case if they could find out what happened to him.

Exiting the park, she pulled out her phone and summoned the car service again. Hopefully The Wolf Pack would be more enlightening than the park had been.

The car ride was brief, and she spent most of it looking out the window, reacquainting herself with the city she'd lived in her whole life but felt as if she had been absent from a long time. They told her she had only been out for four days, but she felt like she had been gone a lifetime.

When they pulled up in front of The Wolf Pack, the bar was in full swing even though it was only about nine p.m. Eldalyn looked down at her casual Capri leggings and tunic top—hopefully people wouldn't immediately recognize her.

Walking in the door, Eldalyn breathed in the smell of wood and alcohol mixed with human sweat and the vague scent of smoke. She felt her shoulders relax and her mind open for once.

Memories began to trickle in slowly.

Eldalyn looked around the room, letting her eyes caress every aspect of the dive. Her eyes came to rest on the petite brunette behind the bar. *Cam*, her mind whispered. Yes! Cam! Eldalyn had been living with her. Eldalyn had wanted to live closer to work to save time on the commute, and Cam had offered to let her rent a room in her house for cheap.

Cam had been her best friend! It was coming back to her. They had gone out to eat breakfast or lunch multiple days a week, and she distinctly remembered them heading to Barnes and Noble one rainy day and purchasing twenty books which they had been planning to each read in turn, sort of a private book club.

Then another memory came through,

Cam hugged Eldalyn. "You know you always have a place here with me."

Eldalyn pulled back lightly from their embrace, feeling a slight pang of loss at the thought of not having her best friend to come home and talk to every night. "I know. You've been great—the best friend I've ever had."

A tear slipped out of one of Cam's sea glass blue eyes, "You won't forget me, right?"

"Never!" Eldalyn laughed. "I'll still see you at work every night. You aren't getting rid of me that easy."

Cam laughed and wiped the tear from her eye. "You're right. I'm acting like a sissy. You're moving out, not walking the plank." Both girls began to crack up at the pirate reference. Eldalyn embraced Cam once more.

"Can you help me lift the box over there?" Eldalyn whispered in her ear.

"And here I thought you were about to continue our heartfelt goodbye; instead you're just using me as you work horse," Cam laughed as she responded sarcastically. But regardless, she moved away from Eldalyn and went to pick up the box of books in the

corner of the room. "Shouldn't Tyler be helping with this? Where is that idiot anyways?"

"He's not an idiot, and he's busy."

"Doing what?" Cam responded skeptically.

"Busy not helping me move obviously." Both girls giggled once again as they headed down the hall towards the front door of the apartment.

Eldalyn opened her eyes. So she had moved out before the attack. And it was time to find out why. As she began to cross the room she caught sight of Mike. Another memory came through.

He had loved Cassie. But she wouldn't give him the time of day. She had insisted she was dating someone else but wouldn't tell anyone who it was. Eldalyn couldn't be sure, but she had her suspicions that it might have been Cam who broke the news. When Mike found out, he had been enraged, slapping Cassie across the face and throwing martini glasses at the wall. There had been so much force behind the slap, Eldalyn remembered watching the pink handprint slowly begin to show across her friend's flawless face. Someone—probably one of the patrons—had called the police.

They had to close early that night; all the employees had hung their heads in shame when they asked the customers to pay their tabs and leave. Eldalyn had lost out on a lot of money. Cassie had quit in order to avoid causing any further disturbance, and had told Eldalyn not to worry about her, that she would find another job—maybe acting or modeling. Although her friend was optimistic, Eldalyn had worried as she'd watched the handprint transform from a red mark to a deep purple bruise. She didn't know much about the performance world, but she knew Cassie wouldn't get a job while she still looked like that. After a few weeks with no prospects on the horizon, Cassie had gone home to visit her mother, hoping that would lift her spirits. Even then Cassie hadn't spilled the beans about her mystery prince Charming.

"I'll be back soon, I promise." Cassie hugged Eldalyn tightly.

"If you need anything, you call me, okay? I still want to meet this mystery man." Eldalyn let go of Cassie and helped her load another bag in the back of her Jeep.

"You will, soon."

Eldalyn smiled, and the girls embraced once more before Cassie climbed into the Jeep and started the engine. Eldalyn waved at the retreating vehicle as Cassie drove down the street.

Eldalyn let out a breath she didn't know she had been holding. Cassie hadn't come back—she remembered that now. She was supposed to be gone for two weeks, and that had turned into a month, and then six. She had finally called Cassie's mom in concern. That must have been when her mom filed the police report. Now it made sense. Eldalyn needed to call Officer Gutierrez, even if she just got his voicemail. Something bad had definitely happened to Cassie.

The room was pounding with country music when suddenly a more sultry song came on and the bar started to line with girls who were about to dance. Eldalyn figured she would call Officer Gutierrez, and then she would go find Cam.

She turned towards the bathroom, picturing all the times she had walked down this hallway wearing various costumes, and in various emotional states. Working here had been a blessing for her, and also a curse.

She remembered the leers, the jabs, the men flirting shamelessly. She'd gone from a cocktail server to almost head bartender, second only to Cam. She'd found her wings here, transformed from a shy caterpillar to a butterfly. And she had planned to go to college. That's what all that money was for in her bank account. Cam had helped her register.

"Computer Programming?"

"What's that?" Eldalyn asked as Cam clicked on the little icon next to the class list.

"It's about working with computers. You need it for a business degree."

"Have you taken it?" She looked up at Cam, her eyes filled with questions.

Cam laughed. "My degree is in landscape design."

Eldalyn joined in her laugher. "Touché."

"Pizza?!" Cam called from the kitchen.

"You know I'm not eating carbs right now!" Eldalyn shouted back.

"Your loss!" She heard the distant sound of Cam grabbing her keys off the hook where they kept them in the hall and a door slamming shortly after that.

Eldalyn felt a tear of joy roll down her cheek as she remembered she had gotten her GED thanks to Cam. Pushing open the bathroom door, she made a beeline for the paper towels so that no partially drunk girl in the bathroom would think she needed comforting.

She couldn't believe it. She had finished her GED at last. She remembered now—she had taken classes online on Cam's computer, and she had gone to take a test in the spring of this year. The striking image of a beautiful sunny morning suddenly filled her mind, and she saw herself driving into an empty parking lot except for one other woman who looked to be about forty years old.

Retrieving her phone from her pocket, she pulled up the number that Officer Gutierrez had called her from that morning and pressed *DIAL*. The phone rang four times before going to voicemail. Eldalyn cleaned up her face while she waited to record her message.

"Officer Gutierrez this is Eldalyn, Eldalyn Wren," She could hardly contain the excitement in her voice, "I'm at The Wolf Pack, and well, I found out some information, and I remembered a bunch of stuff. Not everything, but too much for me to say in this message. I also found out something interesting—"

Suddenly, the door on the wheelchair stall slammed open and a man walked out. Eldalyn jumped, immediately thinking that perhaps she was in the wrong bathroom, but she looked around and there were no urinals. The man must be drunk. She gave him a once over in the mirror; he looked to be about thirty years old, in good shape with broad shoulders and a tall stature—so tall that Eldalyn had to look up in the mirror to see his face. And when she did, a cold realization fell over her.

It was the man from her dreams.

"My Eldalyn, I knew you would return."

The phone fell from her fingers with a crash.

Eldalyn remembered everything.

OFFICER MARCUS GUTIERREZ

JULY 21, 2014

Marcus Gutierrez stepped out of his truck in the precinct parking lot, taking a deep breath before he headed up to the door.

Although he loved his job, it was cases like these that were making his hair go prematurely grey. It didn't matter that he went home at the end of the day; he inevitably couldn't put the evidence down, no matter what case he was working on.

He had spent the entire night before going through Eldalyn's bank records with a fine-toothed comb. He'd been up until nearly two a.m., yet he still felt he hadn't found anything worthwhile. The bank records had been surprising in one regard—he hadn't realized that a woman could make that much money bartending, and that was only the amount she deposited. It didn't account for the money she had left to spend in cash.

Eldalyn's account had just over forty-eight thousand dollars in it, certainly enough to get her started with a new life. At first he had thought perhaps someone had been putting money in her account, but he had checked with the bank and all the deposits had been via ATM and she was the only one with a card for her account. Just to be sure, Gutierrez had requested the ATM camera tapes but was told they were only kept for thirty days. All the debit card purchases and charges on the credit card were of no suspicion; they were typical of any twenty-two-year-old girl: charges for various clothing and shoe stores as well the occasional café. She'd had money, but been very conservative with it.

Entering the building, Gutierrez waved at the front desk girl who smiled and waved back. Stopping in the break room, he filled a cup to the brim with coffee. He'd only gotten four hours of sleep. Something about this case was plaguing his mind both waking and sleeping. They were missing something, but what?

He sat down behind his desk and pulled out a notepad and pen. Cathey wasn't due in for another hour, and Gutierrez hoped to have at least gotten some more information by then. Opening his email, he scrolled through his inbox looking for one from the DMV, only to hang his head when there wasn't one there. When she had first told him about her suspected car, Gutierrez had run her info through a database only to come up empty. That could only mean one thing: the car she was paying for wasn't even in her name.

Their system was built to look up cars by people's names, or, people by car plates. So he had contacted the lender to obtain the information they had about the car, as well as the DMV to see if they had a record of a car insured in Eldalyn's name. But thus far, nothing from either.

Picking up his handset to call the idiots at the DMV first, Gutierrez noticed his *MESSAGE* button was flashing. He generally only gave this number out to investigation victims, so it must be regarding one of the open cases that were sprawled across his desk. Gutierrez pushed the blinking button and quickly typed in his passcode.

"Officer Gutierrez this is Eldalyn, Eldalyn Wren." He noticed she sounded happier than the Eldalyn he had met in the office—actually, happier than any other time he had had contact with her. "I'm at The Wolf Pack, and well, I found out some information, and I remembered a bunch of stuff. Not everything, but too much for me to say in this message. I also found out something interesting—"

His pen froze on the notepad where he had been taking notes as he listened to what followed. He heard a male voice, then a crash which must've been the phone dropping, followed by what sounded like a struggle.

He played the message again. And again. After the third time, he listened to the message details: July 20th at 10:40 p.m. He slammed his fist down on the desk. Nine hours had already passed; he needed to move, and fast. Gutierrez immediately pounded in the three-number extension for the crime scene tech division, barking into the phone at the person who answered that someone needed to come to his office pronto; they would need to record this message and begin analyzing it.

Not even pausing to hang the phone up, he frantically and repeatedly hit the button to end the call, and then dialed his partner who answered on the third ring.

"I'm not on the clock till eight thirty, Dude!" Cathey said, clearly irritated. Man, he was not a morning person.

"I don't care. Get here as fast as you can. Our assault case just turned into a possible abduction."

"What?! No..." Cathey said in disbelief.

Gutierrez didn't have time to listen to the response, much less to explain. "Just come, now," he unapologetically instructed his partner and hung up. Next he dialed his chief's extension. Thankfully he too answered, and Gutierrez quickly explained the situation; his boss said he would be in his office in less than five minutes.

Without taking a breath, he looked up the number for The Wolf Pack, and while the line was ringing he logged back onto his computer to put out an alert to all the cops in the area. He would need to provide them with Eldalyn's full name, physical description, the photo from her driver's license, and as soon as he knew, also let them know what she was wearing last night.

The number for The Wolf Pack went to voicemail just as the tech arrived to pull the message from his machine. He was a young, red-haired man Gutierrez had never seen before. He had been hoping they would send one of the more experienced techs, but it was still early in the morning, and there was no time to waste.

"Abduction, the woman in the message is an assault victim—Eldalyn Wren. Says she was at The Wolf Pack, and an unidentified male either kidnaps or attacks her during the course of the message." The tech scribbled everything down, including Gutierrez's passcode, and began the process of ensuring that the line could be traced.

"I called the place to see if the phone was found or turned in," he hurriedly said to the tech. "No answer there yet, but it's a little early for a bar to be open. If they have it or it can otherwise be located, I'll have someone bring it to you."

Grabbing his jacket, Gutierrez headed for the door, meeting Chief Carlson in the hall. He gave him a quick rundown of what happened as he walked towards his car, waving Cathey over as his partner pulled into his assigned parking spot. Chief Carlson headed back inside to brief the others, and Cathey ducked into Gutierrez's car in one smooth movement.

"So where are we headed?"

"The Wolf Pack isn't open yet, but I remember when we visited before the manager saying he got there at ten. So I figure we go find the boyfriend first, then head there." Gutierrez backed out of his spot quickly and turned on the sirens.

"Do you think he did something to her?"

"Who? The boyfriend?" Gutierrez glanced over at Cathey who nodded. "Not necessarily. We met him multiple times and the voice that was on the message was different, deeper than his." He was weaving in and out of cars, heading to the apartment Eldalyn had said was Joshua's and where she would be staying until she told them differently.

"But he hasn't called to report her missing. Isn't that odd?" Cathey scratched his head and looked out the window. He pulled out the pad that contained the notes on from all of his interviews with Eldalyn.

"Very—that's why we are headed there first." Gutierrez ran a hand through his hair. "Someone knows something. Someone is lying. I thought it might be Eldalyn before, but now I'm thinking it was Mike, that manager at The Wolf Pack."

"Why do you think that?"

"The message Eldalyn left. She said she had remembered a lot of things. She said she didn't have time to tell me on voicemail, but she mentioned she was at The Wolf Pack. And if that's where her memory came back, I'm guessing some significant things happened there, things we weren't told about on our first visit."

Cathey flipped through his notepad. "I remember that guy being a bit evasive. I thought maybe it was because he was running an underground prostitution business—a lot of those bars are—so I instructed vice to do an undercover sting. They've got nothing so far, though."

"I say we lean on him, and the boyfriend, Joshua. Hard. Something here doesn't add up, and it's driving me crazy. Run back over what we got from Mike before." Gutierrez was less than two blocks from Joshua's apartment, so he slowed down and shut off the lights. If there was any chance he was getting ready to run, they couldn't risk alerting him.

"Well, we inquired about Eldalyn's friends to which he suggested Cassie. Then we asked to speak to Cassie, whom he said he hasn't seen in 'a while'— not very specific. We asked if any patrons took a special interest in Eldalyn that night, to which he said he hadn't noticed."

"You know, I think we were asking the wrong questions."

"I agree. I'll call a deputy to get a patrol car stationed outside The Wolf Pack." Cathey flipped his notepad closed and pulled a report out of his briefcase that he had been planning to show his partner when he arrived at work that day. "I got this report last night from the cops that went and spoke to Jeffery—Jeffery Santos that is." He flipped through the pages of notes.

"Basically, the guy is a huge asshole and thinks everyone should bow at his feet, but he claimed not to remember Eldalyn, at least not by name. But when his memory was refreshed when we showed him a picture of Eldalyn, he called 'whoever that girl was'—and I quote—'*one of those sluts that wanted me in high school.*'" Cathey winced as he said it.

"The statute of limitations isn't up for the rape," Cathey continued, "so Eldalyn could press charges if she wanted to. But it would be a case of 'he said, she said.' Anyways, he got some girl pregnant last year, is living with a different girl now, but raising the other girl's kid." Gutierrez raised his eyebrows. "Complicated sounding, I know, but he's got an alibi for the night of the attack. And although I think he's an arrogant punk, the officers didn't get a vibe from him that he was lying or dangerous—just that he was a 'piece of work.'"

Gutierrez nodded. "Noted." He pulled the car into the underground parking lot, and then into the *Future Resident* parking spot. He figured the management wouldn't try to have a cop car towed. "Let's do this." Both officers stepped into the elevator, and after Cathey quickly glanced at his notepad again, he pressed the button for the fifteenth floor.

JOSHUA

JULY 21, 2014

Joshua was relieved from his chair at work at exactly seven a.m. Usually Bobby was fifteen minutes early, and while it bothered Joshua that he had decided today to be right on time, he really couldn't complain.

Walking into the break room to grab the container he had used to bring leftover gumbo to work, Joshua suddenly felt very light headed. Stopping to brace himself on a wall, he realized he had been up for twenty-one hours straight and he definitely wasn't safe to drive the fifteen-plus (depending on traffic) minutes home. Driving had always been a task that had made Joshua sleepy. Maybe he should take a quick nap in his car before he headed to the apartment.

He wanted to be home with Eldalyn so badly. Joshua had begun to realize that his body physically hurt when he had to spend prolonged hours away from her. Pulling out his phone, he wondered if this was what love was supposed to feel like.

There was no text from Eldalyn, which didn't seem too out of the ordinary to him as Eldalyn had never been as glued to her phone as were most young women her age. It was one of the things he found attractive about her. He dialed Eldalyn's number and the phone went straight to voicemail. That did seem odd; she usually would have left the phone on even if she was sleeping, but Joshua thought maybe she had turned it off if she was especially tired. That or she let the battery die, which seemed to be a common trend these days as she struggled to regain what broken pieces of her memory remained.

Arriving at his car, he left a quick voicemail for Eldalyn, telling her he was going to take a quick nap but should be home around eight. Then he set an alarm on his phone and crawled in the front seat of his car.

He was asleep before his head had barely touched the headrest.

When he awoke to his alarm, Joshua quickly rubbed the sleep out of his eyes and started his car so that he could roll down the window. Once he felt alert enough to drive, he backed out of the parking spot and pulled onto the street.

Glancing at his phone, he decided to call Eldalyn once more and let her know he was on his way, in case she was awake but had not gotten his message. The phone went straight to voicemail again, and Joshua tossed his phone in the cup holder. He would be home soon enough.

After he parked his car in the designated spot, Joshua headed up the elevator, eager to hear if Eldalyn had remembered anything the night before. Being away at night was rough because all he wanted to do was talk and catch up with her, but he also knew he had to get sleep at some point when he had to work later that night.

Arriving at his floor, Joshua turned the corner to notice that his apartment door was open. He felt his face pale instantly. Eldalyn would never leave the door open. He didn't know what her habits were like before the accident, but she certainly had been very meticulous and cautious since the day he had reconnected with her in the hospital.

He approached the door and slowly pushed it open. "Hello?"

Suddenly there was a click and Joshua saw a gun out of the corner of his eye. As quickly as it had appeared, the gun disappeared and Officer Cathey was apologizing, "Sorry Joshua, didn't know it was you."

His relief only lasted for a second because he immediately realized that if the cops were here, there had to be a reason. And it probably wasn't a good one.

"Where's Eldalyn?" Joshua's voice was shaky.

Officer Gutierrez appeared from around the corner of the bedroom. "Funny, we were just about to ask you that."

"Oh God…" Joshua felt his knees go weak and he sank to a sitting position in the entryway. "And I just found her." His voice was barely above a whisper.

"Why don't you start by telling us all of your whereabouts from, say, five o'clock yesterday afternoon until now." Officer Cathey seemed to have no sympathy for Joshua, opting instead to go straight to interrogation mode.

"Easy." Joshua pinched the bridge of his nose—he felt a massive headache coming on. "I was here with Eldalyn until six in the evening. Then I dropped her off at Pet Palace on my way to work at six thirty. I was at work and relieved my coworker at six forty-five. I was then at work all night. My coworker, Bobby, if you need to talk to him—"

"We will."

"—He relieved me at seven this morning. I was too tired to drive so I took a thirty-minute nap in my car and then I came straight here to find this."

"And your boss will testify to this?" Gutierrez seemed skeptical.

"Yes, and you can check the times I clocked in and out with this badge. There's a camera on the door and time-clock machine." Joshua quickly pulled his badge from where he had placed it in his pocket after work. Gutierrez began to scrutinize it while Cathey continued to size up Joshua.

"That sounds like something a guilty person would say." Cathey was also not quite ready to buy Joshua's story.

"Does it? Because I would *never* hurt Eldalyn, not when it took me this long to find her." Joshua ran a hand through his hair, feeling as if he was having a heart attack.

"So, you're admitting that you stalked her, that that's how you 'found' her." Gutierrez seemed to have changed sides now that Eldalyn wasn't around. "You know, I bet you attacked her so brutally the first time so she would forget you were her stalker! Is that what happened, Joshua? Hm?" He was on a roll.

Joshua opened his mouth to interject but Gutierrez didn't let him. "I bet she started to remember things. She probably remembered she didn't like you very much, huh? So you got mad, an 'accident' happened. It's okay Josh—you can tell us."

"Joshua," he corrected. And realizing they weren't going to let up on this line of questioning, he knew he had to start making some correct moves before he talked himself in a corner. "And I'd like a lawyer if you're going to continue questioning me. Please."

"Another thing a guilty man would say." Cathey wasn't as heated or passionate as Gutierrez, but at this point Joshua was their only lead and Joshua could tell they intended to follow it to the end.

"No, I just want you to stop twisting what I'm saying. Now let me call my lawyer and you can take me to the station." He stood up and searched his pockets until he encountered his phone. He couldn't believe Eldalyn was gone, but yet these buffoons were wasting precious time on him. He pretended to scroll through his contacts for a moment even though he knew who he had to call. Typing in the number forever engrained in his memory made him wince, but there was nothing else he could do.

"Hello?"

"Mom?" It was a little more than a whisper.

"Joshua?" This question was rhetorical as she was already talking before he even had a chance to ponder a reply. "Please tell me you're coming home. Your father and I—"

"Mom, I need a lawyer," Joshua interjected and his mom immediately went into work mode. He quickly told her that he was about to be taken into police custody.

"What precinct am I meeting you at?" Joshua repeated what the cops told him. "I'll be right there. And not another word to those officers until I get there."

"I won't, and Mom?"

"Yes?"

"Thanks," Joshua sighed in relief. Calling his mom hadn't gone as badly as he thought. She hadn't been mad or berating, or even on the offensive.

"You're welcome Joshua. See you in ten minutes."

Joshua hung up the phone and followed the officers to their car.

Three hours later, the officers were finally finished with their interrogation and were ready to listen to what Joshua had to say.

Gutierrez in particular had been "out for the kill," as Joshua's mother had put it, but a lot of what he said had held little merit. Once they had corroborated his alibi and retrieved Eldalyn's cracked phone from The Wolf Pack, they took him out of interrogation and let him sit in a *VISITORS* room with his mom and some much-needed coffee. Joshua had already called out for work that evening, both because of lack of sleep, but also because he was worried sick about Eldalyn.

The crime techs were going through Eldalyn's phone now to trace her last steps. They had already sent officers to the Pet Palace to start there. Joshua had wanted to go along, but whether he liked it or not, he was still under a small amount of suspicion. His mom came was sitting next to him on the couch, cradling her own cup of the mediocre police station coffee.

"Joshua, I'm sorry. I don't really understand what happened two years ago, but whatever happened, I really want to move past it. I *miss* you; we all do."

"You know exactly what happened."

"No Joshua, I don't. Believe it or not, I'm not a mind reader."

"Sure seemed that way when we were kids."

His mom's face was filled with a weighted smile. "You were never 'one of the kids' Joshua."

"That didn't keep you from trying to make me one." Joshua pinched the bridge of his nose and leaned back on the couch. "I needed to get out on my own and live my own life. I couldn't keep living under your roof and rules forever. I felt trapped. You didn't even give me a chance, or the option, to make it on my own."

"And I see that now, and I'm sorry." His mother's eyes looked deep into his, and suddenly Joshua felt as if he was five years old again.

"I know Mom." He closed his eyes. He would give his left arm to be able to sleep right now.

"So can we move past this?" She crossed her legs and leaned back on the couch.

"Maybe. But I really can't talk much more about this right now. Can we maybe work on this from afar?"

She looked at him, her eyes brimming with tears, pleading. "Please Joshua, come home," she said softly.

He shook his head. "I'm twenty-three now, Mom. I have my own life. You have to accept that. This is exactly what I'm talking about, I won't be coming home, my home isn't with you anymore. We can exchange numbers and work on becoming friends, but that is it." He could tell this wasn't the answer she wanted, but she recognized that it was the best he would offer. A part of Joshua wanted to ask how the kids were doing, about the new baby, and especially about Juni who he hoped had found her voice. But the fear of heartache kept him quiet. He needed to focus on the present.

"Alright, I guess we can start there. The cops have said you can go home and sleep, but don't leave the state or anything crazy."

Thank god, he could go home. "I won't, don't worry." Joshua pulled out his phone and requested that an Uber come get him. His mother didn't seem to notice.

"Shall I drive you home?" She stood up and pulled her keys— complete with a pink fuzzy pom pom—out of her Prada purse. Some things never changed.

"I'll take care of myself, Mom. You go home to the kids." His mom smiled and leaned into an awkward hug which Joshua tried his best to return. She had saved his butt, so the least he could do is act civil, even if he could still feel his insides boiling with the same anger of two years before. He waved as she walked off.

Joshua tossed his coffee cup in the trash and headed for the door. Officer Cathey had promised to call him the minute they got more information, and it couldn't come soon enough.

OFFICER MARCUS GUTIERREZ

JULY 21, 2014

"Déjà vu," Cathey muttered as the two of them pulled open the archaic wooden door to The Wolf Pack. They hadn't bothered to knock this time.

"Mr. Palomino?" Gutierrez called once they were inside. They heard muffled sounds from the same direction the manager had approached from last time. Only this time, when he emerged from the office he wasn't alone.

A petite but vivacious brunette stood alongside him, and Gutierrez couldn't help but notice her attire. The skimpy dress was most likely for whatever theme night they were having at the club, and it definitely drew attention in all the right places. Gutierrez looked to the side to notice the fact that his partner was also drawn to the woman. Gutierrez figured he shouldn't be surprised; they were both red-blooded males.

"Hello officers, what can I do for you?" Mike crossed his arms against his chest—a sign that he knew this visit wasn't near as welcoming as the last.

Gutierrez smiled. Mike may be a slimy sort of character, but his perception wasn't lacking. "We have a few more questions for you."

Mike's eyes narrowed a slight, almost indistinguishable amount. "Do I need my lawyer?"

Cathey shook his head. "It's your prerogative, but our questions are more to do with an occurrence that we believe happened on this property last night."

He shook his head. "Nothing happened last night. Just business as usual. I don't even think the bouncers had to throw anyone out."

The brunette at Mike's side had been standing by patiently, but now seemed to be bored of the officers' conversation. "Mike, I'm going to go stock the bar. Let me know when you're finished." She looked towards

Mike and flashed a smile. Gutierrez thought he also saw her wink, but he couldn't be sure.

She turned to walk away but Cathey cleared his throat. "Excuse me miss, but I don't know your name."

The woman turned back around, performing a perfect sweeping motion with her hair. She smiled with pronounced dimples that probably served to double her tip money. "Cam, and you can find me behind the bar every day but Wednesday." With a second wink for Cathey, she spun back around and continued her path past the dance floor towards the bar on the far side of the room.

Gutierrez's gaze turned back to Mike only to see that he was glaring jealous holes into Cathey's back. This guy definitely has a problem with keeping his professional and personal life separate.

Mike suddenly seemed to notice Gutierrez's eyes on him and he quickly straightened his posture. "Let's talk in my office."

The officers followed Mike down the hall to a room that wasn't much larger than a walk-in closet. It was outfitted with a single desk that held two computers, a large filing cabinet, and a black safe. There was also a cardboard box of what looked like colorful mixed outfits in the corner. There were only two chairs, but Mike motioned for both of them to sit down. Cathey shook his head and politely declined, stating he preferred to stand.

"Let's get started." Gutierrez pulled out his phone and pushed the record button, stating his name and Mike's name for his record. He could hear the sound of a page flip as Cathey pulled out his notebook behind him. "Mike, did anything out of the ordinary happen at your club last night?"

"Not to my knowledge."

Gutierrez didn't notice any obvious signs of distress, so he figured Mike must be at least telling the truth about that. Wanting to leave the recording running, Gutierrez motioned for Cathey's phone. Already reading his partner's mind, Cathey pulled out his phone and flipped to the recording from the answering machine this morning. He pressed *PLAY*, and the room was filled with the sounds of the attack. When the recording ended, Mike was silent.

"What are your thoughts on that?"

Mike's mouth was agape. "I didn't even see her here last night." His voice had lost all traces of his usual bravado. He actually sounded timid. "But, I did find a couple of phones left behind. We find at least one every night but…" He wheeled his chair over to the safe and began to put in the combination. When the door swung open, Gutierrez leaned over to see cash, as well as various items with sticky notes stuck to them on the shelf. Mike picked up one and read the note, only to set it back down. He repeated this process with a second phone. The third phone he picked up, he read the note and moved to hand it to Gutierrez. "This was found in the bathroom last night during the midnight sweep. It's locked, just like most phones these days."

Gutierrez nodded and pulled out an evidence bag from his pocket, grabbing the phone only once his hand was covered. Hopefully fingerprints were intact. "Thanks. So you don't remember any sort of commotion last night?"

Mike shook his head once again. "None. Like I said, business as usual."

Gutierrez was willing to bet Mike was too busy ogling the girls to ever really notice what was going on in his own club. He looked over his shoulder to find Cathey squinting at something on his phone screen. He was just about to stop the recorder when Cathey spoke up.

"I see you call the cops a lot. Mostly for drunks behaving inappropriately, but I also see we have a couple, more serious calls on here." Cathey continued to scroll. Gutierrez knew for a joint like this, the list would probably go on forever.

Mike gulped. *Bingo.*

"Any specifics I need to know about?"

Gutierrez knew that Cathey was just fishing. There was no way they could ever have time to read every single police report filed for The Wolf Pack.

It worked. "Okay, okay… I had an altercation with an employee once about a year ago. She didn't want to press charges, and then she quit to avoid further issues."

Now they were getting somewhere. "And who was this employee?" Gutierrez prodded.

"Cassie Lane," Mike muttered and looked down at his hands in his lap. "That was the last night I saw her. We agreed to put our differences behind us and go our separate ways."

Cathey raised an eyebrow; he wasn't buying it. "Was this a physical altercation?"

"Sort of, I slapped her once, but I immediately realized what I had done and regretted it. Then I broke a few martini glasses in anger, but that's it. And I never saw her again after that."

Gutierrez nodded to Cathey. So this had been what he was hiding before. Maybe now that he was being honest about this, his story about last night would change. "And you're sure there was no commotion last night?"

"None. The girls tell me when something major happens."

Cathey closed his notepad and motioned towards the door. "Crime scene techs are on their way to check out the bathroom. I know it's probably futile, but it's procedure."

"No problem. Whatever you need." Mike was suddenly very agreeable. Gutierrez almost believed that he really did feel remorse for hitting Cassie.

Gutierrez rose from his seated position and followed Cathey as he made his way across the dance floor to the hall where the restrooms were. The brunette was behind the bar with her back to them, polishing glasses.

They waited outside the bathroom for about five minutes when the crime scene techs waltzed in. As they got to work, Gutierrez turned to his partner. "Do you believe him?"

Cathey nodded. "I really think he seemed sincere. Besides the fact that he is definitely out of touch with his own business. I mean, I may be wrong, but he appears to be more interested in the girls than his own customers."

"I agree completely," Gutierrez replied. "And after coming clean about Cassie, I assume he would have told us something if he knew it."

"Do you think he had something to do with her disappearance?"

Gutierrez thought for a moment before responding. "I'm not sure. I think it's definitely worth looking into, but I really do think the guy seemed remorseful when he spoke about what happened."

The lead crime scene tech stood up from where he had been on the floor under the sink. In his gloved hand was a small black chip. "Most of the evidence is gone, but this does look like it might be something—a piece of something black and plastic."

Gutierrez pulled the bagged phone out of his pocket and inspected it as best he could. Sure enough, there was a chip missing from the corner. He handed it to the crime scene tech to compare.

He nodded. "Appears to be the same, but we will double check in the lab to be sure. I'm going to send my techs with this now and see what they can pull off the phone." He looked around at all the other techs who seemed to be finished as well. "We used a black light to look for fluids, but as you can imagine…"

"This place is covered in them." Cathy finished for him. The tech nodded, and the crew began to pack up their equipment.

"Sorry I don't have better news."

"Don't worry, we didn't expect much anyways. We will follow you guys to the lab." Cathey and Gutierrez exited the bathroom and headed down the hall to the main room. "Think we should interview that bartender?"

"Definitely," Cathey replied as he pulled out his notepad.

When they reached the main room, the bartender was nowhere to be seen. They walked back towards the office only to see Mike working on one of the computers. "Hey Mike, is Cam around?" Gutierrez poked his head in the small room.

"Oh, sorry Officer. I told her she could go home for her break. She'll be back in a couple hours if you want to wait around."

Gutierrez shook his head. "We will be back later, thanks." And with that both officers turned and exited the building, pulling the worn wooden door shut behind them.

JOSHUA

JULY 21, 2014

It was nearly eight p.m. when his phone finally rang with a call from the precinct. It was a relief he hadn't planned to go in to work, because his mind was completely preoccupied with thoughts of Eldalyn and slightly muddled from sleep deprivation.

"Did you find her?"

"Hello, it's Officer Gutierrez, and no, not yet."

Joshua let out a breath. He had been hoping beyond all hope they would have found her by now. "Any sign of her? Or information?"

"Yes and no. We traced her steps and spoke to everyone at the Pet Palace and some people at The Wolf Pack. We also recently found out, from tracking her phone, that Eldalyn apparently stopped at two parks in between."

"Parks?"

"Yes, Ralston Park and the one by the downtown library. They're only about a mile apart."

Joshua leaned back and closed his eyes. She had been following the path of her life as she remembered it. She shouldn't have gone to the parks by herself; she should have known better than to put herself in that situation. "I'm not surprised."

"Why do you say that?"

"Eldalyn and I met in Ralston Park two years ago. I think she was retracing her steps."

"That makes sense." Officer Gutierrez went silent for a moment. "Listen, Joshua, against my better judgment, why don't you meet me at

Ralston Park, and you can show me what Eldalyn may have been looking for there."

"Still convinced I'm guilty?" Joshua couldn't believe they still suspected him even after they verified his alibi.

"No, but you're still a person of interest. Also, I have some information I would rather not share over the phone."

"Okay I can be there in about fifteen minutes." Joshua was already pulling on his shoes and running a hand through his hair to attempt to remedy his obvious bedhead.

"See you there." The line went silent. Joshua couldn't imagine what kind of information they had for him, but if they didn't want to say it over the phone, it couldn't possibly be good.

As he was headed out the door his phone rang once more. He fished it out of his pocket in such a rush he almost dropped it. The minute he saw the number however, his speed slowed. It wasn't about Eldalyn.

"Hello?"

"Hey Joshua, it's your mom."

Joshua sighed in exasperation. "Mom, what is this about?"

He could practically hear his mom putting her hands on her hips. "You said we could exchange numbers and become friends."

Joshua rolled his eyes as he pressed the button for the elevator. "I'm busy right now. I'll call you later."

"I really need to talk to you Joshua."

She was always so dramatic. "Later Mom, I'm really busy right now." And with that he hung up the phone just as the elevator doors slid shut. His life was in pieces right now, and re-involving his mother, which had helped him in the short term, would probably only complicate his life in the long run. He mentally slapped himself and hoped she wouldn't call again.

His hopes were in vain. As he stepped off the elevator his phone pinged to tell him he had a new text message. He immediately opened it, saw the drama his mother was trying to use to rope him in, and immediately deleted it. He really did not have time for this right now.

As he opened the door to his car, his phone pinged once again. Joshua preemptively rolled his eyes, expecting to see yet another text from his mom. Instead it was from a number he didn't recognize. He slid into his car while simultaneously opening the message.

Oddly enough, the text was blank. Joshua looked at the number. It was a local area code. Who would send him a blank text? Without responding, Joshua tossed his phone on the passenger seat and put the car in reverse. He would have to worry about blank prank texts later. Right now he needed to focus on finding Eldalyn.

OFFICER MARCUS GUTIERREZ

JULY 21, 2014

"So before the boyfriend—or whatever he is—gets here, let's go over what we know." Cathey and Gutierrez were sitting in their car at Ralston Park, watching as it cleared out for the night. They hadn't stopped by the park close to the library yet, but they were dreading it. Cops weren't really welcome among the homeless.

They had both changed into plain clothes before coming out this evening, but while Cathey was slender with a non-intimidating build, Gutierrez knew everything from his mustache, to his shoulders, to his stance, all screamed *police officer*. Hopefully he could send the kid out in the first park as bait, with Cathey not far behind; at least the two of them would blend in a little more than he would. The second park he had no choice but to go in himself. He couldn't possibly send the boy into the "drug war's den," as he liked to call the park adjacent to the downtown library. Homeless people liked to go in the library and warm up during the winter. So that meant at night, when the library was closed, they didn't tend to stray further than the park that was right next door. It was very annoying to library patrons; in fact, it kept some of them away. But there was nothing the cops could do. It was a free public library and if you had a card, which most homeless people did, they had every right to be there.

"We know Eldalyn Wren was attacked on July eleventh, and when she awoke she had little, if any memory of the past two years. But she said her age correctly, so she was aware the time had passed."

Cathey nodded. "We assume she was honest, as she genuinely seemed to have no idea what occurred in her life, especially since she has made every attempt to keep you informed the minute she found anything out. She knew she hadn't been living at that house, the origin of the glass confused her, and she knew she didn't have many friends."

"Scratch out that last one. In light of what the kid—what's his face—

told us."

"Trevor." Cathey furiously began editing the notes on his notepad.

"You really need to get an iPad or something," Gutierrez joked.

Cathey just rolled his eyes. "Back on topic. So Eldalyn worked at The Wolf Pack these past two years, but for whatever reason, she continued to come back and visit Trevor at the Pet Palace. And he had a feeling she was lonely."

"But apparently engaged."

"Yes, but that tells us that the engagement wasn't going well. She's a sweet girl, not the type to break it off or cheat. So I'm assuming that the issue had to be the fiancé."

Gutierrez agreed. "And the fiancé wasn't Joshua, as there was no proof of any contact over the past two years. And a relationship leading to marriage would leave some sort of dent in the phone records; it is the twenty-first century."

"The thing that baffles me is, if the engagement wasn't going well, and she was unhappy, why did they buy the place settings? Especially if she planned to back out." Cathey ran a hand through his brown hair and scrutinized his notes, looking for a connection.

"Well here's my theory. Eldalyn had no record of purchasing those things on her account. So my guess is the fiancé purchased them, brought them over to show her, and she ended it, causing him to fly into a rage and beat her." Gutierrez pictured the scene in his head.

"Very plausible. But my question is: where is the ring? And why in the hell break all those plates?"

Gutierrez thought for a second. "Well let's assume he took the ring back. Remember, Trevor said it looked expensive."

"But then we are back to the question of why would he destroy twenty-five hundred dollars' worth of plates?" Cathey pinched the bridge of his nose.

This case was giving Gutierrez a headache too. "I don't know. I just don't understand." Just then, Cathey's phone rang with the tune of the "Imperial Death March." It was their chief, probably wondering if they had made any progress.

Gutierrez listened to the one-sided conversation, cataloging the pieces they had yet to put into place. He had to admit it seemed like they were still in the dark, although they had a lot more information than they gave themselves credit for. At this point they had pretty much narrowed their suspect down to one person: the currently nameless fiancé. If they could find him, he had a feeling their case would break wide open.

Cathey hung up the phone. "DMV paperwork finally came through."

"And?"

"She co-signed on a car. Not sure why she was paying it out of her account, but the car is registered to a Tyler Valderrama." Cathey began to connect the dots.

Gutierrez was faster, "Think he's the fiancé?"

"I think the probability is high, I mean, who co-signs on a car for just a friend?"

"What kind of car?" Gutierrez pulled out his phone.

"The Chief already put out a BOLO, but it's a blue late model Chevrolet truck. Here's the plate." Cathey turned the notepad so Gutierrez could type it into the notes section of his phone.

"So on the phone, the kidnapper said, 'I knew you would return.' So I'm guessing there's a high probability they met at The Wolf Pack. What I can't figure out is if our kidnapper and the fiancé are the same person." Gutierrez had to admit they were missing something big.

"You're right, because if the fiancé attacked her, he would know where she was, right?"

"Exactly. Unless he assumed she died, which could be a possibility. But any seasoned killer would know to check. We need to head back to The

Wolf Pack." Gutierrez was about to turn the key to start the car when he remembered they were still waiting on the kid. Plus, The Wolf Pack wouldn't be in full swing until later, and he had a feeling they would have better luck the more employees they were able to interrogate.

"Also, something I was thinking, when we went to The Wolf Pack the first two times—Mike didn't mention a fiancé or even a boyfriend when we asked."

"Which means he lied, didn't know or—"

"We didn't talk to the right people."

Officer Gutierrez agreed just as Joshua pulled up beside them.

After a few brief questions and dropping the bomb that Ms. Wren had been engaged, Joshua was ready to do whatever Gutierrez asked without question. The kid was shell-shocked, but didn't seem offended, or angered, that Eldalyn may not have told him the whole truth. Actually, he had argued that her omission must've had something to do with her memory loss.

In fact, Joshua was so unaffected by the truth, Gutierrez dropped him a step lower on their suspect list. The man they were looking for was quick to anger, vengeful, mean. Letting something big like this go wouldn't be in his nature. Joshua only seemed to sing praises about Eldalyn, which also didn't sound like their perp, whom was sure to give them an earful when they finally found him.

Gutierrez sent Joshua and Cathey through the park, armed with a photograph of Eldalyn. Joshua was only to show Cathey the places they had met and look for clues in those places. The picture was to ask anyone apparent "residents" or passers-by if they might have seen her here. After they finished with Ralston Park, Joshua was to return to the car and speak to Gutierrez, then head home just in case Eldalyn was to go back there. Cathey and Gutierrez would scope out the next park themselves.

The walk-through didn't take long at all, as the park was small, well maintained, and very empty at this late hour. Gutierrez couldn't see the whole park from his view, but from what he could see, there were only a couple of young adults walking dogs here and there, as well as a wayward teen couple trying to make out on a bench. Nothing malicious. Joshua and Cathey returned to the car in under fifteen minutes.

"Nothing here. One dog walker thought he might have seen her, but he really couldn't be sure when. Says he's lived here for years and takes the same route every night, so he could've seen her years ago or last night, he couldn't distinguish."

"And all the places Eldalyn and I stopped and talked two years ago were clean. If she was here last night, nothing belonging to her was left behind." Joshua hung his head.

Gutierrez debated asking him more questions, but knew it would only serve to waste time at this point. "Alright Joshua, you can go home. We will call you when there's another development."

He opened his mouth to argue, but must've seen the look of annoyance pass over Gutierrez's face, because he promptly shut his mouth and headed for his car.

As soon as Joshua was gone, Gutierrez started the car and headed for the park adjacent to the downtown library, parking nearly a block away. Both officers climbed out and began walking towards the park entrance.

"So nothing at all in the locations he showed you?"

"Nope, I mean it's a park. There could have been, but we are twenty-four hours behind her footsteps. If anything was there, it would most likely be gone by now anyway."

He nodded. "Did he tell you anything of interest?"

"Only that they met in the park, met up a second time there as well and made tentative plans for a date. Then she pretty much disappeared. He found her two years later through his job, as he admitted to us earlier at the station." Cathey seemed dismayed; they had both hoped the park would've provided more information.

They turned the corner and entered the park, surveying the mess of tents and sleeping bags set up just on the other side of the wall. There were people milling about, some pacing, obviously waiting for their drug dealer.

Cathey took the lead, slipping the photo out of his pocket. Playing the part of concerned brother, he began asking people if they had seen his sister in the photo around these parts last night. Many scoffed at him saying she was "too pretty for these parts" or that "a girl like that won't be found unless she wanna be." Some of them asked who Gutierrez was, to which Cathey would inform them he was a concerned uncle. Mentally, Gutierrez scoffed, but he was glad Cathey didn't think he looked old enough to be the girl's—and therefore also Cathey's—father.

After about an hour of asking just about everyone they could find who was awake and sober enough to chat, they finally caught a break when they asked an older black man who had no teeth—from what Gutierrez could only assume was a result of the perpetual use of meth.

"Yeah I know her," the man said, gently taking the photo from Cathey's hand. "But I didn't see her last night."

"Oh really? You're sure about that?" Cathey was using his slightly accusatory tone of voice to try and invoke doubt.

"Sure of it. And if she was here, it was probably to see me."

Gutierrez could hear the alarm bells going off in his head. "What do you mean?"

The old man smiled his toothless smile. "Eldalyn and I have been friends for a long time. She used to come to the library one or two days a week, back when she was just a young'un, maybe twelve or thirteen years old." The man seemed to have a far off look in his eyes. "The men here, well, they aren't so nice to pretty little things like her, and she's the same age as my daughter, Daria, so I always try to look out for her, best I can anyways."

Cathey raised his eyebrows. "And where's your daughter?"

The old man shook his head. "I lost my job back in 2005; the missus kicked me out and I haven't seen Daria since. Eldalyn's the closest thing I have to family."

"Does she come down here a lot?"

"Not recently," the man sighed. "Name's Terrance by the way."

"Well Terrance, do you have a last name?" Gutierrez nearly face palmed at Cathey's rookie mistake; now Terrance would know they were cops.

"What? Are you cops?" Terrance asked. Their silence was all he needed to confirm. "Well, you obviously know you aren't exactly welcome here. But I do want Eldalyn to be found, so let me just tell you one more thing, then I'm done talking to you." Terrance stood up and grabbed his bike that was leaning on a nearby tree. "Eldalyn is a nice girl. She used to check up on me all the time. Except this last year, something changed. She became withdrawn, and didn't want to look me in the eye. About six months ago, the visits stopped. I assume she got a car. But trust me, that flashy job she had was not enough to afford a car and the things I saw her wearing the last time she was down here."

"And what was she wearing?" Gutierrez decided to take the lead before Cathey could screw up even more.

"A diamond ring, and these beautiful teardrop diamond earrings. I don't know if they were real, but if they weren't, they were mighty good fakes." And with that Terrance got on his bike and rode away.

Cathey turned to Gutierrez. "Did the background info on Tyler Valderrama come through yet?"

"Not yet, hopefully any minute now, why?"

"Because I was just thinking, a guy who has his girlfriend, I mean fiancée, finance a car for him, doesn't seem like the type to be able to afford jewelry, even fakes. Or if he has cash, but no credit due to always using cash, there must be a reason. Maybe he was hiding something, and she found out."

Gutierrez nodded. "You're absolutely right. I think we need to get to The Wolf Pack."

Cathey agreed, calling the chief to ask about the background check while they headed to the car. The chief promised they would have it as soon as it hit the desk. They reached their car, climbed in, and Gutierrez hit the lights. This was urgent. Almost twenty-four hours had passed since the girl had been seen, and in the world of crime twenty-four hours is an eternity.

ELDALYN

JULY 21, 2014

Eldalyn awoke to find herself sitting on a wooden chair surrounded by darkness. Her head ached in a familiar way, and her mouth felt as if it were full of cotton. She didn't know how long she sat there—could have been minutes, or hours—but finally her memories began to drizzle in and she lifted her chin to scrutinize the darkness.

She tried to move her arm, only to find it was handcuffed behind her back. Her shoulders felt the pain of being restrained, but it didn't register in her wrists because they were numb. Eldalyn's thoughts were as scattered as a broken bead necklace, and the harder she tried to put them back in order, the more they spread apart.

Next, she began to try her legs, just to discover that they too were restrained. They seemed to be tied to the legs of the chair, or at least that's what she assumed as she couldn't look down to verify. She was still trying to figure out how she got here when a door opened in front of her and cast light into the room.

It was a bedroom, she knew that much. There was a bed behind her that she could barely make out in her peripheral vision. In front of her was a desk with a computer, but it was missing a chair—the chair Eldalyn could only assume she was sitting on. Slowly, her memory of the room trickled back. There were two doors to her right which were a bathroom and a closet. She'd been here before. In fact, something in her mind told her she had lived here at one point. Eldalyn winced as her eyes came back to look directly at the light that was flooding into the room; she apparently had been in the dark for some time.

It took a moment for her to recognize the features shrouded in partial shadows, but as she took in the nose and the shaggy blond hair, she knew.

"Tyler," she muttered, but it was muffled behind the gag that was covering her mouth. Now she knew the chances of getting out of here alive were slim to none.

"Ahhhh, so you do remember me. I was told you didn't remember anything." He reached down and lifted her chin, inspecting her face like a farmer would a show animal.

Eldalyn tried to speak once more, but it was impossible with the gag. Tyler seemed to notice this and pondered for a second.

"If I remove it, and you scream, you'll be dead before anyone calls 911 this time."

She nodded furiously, and he pulled the offending cloth from her mouth. Eldalyn opened and closed her jaw a few times, trying to ease the ache in her muscles.

"Did you miss me?" Tyler gingerly grabbed a piece of her hair and slid it behind her ear. She did her best to lean away from his touch. "Aw, come on Baby, don't do that. You used to beg for me to touch you."

"Things have changed."

"But have they really?" Tyler rested his hand on her leg, and she tried not to grimace. "Look where we are. You, me, here in my apartment, we could have a real good time to—"

"No." It made Eldalyn sick to even imagine where he was going with that sentence. "I left you."

"Correction, you *tried* to leave me. You knew you would come back." He leaned in and began kissing down Eldalyn's jaw. She immediately turned her head the other way, but he just started kissing the other side of her face.

"I didn't come back."

"Well, we could argue about this all day, or, you could just tell me where the ring is." Tyler stepped back from where he was in front of her, rising to his full six-foot, two-inch height.

"What ring?" But even as she said it, Eldalyn knew. The last piece finally clicked back in place.

ELDALYN

DECEMBER 25, 2013

"Eldalyn, babe, are the mashed potatoes ready yet?" Cam called from the dining room of their small, two-bedroom apartment.

"Almost!" she shouted back, stooping to pull the green bean casserole from the oven.

The girls had been living together for almost six months now, and it had been wonderful. It had all started when Cam found out that Eldalyn had been taking a bus and walking almost forty minutes to get to work every day. Cam had ended up being Eldalyn's best friend at work. Although Cassie had been her first and, albeit, oldest friend there, she found it difficult to keep in contact with a friend who never seemed to answer or return her calls.

Cassie was a good friend, but Cam—well, Cam was a beautiful person, inside and out. She had long, partially dyed, brunette hair and a killer body, but she also had a kind and giving heart. She had helped Eldalyn through the awkward phase of starting a new job with little-to-no experience. And now, thanks to her coaching and tutoring, Eldalyn was bartending next to her every night except Monday and Tuesday, the only days she had off.

Not only did the two girls live and work together, but they shared everything. Cam was the first person Eldalyn had decided to tell the complete and utter truth to about her mom, high school, and what had happened with Jeffery. Cam had been very supportive and had helped Eldalyn get into a program to complete her GED. She also had taught her how to save and budget money, so when the time came, Eldalyn would have money for college.

Walking into the kitchen, Cam grabbed four plates down from the shelf above the sink. Their apartment was small, but livable, and neither one could deny that they loved the cheap rent.

"What time is Tyler coming?" Cam spoke over her shoulder as she headed back to the living room where they had set up a card table for the occasion.

"I told him four. What about Justin?" Justin was a bouncer at The Wolf Pack, and he and Cam were dating. But only "unofficially," according to Cam.

"I think I said three thirty since he's bringing the tablecloth and the wine."

"You know Tyler won't drink wine."

Cam sighed and walked back in the kitchen. "I don't know why you cater to his every need and let him push you around like this." Rooting under the sink, Cam pulled out a handle of Laphroaig scotch she had been saving. "Think this will do for 'His Majesty?'"

Eldalyn knew that wouldn't be good enough and she would get an earful tonight, but it was already three and most all liquor stores would be closed on Christmas Day. "I guess it will have to. I'm sure he'll understand."

"What I don't understand is why you date that oaf."

"He's not an *oaf*, and he's really sweet," Eldalyn argued as she checked the potatoes and began to pull them out of the boiling water to mash them.

"Yeah, sweet as a lemon," Cam rolled her eyes and headed back to the dining room.

"You just don't know him that well!" Eldalyn shouted around the corner. She had been dating Tyler for nearly a year now. Ever since her first night at The Wolf Pack when she had served him his customary McCallan 12 straight up, Tyler had flirted with her for about a month. Then he started pestering her and badgering her for a date, and she had been able to resist, until the beginning of this year.

Their first date he had taken her to a nice French restaurant in the shopping district downtown. He had ordered for her, which had been a blessing in disguise as she had never had French food and had no idea what to order. He had picked her up and dropped her off at her house, held doors for her, and held her hand throughout dinner. He had all the makings of the perfect gentleman.

And if she hadn't already been falling for him, he showed up every day she worked, always requesting her and tipping her heavily. About a week later, they headed out for their second date. This time he told her to dress casual, and they headed to an arcade where he won her a large stuffed animal lion that she had sworn to him she had no want or need for. He had insisted she accept something, and so she had asked the cashier for a smaller, and more portable, narwhal stuffed animal.

After that, there was no doubt that she had feelings for him, and they had begun to date regularly. On Valentine's Day, Tyler did something no other man had ever done: he took Eldalyn on a trip.

It was a short trip—a few days in a cabin retreat, most of which they spent talking, playing board games, or in bed. And every night without fail, Tyler would take Eldalyn to a nice restaurant in town and let her order whatever she wanted off of the menu. In the span of only about a month, Eldalyn had come to taste, and enjoy, many dishes from around the world, as well as steak and shrimp—two things she had never had as a child.

Tyler always showered her with praises, telling her how beautiful and hot she was. He always came to visit her at work, and many of those times he would bring flowers. Mike joked that one of these days Tyler was going to bore of wooing her, and Eldalyn prayed it would never happen.

But it sort of had happened. Over the past couple months, Tyler had started coming into The Wolf Pack less and less, until he only came once every week, or even every other week. The flowers also stopped. They hadn't gone on a trip together since the Valentine's one earlier that year. He was still nice, but he no longer told her she was beautiful, and he rarely had her spend the night with him anymore. Eldalyn didn't know much about relationships, but she felt this was the beginning of the end. Eldalyn tried to focus on the good things about dating Tyler, even if they were few and far between, as much as Cam hated her for it. Eldalyn simply found she couldn't tell her heart no when it came to Tyler.

Eldalyn's thoughts were interrupted when the doorbell rang. She set down her potato masher to go answer it, but Cam's footsteps were already reverberating off of the front hall floor. Eldalyn picked up the masher again and thought about what Cam had said.

Tyler had become even more demanding lately. When they first started dating, he wouldn't care whose place they spent time at, hers or his. When she had moved in with Cam, Tyler had refused to come over—saying instead if she wanted to see him she could do so at his place. He also didn't let her pick places to eat anymore. She had made one bad selection, one time, and ever since that fateful occurrence, whenever she suggested a place to eat, Tyler would laugh it off and say, "Wouldn't want to get food poisoning, again." Then they would go to the place he chose. Maybe Cam was right; maybe she needed to stop seeing Tyler. After all, Cam had never been a fan, and she prided herself on being a good judge of character.

It had been quite the argument to get Tyler to agree to come over tonight. Eldalyn had to beg and plead and bargain that it was Christmas and she really wanted to spend it with him and her best friend. And when he had argued that they could both come to his place, Eldalyn had to make him understand that they needed all the things in their kitchen to cook the meal. The disagreement had lasted for days, but finally, late last night as she left his place to return home and defrost the turkey, he had agreed.

Cam walked into the kitchen with both Justin and Tyler on her heels. Eldalyn raised her eyebrows in an obvious question, as they were both early for their planned arrival times, but Tyler just shrugged and said, "Found him wandering around the parking lot." Eldalyn laughed out of obligation, but she could tell Tyler was up to something.

Now she knew in her heart she really couldn't complain. In fact, most days, she loved him. He was her better half…or was he? Eldalyn had been thinking and rethinking their relationship over the past month, and had yet to find a solution. She knew loving someone just most days wasn't really loving someone at all.

The trio made their way to the dining room to set up the table while Eldalyn pulled the turkey out of the oven. Cam returned to help carve it, giving Eldalyn a look that said they needed to talk after dinner. Eldalyn nodded slightly in agreement.

"Dinner is served!" Cam embellished as the two women entered the living room presenting the turkey and the rest of the fixings. Eldalyn set her two dishes down and took her spot by Tyler. She picked up the glass of wine that had been placed in front of her, only for Tyler to give her a condescending look.

This didn't escape Justin's notice. "Something wrong with the wine?"

Eldalyn opened her mouth to tell him that nothing was wrong, but Tyler beat her to the punch. "Eldalyn is cutting back on drinking."

"I only drink on special occasions," she argued. She had never been a big drinker, ever, especially since she had started working at The Wolf Pack when she was not yet twenty-one and hadn't wanted anything to compromise her job.

"And it's too much."

Eldalyn glared at him. This was one of the only times he had seen her drink since Valentines Day, so what could he mean it was "too much?" Rather than cause a scene at dinner, Eldalyn decided to shut her mouth and eat in silence.

Justin and Tyler discussed The Wolf Pack a little, and then Cam and Justin spoke about some things they'd always wanted to do for date ideas. Eldalyn had been listening, but apparently not closely; suddenly they were all staring at her waiting for an answer, and she realized she had no idea what had even been asked.

"Huh?"

"Just wondering if you'd figured out an outfit for the New Year's bash yet," Cam raised an eyebrow questioningly. She knew something was up.

"Not yet, I was going to go shopping tomorrow. I'm hoping for some after Christmas bra sales." Eldalyn shrugged. The Wolf Pack was closed on Christmas, but New Years was another story. They were all required to work, whether they liked it or not; however, they could pick their own outfit.

The rest of dinner passed uneventfully, with Eldalyn barely muttering two words here and there.

After they cleaned the table and did the dishes, the four of them sat around the two-foot Christmas tree to do a mini Christmas exchange. They had all agreed to get small gifts for one another. Cam went first. From Justin she received a pair of fuzzy slippers. Seeing as their relationship was so new, it seemed fitting. Tyler had gotten her some chocolates, and her gift from Eldalyn was a set of the bath bombs with labels for *Relaxation*, *Rejuvenation*, and *Detox*. Cam smiled and hugged Eldalyn enthusiastically.

For Justin there was a case of beer from Tyler—men never know what to buy each other—and a monogramed spatula from Cam. Justin laughed and jokingly said he was going to use it to open his own fast food chain. Eldalyn had gotten Justin a gift card for a Mexican restaurant near the club; she'd had no idea what to get him as she'd only seen him outside of work a handful of times. Cam had assured her the gift card would go a long way.

For Tyler there was a handle of his favorite whiskey from Justin, a scarf from Cam (which Eldalyn could tell was given out of spite), and a pocket watch from Eldalyn. When he opened the pocket watch, he smiled, feigned excitement for what Eldalyn guessed was for her sake, and placed the watch back in the box, not even bothering to wind it.

Cam noticed too, but said nothing of the hours she had spent helping Eldalyn pick out a present for the man who seemed to never be pleased. "Alright Eldalyn, your turn—open this one first." She handed Eldalyn a green wrapped package. She could tell what it was before she even tore the paper.

Eldalyn still pretended to be surprised, squealing in delight that Cam had gotten her her favorite perfume that she had caught Cam suspiciously taking a picture of a couple weeks prior. Next, Justin handed her a box wrapped hastily in newspaper. Eldalyn laughed as she opened a giant bag of skittles.

"Gas station shopping this year, huh?" All Justin did was blush. Everyone laughed.

Finally, Tyler handed Eldalyn a small black box. She already knew it was jewelry. Tyler had given her an expensive pair of diamond earrings for Valentines Day, and Eldalyn suspected this might be the matching necklace, but when she opened it up, her heart stopped.

"Oh, Tyler...." She felt tears brimming up in her eyes. She looked up from the gorgeous diamond ring in her hands to find him on one knee.

"I know I've been distant the past couple of weeks Eldalyn, but I didn't know how to be with you and not blow this surprise. Eldalyn, you're the most beautiful girl I know. Please say you'll do the honor of becoming my wife."

Eldalyn couldn't speak; she was in shock. And without thinking, she glanced at Cam, who looked horrified and shook her head while mouthing "no." Eldalyn had a moment of indecision before she said "yes!" and jumped into Tyler's arms. Justin cheered as Tyler slid the ring on her finger. Cam got up and left the room.

Later that night as Eldalyn went to her room to grab work clothes for the next day, Cam accosted her.

"What the hell Eldalyn?"

"You heard him—he apologized! He loves me!" Eldalyn zipped up her overnight backpack and headed towards the door. Cam blocked her exit. Eldalyn could hear the boys laughing in the living room.

"He apologizes all the time, but still treats you like some sort of second class citizen! And now you're just going to spend the rest of your life wondering every single day if he's going to be hot or cold towards you?" Cam's eyes were filled with tears. "Please Eldalyn, don't ruin your life for your first boyfriend."

Eldalyn hung her head. "Well he's going to be my husband so..."

Cam dropped her arm to allow Eldalyn to pass. "Well, I'm not your mom, but please Eldalyn, something is not right with him. I don't trust him, and I don't think you should either."

Eldalyn was almost past Cam when the last of her sentence stuck. Eldalyn dropped her defenses and stepped back to give Cam a hug. "I promise, Cam. I'll be back tomorrow after work and we can talk more, okay? Have fun with Justin" She winked.

Cam just shook her head. "Now that you're engaged, I probably will only see you once in a blue moon."

She laughed. "See you at work Cam."

"Be safe," Cam whispered as Eldalyn pushed past her and called for Tyler. They left the apartment, letting the door slam shut loudly behind them.

JOSHUA

JULY 21, 2014

He knew he should have returned home after the officers let him leave. But he didn't.

Joshua couldn't sit at home while his girl was missing, and possibly hurt.

News of Eldalyn's engagement had hit him like a ton of bricks. For the first few minutes he had been in shock. Then he had felt betrayed, followed shortly by jealousy. But then the memory of the girl he had spent the past week falling in love with had filtered through. So what if she had been engaged? She obviously hadn't loved the guy; otherwise she would have remembered him in the hospital.

He decided to stop questioning and to start searching; he could ask Eldalyn all this when she was safe.

Joshua walked into The Wolf Pack, handing the bouncer his ID. He had been here once a couple years ago, and—surprise, surprise—it was just as seedy as he remembered it.

He scoured the room taking in his surroundings. It wasn't quite ten, so there were no girls dancing on the bar yet. The room was full of men sloshing their drinks and ordering shots. No one was drunk yet, but the night was still young. There were many girls weaving in and out of tables. Joshua was debating which one he should approach when he realized that Eldalyn had been a bartender, meaning he probably should speak to one of the girls behind the bar.

Making a beeline for the bar, Joshua knocked into one man, causing him to splash his beer all over himself. The guy didn't seem to care and simply laughed it off giving Joshua a pat on the back. He spun around, narrowly avoiding a second collision with a cocktail waitress who was leaving the bar with a tray full of drinks.

"You look lost."

Joshua's eyes met that of the bartender, and he could feel himself blush. "I guess you could say this isn't my usual bar."

"I knew that." The bartender flipped her hair to the side and began making a mixed drink.

"How did you know that?" Maybe this was the break he was looking for.

"I've been working here six years. I know everyone who frequents this bar." Setting the drink down on an empty tray sitting on the bar, she began making another drink. "What's your poison?"

Though a drink did sound like a bit of a relief, Joshua knew he had to stick to his search. "Actually, I just came to ask some questions. Did you know Eldalyn?"

The glass slipped from the bartender's hand, shattering on the floor, and she almost dropped the liquor she had been pouring. "What? H-How?" she stuttered, losing all her confidence in one fell swoop. Realizing she had broken a glass, she glanced down at her empty hand and back at Joshua. He opened his mouth to speak, but she shook her head. Leaning forward as if she was trying to hear him better she said, "Meet me by the bathrooms in five."

Joshua could only nod and head off to where he assumed the bathrooms would be. When he found them, he dropped onto the couch sitting right outside. Thankfully, the music was not beating on his eardrums quite as loudly as it had been in the main room. The bartender showed up a few moments later. Joshua stood, but she swooped in to sit next to him, motioning for him to sit back down.

"I'm only on a five-minute bathroom break so this has to be fast." She leaned in so that someone passing by wouldn't be able to hear. "How do you know Eldalyn? Where is she? Is she okay? I'm Cam by the way."

"Joshua." Joshua didn't know what to say. He figured he should just get to the point. "Well I was kind of well, seeing her, but we've only been on one double date." He mentally slapped himself at how dumb he sounded. "Anyways, I don't know how much you know, but she was attacked about a week ago and now she's missing."

The bartender's mouth was agape. "I heard about the attack, but now she's missing? How?"

He shook his head. "I have no idea, but this is the last place she was seen."

Her eyes grew wide. "When?"

"Last night?"

Cam looked as if she was about to cry. "How did I not see her? First I heard she was attacked, and I went to go visit her at the hospital but I heard she had been released, and the doctor wouldn't tell me where she had gone, and now, now she was here and I didn't even see her. I swear if Tyler doesn't go to jail for this I'll—"

"Tyler?"

"Yeah, Eldalyn's fiancé, or ex-fiancé now I suppose. Wait, Eldalyn didn't tell you about Tyler?"

"No, until recently she had some sort of amnesia from her attack."

Cam grabbed his arm. "Well it was him you know—Tyler—he's the one that attacked her, and I wouldn't be surprised if he's the one that has her now."

Joshua felt his eyes widen in surprise. "How do you know?"

"I just do." Cam must've realized how pompous that sounded because she began to explain. "Something had always been off about him okay? He's been coming here for as long as I've worked here. And at first, he said he had a girlfriend but was all secretive about it. And he said she had money. Then suddenly they were engaged. Then she was gone. He said she broke up with him and went back home to live with her parents, but that just didn't sit right with me." Joshua raised an eyebrow, she continued. "When a girl is unhappy with a guy, she argues, she acts out, they fight. But these two were on cloud nine one day, then she vanished the next. That's when he started pursuing Eldalyn." Her voice cracked as she said Eldalyn's name, and she paused, wiping away a tear, "I couldn't stop her, because she was an adult, but I tried to look out for her. I warned her something wasn't right, but she was too in love to see it. And then—"

"Then what?" Joshua was now on the edge of the couch.

"Then he proposed to her, and well, I hoped he had changed at first. Then a couple months after they got engaged, I finally got a good look at the ring and—" She took a deep breath. "It was the same ring."

Joshua was stumped. "What?"

"Cassie, another girl who used to work here—actually her and Eldalyn were friends." Joshua felt his ears perk up at Cassie's name. "She was all secretive about having a boyfriend. Then one day, the manager and her get into an argument and she up and quits, announces she's going home to see her mom. But that night, as she was leaving, I was in the changing room with her and I saw the ring. She made me promise not to tell." Tears were slipping silently down her cheeks. "Then she never came back. I wanted to say something, but I figured she had just moved home with her mom. She was more Eldalyn's friend than mine." She took a deep shaky breath. "But then I saw the ring. The night Tyler proposed to Eldalyn. And I knew. But Eldalyn, she's so rational. She wouldn't listen. And I had no hard proof for her." Cam was all out sobbing now. Joshua could tell she had held all this back for entirely too long.

"Because, well, I suppose maybe Tyler is just cheap, but why wouldn't you return your ex-girlfriend's ring and buy your new girl a new one? Isn't that just sort of trashy?" Joshua nodded in agreement.

"So this all has something to do with Tyler."

Cam nodded. "I wasn't here the first time the cops came, and I assumed Eldalyn was recovering so she could tell them what happened. If I had known she didn't remember I would have gone to the station myself. Eldalyn is the sister I never had."

Joshua placed a reassuring hand on Cam's shoulder. "I'll find her. I just have to."

"Please call me when you do." Cam pulled out her phone handing it to Joshua to put his number in. After he did, he called himself so he would have her number as well. Then they both stood.

"I will." Cam turned to leave. "Wait!" Joshua called to her. She spun back to look at him. "What is Tyler's last name?"

"Valderrama." She quickly spelled it for him, and with that, she slipped around the corner and out of sight.

Joshua picked up his phone and began to leave the building before he realized there wasn't much he could do with just a first and last name. He was all the way to his car when the text came through. It was from Cam. He opened to text to find an address and a message below that said: *The last place he lived.* Joshua didn't waste any time; he jumped in his car and put the address into the maps app. He would call the police on the way. He couldn't risk losing Eldalyn again.

ELDALYN

JULY 10, 2014

Eldalyn sighed and dropped the swatches of fabric in her hand, letting them float gently down to the table. The wedding was only three months away and there was still so much left to do.

Last week, she had ordered the plates Tyler had specifically requested and had them shipped to her old house, as there wasn't space to store them in Tyler's two-bedroom apartment. Eldalyn would have preferred they register dishes like most couples did, but Tyler insisted they purchase their own. They had discussed moving once they were married; however, they had yet to come to a consensus as to where and what type of dwelling.

She knew she would have to sell that little house she had spent her whole life in. The problem was fixing it up to a state in which it would sell. It was in such a state of disrepair that at this point, she could pretty much only sell it for the value of the land it was sitting on. Tyler was eager to use that money to buy a flashy apartment in the middle of downtown. But Eldalyn really wanted a homey condo or a small house a little further out in suburbia. For now, they agreed to return to the apartment after their month-long honeymoon, and they would discuss it more then.

Eldalyn could hardly wait for their honeymoon. Tyler had left her in charge of almost every part of it, telling her that the budget was pretty much endless. Eldalyn had decided on spending some time in Asia, starting in Thailand then heading north to finish in China. The whole journey would take three weeks, and then they would fly to Hawaii for their last week.

Their relationship had improved since they had gotten engaged and started living together about a month ago. Tyler no longer seemed worried about Eldalyn cheating or sneaking around on him, now that they lived under the same roof. She felt that she could trust Tyler immensely. The "good" days now outnumbered the "bad" days, or at least that's how it seemed to Eldalyn. Of course they still fought, but Eldalyn found it was easiest to just let Tyler have his way. They hadn't yet combined finances, but he had given her a credit card that was attached to his account with which to purchase things for the wedding. It was nice not having to worry about money.

Tyler told Eldalyn he had received a large amount of money from his parents when they passed away, and not only that, but he said that he had started a business which he had already sold. Now he worked part time at a tax office, but he told her that was more just something to do with his time as opposed to a means of income.

She was still fretting over the swatches of fabric when Tyler came up behind her and set his chin on her head. "What's the matter babe?"

"I still can't decide on colors for our wedding."

He pondered for a moment, "Well, did you choose a venue yet?"

She nodded. "The performing arts center. We can rent out a ballroom for the reception and be married outdoors if the weather permits."

"Sounds wonderful." He rubbed her back lovingly. "Well you love the outdoors so much, why not do a couple shades of green? Like a forest green and a lime green with white."

Eldalyn smiled. Actually, that would be perfect. "Thanks, you always know just what to say."

"Have you picked up your dress yet?" he asked, leaning over to glance at her to-do list.

"Not yet. I need to do that tomorrow afternoon." Eldalyn scribbled a note down on the list so she wouldn't forget.

"Well I'm headed out. I'll see you tonight when you get home from work."

Eldalyn smiled. "You know better than to wait up." Tyler laughed in response and gave her a peck on the lips, then grabbed his keys and headed for the door. Turning back at the last moment to give her a little wave, Eldalyn laughed and waved back.

She turned back to the swatches, selecting the shades of green she wanted and tossing the rest of the colors aside. Tyler really did know her better than she knew herself. Eldalyn looked back at her to-do list and realized that if she picked up the dress tomorrow, she would have to store it somewhere for three months where Tyler couldn't see it. This was a major dilemma, seeing as they currently shared a room and a closet. Eldalyn thought briefly about calling Cam, her maid of honor, to store it for her, but then decided against it. She already owed Cam one too many favors.

Suddenly, Eldalyn realized that maybe she could use the spare bedroom. It was on the opposite side of the apartment, so they rarely used it, and Eldalyn had only been in it on occasion to vacuum. She had yet to see Tyler enter it at all. Maybe the closet in there would have room.

Rising from her chair, Eldalyn headed to the other side of the living room, opening the door to the guest bedroom. The room was mostly empty, except for a bed that only had the base sheet on it and a small nightstand in the corner. Eldalyn had been meaning to ask Tyler if she could redecorate this room, but between work and wedding planning, that really wasn't in the cards right now.

She walked over to the closet which had two sliding doors and slid open the first half. It was full of clothes. At first glance, Eldalyn assumed they were Tyler's clothes, but as she looked closer, she realized they were more her size.

Eldalyn thought back to the day she had moved in, but she distinctly remembered fitting all her clothes in her half of Tyler's closet...so who's clothes were these? She rifled through and pulled out a few pieces here and there. They certainly were all close to her size, but they were much more expensive than any clothes she would buy for herself. She looked at the tags and recognized stores she had seen in the mall but never dared to enter. Eldalyn rifled all the way to the end when her hand encountered a zippered garment bag. Slowly, she unzipped the zipper. It caught a few times obviously having been in that closet a while. But as she exposed the garment, she could feel the color draining from her face.

It was a wedding gown.

Her breath caught. She tried to reason; for a split second she thought maybe Tyler had picked up hers and had been playing a trick on her? But Eldalyn knew immediately that wasn't right. This wasn't her dress. She had chosen a modern silk mermaid style strapless gown, and this one had lace sleeves and a high neckline. Maybe it was his mother's? Eldalyn pulled the dress from the bag, and upon further inspection saw a tag hanging from one of the sleeves. When she raised it, she felt the breath leave her body; it read *Cassie Lane.*

Slowly, the shock she felt was replaced by anger. Something was going on here. She began furiously searching the closet for something else, any sort of clue. The floor of the closet was cluttered with sports equipment and the higher shelves were filled with boxes of all of Tyler's old school mementos. Eldalyn began pulling out and digging through each and every box, until finally she found what she was looking for.

In a Reebok shoe box, there was a picture of Tyler sitting on a log with a younger looking Cassie by his side. Eldalyn flipped over the picture to find nothing on the other side; no one bothered to label their pictures anymore. She then found a reel of photos taken in a photo booth with Cassie. And in the photo, there clearly was a ring on her left hand. Eldalyn squinted, and then squinted harder. Suddenly she felt as if she'd been punched in the chest. Cassie appeared to be wearing the exact double band diamond ring Eldalyn currently had on her finger.

Cam had mentioned this to Eldalyn, but she hadn't wanted to believe her. She hadn't wanted to hear about a prior romance. Tyler had always said, "I don't like talking about exes." Was this why? Was he upset that his last girlfriend, coincidentally Eldalyn's then best friend, had disappeared?

Then Eldalyn glanced at her hand. Her ring sparkled in the dim light of the guest bedroom. Why would Tyler give her the same ring he had given Cassie?

She quickly dumped out the contents of the box where she had found the pictures and began digging through the pile of knick-knacks on the white plush carpet. There were coins, a pocketknife, some old action figures, bracelets, and—Eldalyn's breath caught in her throat—there was a red leather wallet with bluebirds embroidered on it. She knew she had seen it before.

As she eased it open, her worst fears were solidified. There was a driver's license belonging to one Cassie Lane.

Eldalyn's mind began to spin a million miles a minute. There were so many thoughts going each and every direction. But she knew one thing, and that was that she had to get out of here.

Shoving all the things she had dumped on the carpet back in the box, except for the wallet and photos, Eldalyn quickly tossed the box on the top shelf of the closet and closed the door, running from the guest room.

She grabbed her shoes and keys and headed down to the car she had purchased with Tyler, climbing in and slamming the door. Tyler hadn't had a car when they met, and he had convinced her since he was paying for the apartment she should be paying for them a car. She nearly slapped herself at the memory of that conversation. She had been such an idiot! Eldalyn started the car then paused for a minute, laying her head on the steering wheel. Taking a deep breath, she thought about what she needed to do first. And that was to get to a police station. Pulling out her phone to find the nearest one, Eldalyn put the car in reverse and pulled out of the parking spot.

As she was driving down the street, Eldalyn realized she could never return to that apartment. If Tyler found out what she knew, she could be next. She hadn't grabbed anything to take with her, but she knew she still had things at her old house. She would go there after she finished at the police station. But she couldn't stay long; he would come looking for her. Eldalyn just couldn't believe that Tyler was Cassie's mystery man all those years ago. She felt the tears start to brim at the edges of her eyes. Cassie was fine—she just had to be. Eldalyn would call her right now. She picked up the phone and dialed Cassie's number. When she didn't answer, Eldalyn hung up. Hopefully Tyler wouldn't come home and immediately notice what she'd found so she could at least stay the night at her house before leaving town. She often worked late, usually until almost three a.m, and Tyler wouldn't notice she was missing until he crawled out of bed at eight or after. Eldalyn had never been a religious person, but she found herself praying vehemently as she turned into the police station. She begged God that this was all a mistake, and the police would call Cassie up on the phone, and she would come collect her wallet, and everything would be fine.

But deep down, Eldalyn knew that wouldn't be the case.

ELDALYN

JULY 21, 2014

Eldalyn didn't remember passing out, but she must have because when she came to she was still tied up, but ungagged, and her neck hurt like hell from the position she had been sleeping in. She would've given anything to be able to move her hand to rub the kink out of her neck.

She was awkwardly trying to roll her head side to side when Tyler reentered the room with a plate of food and something small concealed in his other hand. That's when Eldalyn realized there was something heavy around her neck. She had thought it was just the sleep wearing off, but now she knew it was some sort of collar. Quickly, she glanced again at the small item in Tyler's hand and put two and two together—she was wearing a shock collar.

"Now Eldalyn, you have two choices. Choice one…" He lifted the plate of food. "You tell me where the ring is, and you earn this lovely plate of roast beef and mashed potatoes. Or choice two," he lifted the remote to the shock collar, "I shock you until you pass out. Choose wisely."

Eldalyn thought for a moment. The memory was there, but it was only a filament of what it once was. It was the day she was attacked. That's when she had gotten rid of the ring. She was about to open her mouth and tell Tyler exactly what she had done with it when she realized something: he had only listed two choices, and neither of them involved letting her go. Which meant, he was either going to kill her, or keep her here indefinitely regardless of her answer. She knew too much.

She smirked as she remembered exactly what she had done with the ring. Even if she did tell him, it was way out of his reach, and since she wasn't getting out of here anyways…

"Screw you."

The first shock nearly made her vomit, but she kept her head up and didn't make a sound. The second shock was even stronger, but this time she was prepared. It wasn't until he upped the shock to level three that Eldalyn began to writhe in pain. But she kept her mouth shut.

This only served to anger him more, but he obviously didn't have too many levels left on the dog collar. These things were actually supposed to be humane these days. But with a huff, he turned it up to the highest level. Eldalyn screamed in pain.

When the room was silent once more, she decided she might as well aggravate him more, especially since she was going to die anyways. "You killed her," Eldalyn rasped.

Tyler only laughed. "Killed who?"

"Cassie."

He started to do a sarcastic slow clap. "Well, well, if it ain't Detective Eldalyn Wren on the job. I'm surprised it took you this long to figure it out." Tyler began tossing the remote for the collar up and down in his hand. "No one missed the dumb bitch anyways. She's honestly more use where she's at now that she was when she was alive."

"Where is she?" Eldalyn felt a tear sliding from the corner of her eye. She only wished she could wipe it away before he saw it—too late.

"Why? You want to know where you are headed too?" He laughed then, probably thinking that scaring her was a good idea, because then he continued. "She's in your favorite park right next to that brick wall. There's some sort of bush feeding off her now. Good news is, there's a spot for you too, right next to her."

Eldalyn was shocked. "How did you know I—"

He began laughing once more. "You think I'd just out of the blue start dating some strange girl who barely even talked? You don't think I would check into her a little more first? I thought you were at least a *little* smarter than that."

"You followed me?!" Eldalyn's voice broke as the realization of the full depth of Tyler's obsession settled in.

He nodded. "Multiple Times. Ever since that first night you worked at The Wolf Pack. You were so beautiful, and well, I knew Cassie would bore me one day. So I kept tabs on you until I did away with her, planning to approach you. Then I saw you talk to that other boy, and well, you know, I couldn't let him take my woman."

"I wasn't your woman."

An evil smile spread across his face. "Yes, you were, and you still are; you just don't know it yet."

Eldalyn realized in horror that Tyler had been following her, obsessed, for months. And he knew about Joshua, but maybe he didn't know that Joshua was back in her life. Hopefully he was safe.

Tyler didn't seem to notice that Eldalyn no longer cared where this story was going, because he continued on. "I had to up the ante, start wooing you quicker. And luckily for me, you didn't head back through that park to meet that guy anymore. I would hate to think what I would've had to do to the poor chap if you had started dating him instead..." Tyler trailed off. As if remembering she was there, he suddenly leaned over and touched her face. "You're way too good for him baby."

Eldalyn recoiled at the pet name and moved her neck just enough so she could bite the finger touching her face.

Tyler roared, jumping to his feet shoving the gag back in her mouth. "I told you to behave!" A sick smile spread across his face as he observed Eldalyn choke on the gag. "You're just like her. When I was a little boy, my own mom would call me 'trailer trash.' She would go on and on how I didn't even deserve to live in her house. She hated that she got stuck with me. She was convinced I ruined her 'perfect little life,' as she put it. One day I brought home this cute girl from school, and do you know what the bitch did?" He paused waiting for Eldalyn's response. Mentally, she began to knit together the true depth of Tyler's deception in her mind.

As he glanced again at the gag in her mouth, she could tell he was getting a sadistic satisfaction out of the control he had over her. With a smirk, he continued his story. "She chased her away. Told her I was a monster and that she was too good for me. That's when I ran away. And you're just like her, aren't you? You thought you were too good for me. But you're wrong." Noticing that Eldalyn was starting to zone out, he slapped her hard across the face.

Eldalyn let out a yelp which was muffled by the gag. This only served to excite Tyler more. "You know, I'd hoped you'd learn to love me, but regardless, this arrangement could be much better. Tell me Eldalyn, am I still the one in your will?"

She felt her eyes go wide. Had she written a will? If she had, when had she done it? She squinted her eyes trying to remember.

Tyler knew exactly what she was trying to do. "Oh yes, you have a will, remember? We had them done, both of us, as a couple, a few days before you pulled your little stunt." He paused and began to pace around the room. Eldalyn followed him with her eyes, trying not to move her neck which was already sore.

"You know, I was running a little low on Cassie's money anyways… this would be a good time to cash in on yours…" As if realizing Eldalyn was still listening, he muttered a few more words under his breath, shocked her again for good measure, then left the room, slamming the door behind him.

Eldalyn's throat burned where the collar was touching it. She tried to move her head, just to reposition it a little, but it didn't seem to be doing anything at all. It was on too tightly. She couldn't believe this monster had been watching— no, plotting—for years. He wanted her to worship him; wanted to possess her as if she was some sort of trophy. And then, when he was done, he was set up to receive all her money and property. How had she been so stupid to get involved with him? And Cassie—oh poor Cassie—all this time she had been planning her wedding, it had been using Cassie's money.

Trying to think about something other than the pain, Eldalyn went back to the issue at hand. She wanted to live. And neither obeying Tyler nor sitting here in silent protest were going to make that happen. Tyler had to leave sometime. He'd never had a serious or regular job, but if he didn't show up at certain bars on certain days he would be missed. And when he left, she would have to make her move.

To make sure her plan would work, Eldalyn did a little trial move. She leaned all the way back in the chair, lifting her legs a little bit until the two front legs of the chair came off the ground. She leaned back forward quickly as not to tip herself backwards. Then Eldalyn tried to lean forwards, to see if she could get the back legs off the floor. The way her feet were tied to the bottom of the chair was awkward, but Eldalyn found she could place them flat on the ground and stand. In an awkward squat, with a chair and her arms behind her back, Eldalyn tried to take a step. She found her legs we bound much too tightly, and it was too awkward to allow step-like movement. But she could hop. After a couple trial hops, Eldalyn figured she had as best of a plan as she was going to get. But she still had the problem of not knowing when he would leave.

The apartment walls were somewhat thin, and Eldalyn could faintly hear the TV from the living room down the hall. She knew from when she lived here that Tyler usually kept it louder than that, but he was probably listening to her making sure she didn't try anything. Tyler had always been glued to the TV, when he was home anyways. He spent most of the time they had lived together at bars and clubs, only returning home when he was adequately drunk enough to yell at her and conveniently forget it in the morning.

Looking back, Eldalyn could see nothing but his duplicity. One moment he was loving and sweet; the next, a tyrant. Why had she agreed to marry him in the first place? Cam had been right—she should have stayed away.

Eldalyn sighed and leaned her head back, closing her eyes. She was taking a chance in hoping he still had the same habits as before, because she knew once the TV shut off and she could be reasonably sure he had left the apartment, she would have to make her move. Otherwise he was bound to find out what she did to the ring, and when he did, her life was over.

OFFICER MARCUS GUTIERREZ

JULY 21, 2014

They were walking into The Wolf Pack when the phone finally rang. Gutierrez glanced down and saw it was the boss and motioned to Cathey to continue inside while he lifted the phone to his ear.

"What do you have for me?"

"Hey, hello to you too." The chief paused for dramatic effect then continued on without necessarily waiting for an answer. "Anyways, we got the paperwork back on Tyler Valderrama, and I can tell you, we've got to bring him in ASAP. If he doesn't have the girl, he's a suspect in the disappearance of Cassie Lane in this county and another disappearance in Orange County California. He was seen with both victims shortly before they disappeared. And recently some evidence was brought into our office that was finally a break in the case."

Gutierrez couldn't believe his ears. He had just looked into Cassie Lane not a week before and Tyler's name hadn't come up at all. "What evidence? And when?" Gutierrez wished Cathey was here with his notepad.

"That's the thing, the evidence was just brought in about ten days ago. It looks like his current fiancé had been looking through some things and found a picture and the wallet of one of the victims. And not only that but she turned over a ring that had been seen on both victim's fingers. And get this, Tyler had then given it to her; they were engaged. Anyways, the fiancé—"

"Eldalyn Wren…" Gutierrez finished for his boss.

"Was attacked two days later, but the evidence hadn't been entered in the electronic system yet. Since it was a cold case, it was at the bottom of the pile and was entered only hours after you ran the check on her. Who knew that a current assault case would be part a suspected missing persons cold case?"

- Gutierrez didn't like where this was going. "Who took her statement?"

"A new hire. He didn't get in any hurry because it wasn't an active case."

Gutierrez rolled his eyes; the system really needed to work on its efficiency. "Please tell me the ring was at least sent to the lab or its origins were investigated or something."

"Yes, the ring has been in the lab all week. The only DNA found on it was Eldalyn Wren's, but they did trace it back to a store in Orange County, but get this, it was purchased in 1940. And not by our perp."

"Who bought it?"

"The grandfather of our missing victim in Orange County: Oliver Fleming. They called him up only to discover he passed away in 2011. However, he had purchased the ring and given it to the man who wanted to propose to his namesake, his granddaughter Olivia. His widow says that Tyler Valderrama dated Olivia from 2005 to 2008. When he came to Oliver and told him he wanted to propose to Olivia but didn't have the money to do so, the grandfather gave the family heirloom ring to Tyler. The Flemings are well off; it's worth about fifty thousand dollars." Gutierrez let out a low whistle. "Tyler and Olivia were engaged from 2008 to 2009, when suddenly, Olivia disappeared."

Gutierrez switched over to speakerphone and began typing everything the chief was telling him in his phone.

"The local authorities investigated for a year, but there was no trace of the girl. And Tyler had a rock-solid alibi, so he wasn't charged. They monitored her credit cards and accounts, and there was no activity. They officially labeled it a cold case in 2011." He took a deep breath. "And that's when it gets weird… right as it was labeled a cold case, there was action on her cards again—deductions from her large trust fund. But still no sign of Olivia. The authorities didn't notice, nor did the family since Oliver had been the one monitoring those kinds of things, and he had passed away. His widow claims the devastation of losing his only granddaughter killed him."

"And where did these deductions from the trust fund take place?" Gutierrez looked up just as Cathey exited the club and walked up to his partner's side, notepad and pen in hand.

"Well, this is where things *really* get weird. They've been in the tri-state area, with deductions in Kansas, right here in Colorado, and some in Utah. But they rotate, as if the person doing the deductions is on a route of some sort."

"You think it could be a truck route?" Cathey piped in, without even knowing the context of the discussion. It wouldn't be the first time a trucker had committed murder.

"I checked; no indication of any common truck route. But there are a few railroad routes that almost line up. I've got someone verifying the dates with Union Pacific now."

Gutierrez looked over at Cathey. "Either way we better get to Tyler as quickly as possible. Do you have an address?"

"Already texted to your phones with the full report on Mr. Valderrama and I dispatched a squad car to back you up before I called you. They should get there the same time as you. Already called the ADA too, and she's finding a judge who's awake to sign the warrant now."

"Thanks Chief." Gutierrez hung up and looked at Cathey. They both climbed in the car and Gutierrez started the engine and flipped on the lights. Gutierrez began filling Cathey in on all the information he had just received from the Chief. Cathey listened intently, jotting down multiple notes. When Gutierrez finished, he asked Cathey if he had had any luck in the club.

"Yes and no. The first time we were here, we missed talking to Cam, one of the bartenders who claims to be Eldalyn's best friend. She was very forthcoming with me about Eldalyn's life prior to the attack. But what I don't understand is why the manager didn't point us in her direction the first time we came by."

"There are too many things in this case that don't line up." Cathey scratched his head as he looked at the notepad in his lap.

"You're telling me." Gutierrez turned onto the street.

"There is one thing Cam told me. Joshua was here just before us, and she gave him the address that she had for Tyler."

"Oh *great*. So he's going to be there in the crossfire."

"No, get this—it's different than the address the chief just gave us. I called myself for backup to the address the bartender gave me. So they'll meet Joshua there. They've been warned there's a civil vigilante on the loose."

"Two addresses? Who is this man?" Gutierrez could hardly believe the web that was being weaved in front of his eyes.

Cathey was silently scrolling through something on his phone. Finally he looked up and filled in Gutierrez. "The report in my email only shows a history for Tyler Valderrama back to 2005 when he appeared as Olivia Fleming's boyfriend. Prior to that there is no record of him."

"So it's a fake name."

"Exactly."

"Any record of a job?" He was pushing the speed limit but he didn't care.

"It looks like odd jobs here and there—most recently a seasonal job this spring in a tax office. One of those 'help you file for cheap' places where they just punch your information into a website and charge you exorbitant fees. But I was thinking, the hours there are flexible, and it looks as if he didn't have a car other than the one Eldalyn was paying for. Do you think he was hitchhiking on the train to get across state lines for cheap?"

"I mean, it would be a bit chilly in the winter, but I suppose it's possible." Gutierrez scratched the barely-there hair on his chin. They needed to get to Eldalyn and fast. He had a feeling this guy wouldn't hold out much longer.

Gutierrez flipped off the lights as he pulled onto the street where the address the chief gave them was located. No purpose in giving Tyler a heads-up if he was indeed at this address.

He pulled up next to the other squad car that was already parked in front of the building. Cathey motioned to the other cops to follow them. They all pulled out their weapons and headed up the stairs.

Once they reached the door of the apartment, Gutierrez knew something wasn't right. It was absolutely silent, and there was a pile of mail by the door. Tyler hadn't been here in awhile. He holstered his weapon, but Cathey and the two backup officers kept them out. They were in a rougher part of town with no on-site manager to ask for keys. Gutierrez kicked the door to find that the lock was weak and it swung open easily.

The inside of the apartment was in a state of disarray. There was barely any furniture, and the furniture that was there was old and worn, and some partially destroyed. The place was dusty. The entire kitchen was covered in dust at least an inch deep. Cathey cleared the bedroom then returned to the kitchen. "There's no one here, and I would guess no one has been for quite some time."

"I agree." Gutierrez opened the fridge to find it was dark and no cold air flowed out. "No one has been here in ages. But when he left, he must've known he wasn't coming back."

"So why did he keep this place?"

"There's only one reason killers keep places they no longer use. There's something here that they still need or want. Get crime scene techs out." He turned and headed towards the door. The two backup officers were already pulling out drawers and searching cabinets. "We've got another address to get to."

Gutierrez only hoped they wouldn't be too late.

JOSHUA

JULY 22, 2014 JUST AFTER MIDNIGHT

The apartment building Joshua pulled up in front of was definitely nothing like his own. Unlike his, which was all indoor with a parking garage and all the amenities, this place looked like a converted motel, with all the doors facing the outside and paint chipping from every surface in his view.

Joshua walked up to the door labeled *310*, wishing he had some sort of gun on him. All he had was a pocketknife, and if the guy who had Eldalyn had a gun, it would be no use. He had called the cops on the way here, telling them where he was going and why. They had told him to wait in the car and let them handle it, but they weren't here yet and he couldn't stand it if he lost Eldalyn again permanently.

He tried the doorknob. It was locked. Joshua knew better than to try and kick it in; he was no karate kid. Instead he flipped out the thin rod of his pocketknife and began trying to jimmy the lock. This place looked old, and the older the lock, the easier it was to pick.

As a child, Joshua's mother had often locked herself out of the house. With so many kids to look after, no one could really blame her. When Joshua was really young, his mom would hoist him through a small window above the washing machine and he would unlock it from the inside. But as he had gotten older, and too big for the window, he had learned to pick locks with various things from his mother's purse: bobby pins, paperclips, and whatever else was small and rod-shaped. Luckily, his mom had gotten a keypad lock several years ago, and Joshua's lock-picking skills were no longer required.

It took a few minutes, but Joshua finally heard a click. Holding the rod in place, Joshua eased a credit card from his wallet and slid it between the door and the bolt. Then he pushed the door open.

The apartment was dark; but then again, it was the middle of the night.

Joshua heard no sounds of movement, but that didn't mean that the guy wasn't here and was just asleep. He didn't want to chance waking him up, so he eased around the living area without turning on the lights.

As his eyes adjusted to the darkness, he could see the TV along one wall, surrounded by furniture, and the kitchen to his other side. A black abyss that must be a hallway lay ahead. Joshua kept his back to the wall and walked on his toes, hoping the slight creak of the old floors wouldn't give him away.

He came to the first doorway opening and peered in. It was a bathroom. Joshua began to ease past before he realized this guy could be keeping Eldalyn anywhere, so he stepped into the bathroom and peered around the shower curtain.

It was empty.

Joshua turned and headed back to the hallway, hitting his foot on the door jam. He winced in pain and bit his lip to keep from crying out. He couldn't help but think what a cliché he was right now—trying to be the hero, sneaking around in the dark, and jamming his toe on the way.

He came to the next door frame. This door was closed, as quietly as he could, he twisted the knob.

As he peered into the darkness it took him a minute to decipher what he was seeing. It was a bedroom, with a single window that was covered with dark curtains, but a line of light came through the bottom where the curtains didn't quite reach the windowsill. There was a bed, and on it a sleeping form. Joshua stepped back into the hallway, pressing himself against the wall. His heart was racing and he could barely breathe. But as he peeked around the corner once more, his eyes were drawn to something in the middle of the room. At first he had thought it was a pile of clothes on a chair; then he realized it was a hunched over form.

It was Eldalyn.

Cautiously, so as not to wake whoever was sleeping on the bed, he tiptoed over to her side and knelt down, softly touching her knee. She startled awake but made no sound, as there was some sort of gag in her mouth.

She made eye contact with Joshua and her eyes widened. She looked quickly from the bed, back to Joshua, and shook her head in despair. Joshua put his finger to his lips, motioning for her to be quiet, and pulled the sock out of her mouth.

He ran a hand down the side of her neck and his hand encountered something thick around her neck. Joshua didn't know what it was, but knew that regardless, it did not belong there. He quickly unclipped it from her neck and dropped it to the floor.

Joshua began inspecting the way Eldalyn was tied to the chair, and he realized immediately it was not going to be easy to get her out. The guy had used bike wire to tie her up, and it was locked with a combination lock. He groaned internally.

He looked up and his eyes met Eldalyn's once more. She mouthed something to him. He raised his eyebrows, and she mouthed it again. It looked like "save yourself, get out." But Joshua shook his head, touching Eldalyn's face. He wasn't going to leave her here.

Suddenly, a light flicked on and Joshua head a distinct click.

He turned his head to the side to find Tyler sitting up in bed with a revolver pointed at his head. This is exactly what he had been afraid of.

A menacing grin spread across his face. "I knew it. This entire time! I knew you were a cheating bitch! Just like the rest of them!"

Eldalyn's voice was hoarse, but she spoke before Joshua could open his mouth. "Don't listen." It was all she managed to say. Joshua glanced back at her to see her eyes fixed on him. She was talking to him not Tyler.

"She didn't tell you, did she? She was engaged to me! This whole time that she was dating you! How does that feel? Huh?" Tyler was raving now. He stood from the bed and began walking over to Joshua wearing nothing other than boxers. He knew that he needed to have the element of surprise on his side. When Tyler was only a foot from where Joshua was crouched, he made his move, lunging for the hand with the gun with his arm outstretched, his pocketknife clasped in his fist.

Everything seemed to happen simultaneously after that. The gun went off, there was a scream, and Joshua felt a searing pain in his shoulder. He rolled to the side. He'd seen it in movies, read about it in books, but nothing compared to the actual feeling of being shot. He lay there unmoving, biting his lip as his arm was on fire.

Sirens came in the distance. They were coming there—they just had to be. But then, when the sirens were still a long way off, they stopped. Joshua's heart fell in dismay. He knew that in most movies, this is the part where he valiantly got up and saved his girlfriend's life, but he couldn't find it in him to move. The pain was just too great, and his arm seemed unmovable. He just lay there.

"Please, Tyler, look, you killed him. We can be together. Let's go, quickly, before the cops arrive!" Joshua couldn't believe what he was hearing for a moment, but then he recognized the hint of sarcasm in Eldalyn's voice. She was trying to get him to untie her.

"Ha! Stupid girl. You think I'm just going to leave him here for the cops to find? Fat chance. He will have an honorary plot across the park from you!"

Joshua felt the floor vibrate ever softly as Tyler walked his way.

"No wait! Tyler, please come here babe." Eldalyn was using her sweet voice now. She knew that he wasn't dead. Tyler's footsteps stopped and receded in the opposite direction. Joshua heard him pause and heard some noises he couldn't place.

"Ow! You bit my tongue! That's it. You're DONE! Do you hear me? DONE!" Tyler screeched, and a commotion of some sort followed.

His thoughts began to get fuzzy and for a moment the life in front of him faded away. He was in a kitchen, with a three-year old Juni and pasta all over the floor. The corners of the kitchen began to fade, and Joshua quickly realized he was losing consciousness. He wasn't sure when, but at some point he had closed his eyes and now it seemed an impossible feat to reopen them. His body didn't want to respond to the commands he was giving it. His vision began to fade back to the kitchen. *No!* He was not going to let himself lose consciousness! With all the force he could muster, he managed to get his body to open his left eye. Once he was again in visual contact with the scene in front of him, opening his right eye came much easier. With both eyes open and his mind back in the present, Joshua suddenly noticed the complete silence in the room. When Joshua rolled over just a bit to look over his shoulder, he noticed the chair, Eldalyn, and Tyler were gone.

He struggled to his feet. He didn't think it took that long to right himself, but by the time he was standing he looked up to find a police officer pointing a gun at him. He raised his good arm and tried to hurriedly explain. "I can't raise this arm, I've been shot. I'm the guy that called you! I'm Joshua Williams."

The cop lowered his gun slightly but didn't put it away. "Where's the girl?"

"She was here. Tyler took her. And I think I know where they're headed. Please, call Officer Gutierrez. He knows me."

"No need." A voice came from around the corner as Officer Gutierrez came into view. Behind him a paramedic rushed in and began putting pressure on Joshua's arm. "What happened?"

"He had her tied to a chair, right there," Joshua pointed. "He shot me, then she tried to distract him so he wouldn't kill me. Then she pissed him off, and he said he was going to kill her. He's taking her to the park, I think, the one we met in." This was all the time it took the paramedic to put him on a stretcher and rush him down to the waiting ambulance. As the doors closed, he could see Cathey and Gutierrez climbing in their squad car. Hopefully they weren't too late.

He realized the medic was saying something to him. "Sir?"

"I'm sorry," Joshua responded, realizing she had been saying something to him. "Could you repeat that?"

"I was saying, is there anyone I should call?"

He nodded. "Take me to Briar Medical Center and ask for Dr. Williams please. He's my dad." The medic nodded, and Joshua leaned back and closed his eyes. He'd never been religious, but he hoped that if there was someone up there, that he was looking out for a certain Eldalyn down here.

ELDALYN

JULY 22, 2014 ABOUT 2AM

He was raving like a lunatic as he half-carried, half-dragged a re-gagged Eldalyn through the park, still attached to the chair. In his other hand he carried a shovel. Her feet were slick with blood as the bounds attaching her feet to the chair were jarred and tightened with the motion. She hoped Joshua was safe.

Eldalyn had never seen the park this quiet. It must be the middle of the night. She looked around for anything that could help her get loose. She began to struggle against the handcuffs, which betrayed her and made a clanking sound as she tried to slip her hand out. Tyler spun around in anger at the sound.

"What is it with you women? Why can't you just listen and do as I say!" he roared, punching Eldalyn straight in the nose. She heard a crack and immediately tasted blood. Satisfied, Tyler turned around and resumed dragging her to whatever spot he had designated in his twisted mind. Eldalyn's eye burned with tears as she thought that her friend was here somewhere, six feet under. She looked up to fight them back, her eyes coming to land on the night sky. She just needed a chance.

That's when Eldalyn noticed how slick her wrists had become with sweat. Or maybe it was blood, or both. It was painful, but she could move the cuffs slightly. Maybe it was enough.

Tyler set the chair down by a row of bushes, muttering to himself as he began to dig. Eldalyn watched as he dug quickly; he was much stronger than she had realized. She knew this was her only chance.

Wiggling her wrists, she felt the skin that was cut shift as she got the metal portion back on her unmarred skin. She was still struggling with the second cuff when she heard sirens in the distance. They were coming. Joshua had told them where she would be. So he was alive. *Thank God.*

Tyler heard the sirens too. He suddenly became frantic, and picked up Eldalyn, chair and all, and tossed her in the hole he had dug. But even though the hole was barely two feet deep, Tyler began shoveling dirt over Eldalyn as quickly as he could.

Eldalyn was perplexed. He had to know that this wasn't going to work. Something was wrong. He was falling apart.

Tyler dropped the shovel and began pushing dirt on her with his hands. Eldalyn closed her eyes and mouth, trying to inhale as little dirt as she could. She was barely covered with a light layer of dirt when Tyler cursed, realizing Eldalyn was protruding much too far out of the ground.

Quickly, he detached Eldalyn's legs from the chair, leaving her hands cuffed behind her back, and threw the chair off to the side. Then he tossed her roughly back into the dug-out place. Eldalyn tried to catch herself, but she felt her head come into contact with the rough ground. Stars danced before her eyes, but she fought the urge to pass out. She closed her eyes and once more held her breath as dirt was piled on her. She still wasn't in that deep and she hoped it was shallow enough that she would be able to breathe.

Eldalyn began to struggle once more with her handcuffs, finding it harder to slip them off now that there was dirt in the mix. She was so busy trying to get the handcuffs off that she barely noticed when it became silent. She held her breath and tried to listen—there was no sound. Tyler must've gone.

She tried in vain to sit up. Not only was it difficult in her weakened state, but the dirt covering her was suddenly much heavier than she anticipated. She then tried to move back and forth, and found while that was easier, it still didn't help much.

Suddenly, she heard voices. She felt the fear creep back into her until she rationalized that voices would mean that someone other than Tyler was here. She forced herself to relax as she let what she assumed were the cops removing the dirt from her. As she felt the weight lift off her mid-section, Eldalyn sat up and attempted feebly to open her eyes, which proved to be impossible. She waited patiently for the handcuffs to be removed.

But no one moved to get them off her. In fact, no one touched her to help her at all. Something was very wrong.

"Oh Tyler, what have you done?" It was a female voice. Eldalyn's breath caught in her throat.

"She just wouldn't shut up!" Tyler sounded rushed and frustrated. Or maybe it was embarrassment. Eldalyn couldn't decipher based on his voice alone and she still couldn't open her eyes.

"You have to stop doing this. I can't keep cleaning up your messes." It was the female voice again. And it sounded sort of familiar, but Eldalyn couldn't quite place it. "Hurry up! Grab her before the cops come!"

She felt herself being lifted up and tossed over presumably Tyler's shoulder.

"You were supposed to leave her alone," the female voice muttered once more.

The jarring moment help loosen the dirt from her eyes and Eldalyn began to blink furiously to dislodge the rest of it. When she did, she was in utter shock at what she saw.

"Hello Eldalyn."

It was Cam.

"Cam?" Eldalyn squeaked. She felt as if all the air had been forced from her lungs, and although her stomach was empty, she felt a sudden urge to vomit. She pinched her eyes closed and opened them again, hoping she would find another face staring up at her.

But Cam was still there. "Why couldn't you just stay away from him, Eldalyn? I asked you… no, I begged you." Cam pinched the bridge of her nose and squeezed her eyes shut as Tyler began to move in the direction of the car. "If you had stayed away from him, none of this would have happened."

"Cam," Eldalyn whispered. It was all she could muster. She felt as if her heart was on fire. She closed her eyes again so she didn't have to see her friend's betrayal any longer. Against her will, she felt tears slide down her cheeks and all the fight left her. "How long?" She knew she probably didn't want to know the answer, but she wanted a gauge of her own stupidity.

Cam looked confused. "How long what?"

"Have you two been—"

She cut Eldalyn off. "What? No! Eldalyn, Tyler is my brother."

"Wha-at?" she stuttered. She couldn't believe her ears.

"And my name isn't Cam, its Olivia, Olivia Fleming." The smile that spread across Cam's face was foreign then. It was a mix of a sick sense of satisfaction and pride, both of which made the hairs on the back of Eldalyn's neck stand up.

"Why would you lie about your name?" Eldalyn questioned, but before she even finished the sentence, she realized there was only one reason people lied about their identity.

"So no one could find me."

The two of them continued to bicker all the way to the car. And the way their banter went back and forth, Eldalyn couldn't believe she hadn't noticed before. They were comfortable with each other. It the same way that married couples became after cohabitating for a number of years.

She was woozy, from either the beating or the lack of food—she wasn't sure—but following their conversation was becoming increasingly more difficult the more she tried to listen.

"We can't go back to my place. The cops are already there, thanks to your idiot ass." That was Tyler. He was in the passenger seat, so apparently Cam was driving.

"I already went over this; you weren't supposed to be there! You told me you only needed a few hours to find out where the ring was, then you were going to get rid of her!" Cam was obviously stressed, and not happy with Tyler's actions.

"And I told you that I just couldn't do that!" Tyler was just as agitated as Cam, but he certainly didn't seem as worried. In fact, the confidence was still rolling off him in waves.

Cam let out a huff and Eldalyn felt her weight shift to one side as the car turned. "We can't drive around forever. I guess we have to go back to the old place."

"What about your apartment?"

"I told the cops she had been living with me! They're probably already there checking it out!" Cam yanked the wheel hard and Eldalyn felt herself almost fall off of the back bench seat. The way her hands were tied, it was impossible to right herself, or even try and hold on.

"You're too paranoid. They don't even know you're involved." Tyler looked back to check on Eldalyn, smiling wryly when he saw her eyes were now open. He reached over to touch Eldalyn's face and she shuddered. His fingers were dirty and his nails caked with dirt. "Can't we just take her with us?"

She sighed. "No Tyler. She knows too much. There's no option now."

"You're her friend, maybe you can talk to her."

Cam shook her head. "Our friendship ended the minute she found that picture Tyler. Speaking of 'idiot asses,' why didn't you burn them?" It seemed as if Cam was talking in a loop, her increasing anger with Tyler evident in her voice. Eldalyn was still baffled by their relationship. How had she not seen this coming?

And why Cam hadn't just told her that Tyler was her brother? With a wince, Eldalyn realized that if Cam had mentioned Tyler being her brother, she may have been even more ecstatic to marry him in order to be Cam's sister.

Eldalyn had been an idiot. And now, all she had was her regret to ponder.

OFFICER MARCUS GUTIERREZ

JULY 22, 2014 ABOUT 4AM

Cathey sat staring at the partially dug hole. The night breeze whistled past his hair. "We're missing something."

Gutierrez shook his head. "I know." He surveyed the area, taking in the chair tossed to one side and the bike lock chords still lying in the freshly dug dirt. Everything had been done in a hurry. There appeared to possibly be blood on the ground, but there was no Eldalyn in sight.

"You know, something's been bothering me about that apartment." Cathey scratched the side of his face and looked over to Gutierrez. "When we were searching it, granted it was devoid of most everyday items, but looking at what was left of the furniture and the dishes in the kitchen, I got the distinct feeling that—"

"That what?" Gutierrez wondered where this was going.

"That a woman lived there."

"One of our victims?" Gutierrez pulled out his phone and looked at the notes he had typed in earlier.

"I don't know. But Tyler doesn't seem like the type of guy to have what was a white couch with pink accent pillows." Cathey also pulled out his notes and began flipping through the pages. "There's something else that baffles me."

"What's that?" Gutierrez stepped aside as the crime scene techs arrived and began roping off the area.

"That bartender at the club... I mean, I'm sure some people are more open than others, but really, what bartender knows a patron's address? Even if it's her friend's boyfriend, I mean, do you even know the address of any of your friends?"

"You're absolutely right. She's given us more information than we've gotten from anyone other than our own research. Which can only mean one thing—"

"She's involved," Cathey finished for him. Gutierrez whipped out his phone and began to dial the chief as Cathey continued flipping through his notes looking for a last name. When the chief didn't answer, Gutierrez looked at the time on his phone and realized it was nearly four in the morning. Without leaving a message, Gutierrez changed routes and dialed the station, hoping at least one of the night cops was in.

Thankfully the odds were on his side tonight.

"Hello?"

"This is Officer Gutierrez, badge number 6403. Who am I speaking with?" Gutierrez motioned to Cathey to finish up with the crime scene techs and meet him in the car. Then he turned and headed there himself.

"Ferguson, what's up?" Gutierrez was glad to hear it. He and Ferguson had started at the department at the same time. However, Ferguson was a family man and worked nights so he could stay home with his toddler during the day while his wife worked her day job.

"Ferguson, man am I glad it's you. Listen, I need you to tell me what comes up when you put in Cam Johnson. She's an employee at The Wolf Pack, probably about twenty-five years old, brunette hair..." He heard typing in the background as he presumably typed the name into their system.

"Well, this is weird."

"What is it?" Gutierrez was getting into his car just as Cathey began walking towards him.

"I mean, nothing illegal, but definitely odd. I have a Cam Johnson that matches that description, but she received her first driver's license at the age of twenty-five. When she applied for her license she claimed she hadn't had one previously, which according to our system, that may be correct—this is the only license registered to a female of that age. Lots of 'Camille's and

'Cameron's though, which might be worth looking into. But if you ask me, I doubt that if she had a former license, she would change just the first name and not the last."

"So you think she could have another name?" This is not what he wanted to hear. It would make tracking the bartender down even more difficult.

"Most likely, I mean, what female in a city with only buses for transportation gets her first license at twenty-five? Something doesn't match up." Cathey opened the door and slid into the car.

Gutierrez sighed. "Well, what's the address on the ID?"

As Ferguson began to rattle it off, he felt a sinking feeling in the pit of his stomach. Once he got to the apartment number, Gutierrez knew. "The apartment we searched." He shook his head and started the car. Cathey deduced immediately what had just transpired and used his phone to call the crime scene techs. As Gutierrez hung up on a confused Ferguson, he could hear Cathey yelling at the crime scene techs that had been combing the apartment to clear out and move their vans around the corner. They must've begun to argue because he told them to just do it and they could complain later.

"So what's the deal with Miss Johnson?" Cathey pulled out his note pad while simultaneously snapping on his seatbelt as Gutierrez gunned it out of the parking lot.

"Well, Miss Johnson suddenly appeared in this area asking for a license in 2009."

"Are you thinking what I'm thinking?" Gutierrez glanced over at his partner, and he could literally see all the pieces fall into place.

"Are you thinking that Cam Johnson suspiciously appeared right when Olivia Fleming fell off the map? Do you think they could be the same person?

"Possibly. And now I'm wondering, if they *are* the same person, what she's doing with Tyler. Do you think this was some sort of joint plot to abduct and kill women?" Cathey didn't like the sound of that, and honestly, neither did he. Something sounded off.

"But why the disappearing act for her and not him? Wouldn't he be the one more concerned about being recognized?"

They both sat deep in thought for a moment before Cathey spoke up. "Unless it's like we originally thought, and Tyler Valderrama was a fake name all along."

Gutierrez nodded in agreement as they sped through the exact same streets as they had earlier that evening. They both remained silent the rest of the drive as they ran through scenarios of how this killing team had come to be. As they pulled around the corner onto the street where the apartment was located, Gutierrez shut off the lights and siren, both of them hoping their hunches were right and they had brought the girl back here.

As they pulled into the parking lot, they both checked their guns to ensure they were loaded with safeties off, and then stepped out of the car as silently as possible. Gutierrez motioned to Cathey to take the stairs to one side of the complex while he eased up the other. As they arrived on the second floor, they both unholstered their weapons and held them in attack mode. They eased towards the wall, walking along it until they were both on opposing sides of the door in question. Cathey cocked his head to one side and pointed to his ear. Gutierrez held his breath, and that's when he heard the raised voices from within.

"Oh god, the cops have already been here! This isn't how I left it!" It was a female voice Gutierrez could only guess belonged to Miss Johnson.

Her comment was followed by a groan. "I don't know I don't know... okay...giving me a headache." It was a male voice—had to be Tyler. Gutierrez couldn't tell if they had Eldalyn with them. He had to confront the fact that this could all be in vain, and they could've already killed her. But he had to hope she was still alive.

"I'm always cleaning up your stupid messes...First it was that blonde girl, who I told you was trouble, and then I specifically said not to touch Eldalyn...you left all that stuff where she could find it...burn it! And for God's sake why couldn't you buy a new ring...given you the money!"

There were a few muffled sounds that followed the yelling. Gutierrez tried to lean towards the bottom of the door to get a better idea of what they were dealing with. He preferred to know if there was a live hostage in there before kicking in the door.

"You don't understand…She…She was the one…can't always ask you for money sis…embarrassing." The male voice sounded forlorn, and suddenly Gutierrez wasn't so sure they were dealing with a hostage situation at all.

The female voice continued to fade in and out. Gutierrez guessed she must have been pacing. "That's what you said about the first one…what happened there…girls don't want a guy…the truth okay? It'll be you and me…Stop messing with the program…to be rich?" The female voice was still raving, but it began to fade even more as if she had stopped pacing and was walking further away from the door. Gutierrez motioned to Cathey to cross the door frame and get behind him. At this point he was assuming their hostage wasn't there. It was time to bring down a pair of killers.

"I just want something more." The male voice waivered and a muffled thump followed. Gutierrez put his hand on the doorknob and slowly turned. It was unlocked. He eased open the door and looked through the small gap. The woman was standing behind the couch while the man was sitting on it. He could only see two people, and he held up two fingers to inform Cathey.

"And when grandma kicks the bucket, you'll get it!"

"No, you don't get it, I don't want any more money."

"What do you mean you don't want more money? The only reason you went through the adoption databases to find me was to find money! And this whole plan, this was your dream!" The woman sighed. "It's a little late to say that now, we are up to our ears in this…You know what? I'm done. I'd hoped the cops would find you and eliminate you on their own, so I wouldn't have to do it. You're dead weight, and I'm tired of dragging you everywhere with me only for you to cause trouble."

"Wha—What do you mean?" The male voice was nowhere near as

pronounced as the female's.

Gutierrez looked around the corner once more but couldn't tell if either of them had a weapon.

The female voice began to speak again in an even more berating tone. "All this money was supposed to be mine! The inheritance, the heirlooms, everything! Then you show up out of the blue to claim your birthright. I knew the only way to make sure I still got the money was to convince you to be quiet and play along with my plan. I just didn't plan on you being around this long. I assumed your ass would've been arrested by now."

Gutierrez eased the door open a little further, but it was too far. The woman went silent and began to turn for the door. Gutierrez went for it, stepping into the room.

"Put your hands up!" he yelled.

Two things happened simultaneously. The woman began to move her arms as if she were going to do as instructed, but instead stopped, a gun leveled at Gutierrez's chest. Tyler also stood from the couch, a gun in his hands. Gutierrez noticed a form lying on the living room floor. He couldn't be sure, but out of the corner of his eyes he thought it was possible it could be their hostage.

"Not on your life," the female hissed, and as an unconscious reaction, Gutierrez fell to the floor, Cathey not far behind him. Her gun went off and a bullet whizzed above his head.

Rolling to his side behind the island in the kitchen, Gutierrez barely had time to recoup before the second shot flew over his head. He peeked up for a moment before he returned fire. When he ducked down once more, he radioed to the backup and let them know shots were actively being fired.

Preparing to fire a second round, Gutierrez peeked up again to find the woman wasn't in his line of vision. It was only Tyler, and he was hunched on the ground grabbing his side. He looked to his left and found Cathey cautiously inspecting the same scene he was. They both began to look around for the woman who had seemingly disappeared. Gutierrez stood, and Cathey covered him as he headed towards Tyler, kicking the gun out of his reach on the way. Just as he reached him, their backup came around the corner.

"This is only one. Second is a female, five foot six, brunette, considered armed and dangerous," Gutierrez rattled off as he handcuffed Tyler. After he was sure he was secure, Gutierrez moved to inspect the figure on the floor. It was a woman, and it looked to be Eldalyn Wren. Her eyes were closed so he placed a finger on her neck to check for a pulse. It was there and racing wildly. He looked back at her face to find her looking at him.

"Is Joshua okay?" she rasped out.

"He was alive last time I saw him, yes. Just how are you doing young lady?"

"I've still got my memory this time, if that's what you're asking." And she flashed him what he assumed was supposed to be a smile but winced in the process.

They were suddenly surrounded by EMTs who immediately went to work on the handcuffs binding Eldalyn. One of them took one look at the handcuffs on her wrists and shook his head. They weren't standard issue, and they would either need a key or they would have to saw them off. As they tended to her ankle wounds, Eldalyn motioned for Gutierrez to come closer.

"It was weird—" she rasped, stopping because she seemed to be out of breath.

"What was weird?" Gutierrez leaned in closer to try and hear Eldalyn in the midst of the commotion. She winced as they put some sort of solution on her ankle wounds. Gutierrez placed a hand on her shoulder, trying to be comforting in the only way he knew how.

"I lived with them both and never saw this coming. Th—They don't even look alike." Eldalyn's voice faded out. Gutierrez knew the talking was causing her pain. Her outburst had spawned nothing but questions, but he knew he would have to wait to interview her later. It was obvious from the sound of her voice that she was too weak now. He removed his hand from her shoulder, stepping back to search the room for signs of his partner. Two more EMTs approached Eldalyn and fitted her with a neck brace and back board as they prepared her for transport.

Not seeing his partner anywhere in the apartment, Gutierrez followed the EMTs as they lifted Eldalyn and gingerly carried her down the stairs and towards the waiting ambulance.

As they slid the stretcher into the vehicle, Eldalyn's panicked eyes met his and she opened her mouth to say something, but all that came out was a strangled gasp. Gutierrez motioned for Eldalyn to rest. "It's okay, Eldalyn. We can discuss it later," he reassured her.

She shook her head and opened her mouth once more. What came out was a little more than a whisper, but Gutierrez could tell the implications of the words hurt physically as well as emotionally as they tumbled out. "Cam—sh—sh—she just wanted money." Eldalyn's voice faded out as her eyes closed slightly. Gutierrez couldn't tell if this was due to her injuries or shock; the doors of the ambulance shut in his face. He turned and surveyed the parking lot to see Tyler being pushed into another ambulance on the other side. Officers were still searching the apartment building, but just as he feared, there was no sign of Cam—if that really was her name.

Gutierrez walked back to his car and ran his hand through his hair. He spotted Cathey, who seemed to be deep in conversation with another officer about ten feet from their cruiser. He leaned on the car and took a deep breath, patiently waiting for his partner to finish up. With a small, exhausted smile, he took another deep breath. These cases were making him nothing but old.

Finally, Cathey wrapped up his conversation and approached the car. Always the pro at reading body language, he seemed to understand why his usually stoic partner was standing by the car taking deep breaths of the cool night air. "At least you saved her," he reassured him, flashing a half smile that Gutierrez could barely see.

"But she got away," he said dejectedly as both officers slid into the car and headed back to the station.

JOSHUA

JULY 22, 2014 IN THE EVENING

He must've drifted out of consciousness, because when he awoke again a preteen girl was looking down at him. It took him a minute to recognize her.

"Miki?" he asked.

"Joshua!" Suddenly, there were more faces in his view—a teenager who somewhat resembled Marc, and a young girl who was clearly Juni. And his mom was in the background holding a toddler. He smiled.

Marc and Miki both began speaking at once. "Joshua! We missed you so much!"

"Joshua, I have the room next to yours now! We can have a man cave in the basement!"

"And you have to meet Mari! She's a pain in my—."

Joshua smiled at the two of them and looked over at Juni. His mom answered his unspoken question. "She still doesn't speak, but we use sign language regularly. They hope it's just delayed speech still. Her vocal chords and hearing appear normal. Brain scans are next if she doesn't start talking soon."

"Well I'm very glad to see all of you." Joshua looked around the room and noticed someone was missing. "Where's Dad?"

"On his way," his mom reassured him before the kids began talking over each other again.

"When are you coming home?"

"We can watch my new favorite movie together! And Marc can make his special popcorn recipe for us!"

"Whoa, wait you guys." Joshua made eye contact with Marc and Miki.

"I love you guys and miss you a lot, but I'm an adult now. I have to live on my own and have my own life." Miki's face fell, while Marc tried to play it cool. "But I will come visit one of these days, I promise." He looked up to meet his mom's smile. It was a good compromise.

Just then his father walked in and his mom herded the kids out of the room. "Hey Joshua. You gave me quite the scare."

"Sorry Dad." Joshua smiled before remembering why he was here in the first place. "Where's Eldalyn?"

"That's my son, not even asking about his own condition, more worried about his girlfriend." He smiled at his son.

The fact that he wasn't answering scared Joshua. "Dad?"

"She's fine. Well as fine as she can be. Dehydrated and in need of a few stitches, but she'll survive. She'd been asking for you, but we told her you were resting."

"How long was I out?"

"Only a couple hours—mostly from blood loss. Your humerus was broken, so we did put you under to set it. We pulled the bullet out. You'll be bedridden for a couple weeks, but you'll be fine."

"Can I see Eldalyn please?"

Joshua's father laughed. "Alright, let me go get her for you. But please, don't scare us like that again son."

"I won't, Dad." Dr. Williams turned and left the room, only to return a moment later with a nurse wheeling Eldalyn in a wheelchair. She smiled as soon as her eyes found his. The nurse wheeled her over to the side of the bed and left the room. Joshua's father followed suit, closing the door behind him.

"Dare I say, the roles have been reversed. Now it looks like I have to take care of you." Eldalyn smiled the beautiful smile that Joshua had become accustomed to seeing.

"I would say you are correct." He leaned over the side of the bed and she knew what he wanted. Their lips connected. Joshua pulled away first. "My dad said you have stitches?"

Eldalyn held up her hands to show her bandaged wrists and then leaned back to show him her bandaged ankles. "Whatever I was bound with cut pretty deep, but they're no bullet wound."

"Sorry, I'm no hero."

"Don't say that." Eldalyn slapped his arm gently, wincing as her wrist moved. "You're *my* hero. Not every guy would enter the bad guy's apartment without waiting for the cops."

Joshua smiled. "I couldn't stand the thought of him having you a moment longer."

She smiled back. "He's all bark and no bite."

He looked down at his bandaged arm. "Apparently we remember things differently. Eldalyn listen, I lo—" He was cut off as a herd of children entered the room carrying various things to give their brother. They stopped short when they noticed the woman in the wheelchair next to his bed.

"Who's that?" Miki said with an attitude that Joshua knew would only intensify in the next couple years.

His mother looked as if she was about to scold Miki on her tone, but Joshua spoke first. "This is my girlfriend, Eldalyn."

As soon as she had a name she became the new shiny object in the room, and Juni and Miki moved to inspect her. Marc gave Joshua a look with one eye raised. He'd never introduced his parents to a girlfriend before.

Joshua's mother came around the side of the bed. "Your dad says you can be discharged, but only if you have someone to take care of you. We still have your old roo—"

"I'll take care of him," Eldalyn interrupted. She made brief eye contact with his mom then looked back at Joshua. "It's the least I can do. I owe him so much after all he's done for me." She reached her hand out and took Joshua's, and he felt a smile spread across his face.

"If you're sure..." His mom would never give up on trying to get him to come home.

"I am. The doctors are ready to discharge me now. They even scanned my head and despite all odds, my concussion actually healed nicely despite the kidnapping. They said I could drive again."

"That's great." Joshua smiled at her, wishing they were alone so he could finish their earlier conversation, but it would have to wait. He turned to Miki and asked her about school. He had to admit it was nice to see his family again. He reached over and grabbed Eldalyn's hand with his good arm. She turned to look at him and smiled in return. Out of the corner of his eye, Joshua could see his mother silently appraising Eldalyn.

Miki was still talking, but honestly Joshua hadn't been listening. He was too busy inspecting the look on his brother Marc's face. Something was up there, and he made a mental note to ask about it later. The conversation was interrupted when there was a knock at the door.

Joshua glanced up expecting to see his father, but instead the assuming figure of Officer Gutierrez filled the doorframe. "May we come in?"

"Of course," Joshua answered, and his mother made a motion to clear the room. Eldalyn made a move to stand up to leave the room, but Officer Gutierrez motioned for her to stay seated as he walked in with Cathey behind him.

"We need to talk to you as well, Miss Wren. It will save us time to discuss this with both of you right now."

They both nodded as the officers took up residence in the hospital room and closed the door behind them. They turned to Eldalyn first.

"So Eldalyn, we need to know everything you remember about Cam."

She thought for a moment, scratching her chin absentmindedly. "Well,

I met her at The Wolf Pack, where she had been a bartender for a few years. I guess we never really talked about her past, and I never asked. We always just talked about my past and my life—which I guess is odd now that I think about it." Eldalyn stood and walked over to the window. Even though she had been wheeled in in a wheelchair, it was obvious she was well enough to walk without it. In fact, her footsteps were perhaps the least shaky that Joshua had ever seen.

"When I first came to in the hospital, I had a dream about her. I just couldn't remember her name. And in my dreams, she would always fade into Tyler's face. I guess I could never see the resemblance, but she confessed to me that they were brother and sister. Why she never told me, I have no idea."

"You were dating, and at one time engaged to Tyler, correct?" It was Cathey who spoke up.

"Yes, and that's the weird thing. She was always so against the relationship, but I never saw it as being in a sinister way. But now I see that she saw me as a threat. And she never said a thing. I lived with her, and she said nothing when I moved out to live with Tyler."

Gutierrez nodded. "There was a lot she wasn't telling you. Anything else? Did she ever mention any other places of residence? Any family? Friends?"

Eldalyn shook her head. "I don't think so, and if she did, I don't remember. She dated Justin from The Wolf Pack for a while, but I have a feeling it was just for show. She didn't really seem that into him, or any guy for that matter."

Both officers nodded simultaneously, but it was Gutierrez who spoke once more, pulling up a picture on a tablet which he handed to Eldalyn. Joshua tried to peek over her shoulder, but winced as he tried to sit up. His shoulder was still in a lot of pain. "That's her before she dyed her hair dark. Cam's real name is Olivia Fleming, and she disappeared from her family home in California in July of 2009."

"What?" Eldalyn's mouth dropped open as she looked closer at the tablet in her hand. Joshua could just make out a blonde woman in what looked like a summer dress.

"She and Tyler were engaged. Well, we can't tell if they were really engaged, or if it was just a ploy to get money. Either way, we interviewed Tyler earlier today, and Olivia and Tyler are indeed half siblings. They share the same mother. Tyler says he found out when he turned eighteen and could obtain access to the adoption records; he then went to California to find Olivia. He says when he found her, she told him all about the large trust fund she had, but couldn't touch it until her grandparents died. The grandparents also had a sizeable estate that Olivia told Tyler she was set to inherit in addition to her trust fund. Tyler says that no matter how evil Olivia may be, she couldn't deal with the thought of killing the grandparents who raised her. But she sure didn't have a conscience about robbing them blind. We asked Tyler to elaborate on why they decided to work together, but it seems Cam-slash-Olivia kept him in the dark about some of her reasoning to choosing him as her partner in crime. Cathey and I have our own assumptions but nothing concrete."

Gutierrez took a deep breath before continuing. "It was then that they hatched the fake engagement and disappearing act to get as much money out of the grandparents as possible before they left town. He says they did it for the rings and cash they were given for the wedding."

Joshua looked back at Eldalyn who was quivering with what he assumed was shock. Cathey stood up and walked over to her, gently grabbing her arm and leading her back to the wheelchair she had recently vacated. After she was seated, Gutierrez continued.

"I don't know where their plan went wrong though, because once they came out here, they began accessing the trust fund without waiting for the grandmother to die. Cam—or Olivia, rather—was keeping the bulk of the money and feeding Tyler enough to pay for living expenses and keep him placated. Tyler couldn't work a job because he hadn't been able to get a fake ID like Cam. I'm not sure if it was coincidental or purposeful, but then it sounds like Tyler started to go after your friend Cassie. We can't be sure, but perhaps due to being abandoned as a child, he has some major separation issues. Because she tried to leave him just as you did, and it didn't end up so well for her."

Eldalyn smiled sadly. "Did you find her body?"

Cathey nodded. "Right next to where he tried to bury you."

"Anyways," Gutierrez interrupted, "when we brought him in, Tyler was a mess and all ready to confess everything that had happened with Cassie. We can't be sure, because his lawyer is negotiating a deal with the DA, but it sounds as if Cam was the brains of the operation. Cam is the one that buried Cassie in the park. In Tyler's confession, it sounds like she showed up as he was attacking her, just as he did you Eldalyn, and she didn't want to risk them being found out, so she directed Tyler to take her there and she buried her alive there."

Gutierrez took a shaky breath as a single tear slid down Eldalyn's cheek. "Tyler says she was there the night he attacked you. He says she was the one who broke all the plates in order to distract us from why they had really torn apart your house, but thankfully, instead of burying you too, she left you behind. We aren't exactly sure why she did that, other than the idea that maybe she thought you were already dead, or close enough that there would be no saving you, and it would just appear you were the victim of a robbery gone bad. When people started asking around about you, we believe she realized her mistake and began to get nervous and tried to frame Tyler. And when she saw you walk into The Wolf Pack that night, she knew something was wrong and alerted Tyler to come get you and do away with you for good this time. He said he was supposed to get the ring back, which he wasn't supposed to give you in the first place since it was evidence tying him to Olivia, and kill you. But he just couldn't, and that's where Joshua entered the picture."

Eldalyn smiled and looked up at Joshua, putting a hand on his arm. He smiled and put his hand on top of hers. "So I don't get it—why did Tyler give me the ring in the first place?" Eldalyn looked at Officer Gutierrez with a quizzical look in her eyes.

"We aren't really sure. And honestly, I don't think he is either. He says he wanted to marry you because he knew about your sizable bank account and the property in your name, but when we asked about why he gave Cassie, and you, the ring, he just shrugged. Honestly, I don't think the guy is a genius."

Joshua smirked, which didn't escape Cathey's notice. "Which by the way, Joshua, you will need to testify to what you saw at Tyler's trial, if there is one, that is. But as long as the judge accepts whatever deal his lawyer cuts with the DA, he will plead guilty, which will save us all the trouble of a trial." Cathey smiled.

"What about Cam?" Eldalyn looked at Gutierrez expectantly.

"That's why we are here. During the gunfire and all of the commotion, she managed to get out of a fire escape in the back of the apartment complex. We aren't sure where she would have gone. We believe she has contacts in the railroad; she's been using the rail system for years to travel to small towns with less security, and conveniently less cameras, to pull money out of her trust—without her grandparents', or even Tyler's, knowledge. We've only spoken to a couple of the smaller banks of the branch she visited, but it sounds as if she may have been dressing up as her estranged mother and using her mother's old driver's license, which she stole when she 'disappeared,' to access the account and withdraw funds early. The grandparents had put Olivia's mother's name on the account a few years before as they had begun to age and they'd wanted her to monitor the disbursement of funds. Turns out, Olivia's mother hasn't been seen in some time either. Which is another matter we are looking into."   Gutierrez scratched his head, clearly in deep thought, before continuing. "Anyways, somewhere along the way, perhaps after the incident with Cassie, Cam realized that Tyler wasn't all there and that she really didn't need him anymore. We think she tried to set him up for your attack, Eldalyn, but for whatever reason, something went wrong with that plan. Then, when we started sniffing around The Wolf Pack, she decided she would play hero by giving us Tyler. What she didn't count on was Tyler calling her in a panic when he had you in the car and basically, we believe, she became scared he would get caught and tell us everything. I think she had hoped to flee town while Tyler took the fall, but his phone call made her realize how truly unstable he was and she decided to go help him, or very well maybe to go kill you and him both. We aren't sure since we obviously foiled any plan she may have had."

That's when a question bubbled up in Joshua's mind. "What about their parents?"

Cathey shook his head. "We are still trying to figure out exactly what happened, but both Olivia… Cam, and Tyler were born out of wedlock. which must've been a huge embarrassment to the Flemings as they were of high stature in the community. Olivia was raised by the grandparents, but for whatever reason, Tyler was put up for adoption. He was adopted by a family with the last name Johnson, which is why Cam chose that as her fake last name. It turns out the family he was adopted into fell apart after a couple years and ended in divorce. His childhood was not pretty, and when he found out how Olivia had been raised, I guess you could say he became very jealous. And Olivia, well, we speculate that she has limited knowledge of the legal system and thought perhaps Tyler could claim part of her inheritance. This isn't true, but it's the only way we could figure she would have motive to work with Tyler on their marriage scam. We've also interviewed the grandmother and have found there are indeed other people listed in her will to receive sizeable portions of their estate besides Olivia, and we suspect she either didn't know, or did know and that's why she didn't let Tyler tell their grandparents he was her half brother. All out of fear he would be added to the will—which already has about six other names of people benefiting from the Flemings' deaths—and here we are back at their plan to squeeze the grandparents for money and disappear. As I mentioned before, Olivia's mother hasn't been around in nearly ten years. The grandparents claim she was always a flighty, free–spirit type and her disappearance didn't alarm them. But she is one of the few people listed on the estate in addition to Olivia.."

A small frown stole over Eldalyn's features. "All this for money?"

Gutierrez nodded. "I know. Greed really is a deadly sin."

She nodded. "I guess I had just hoped there was a deeper reason for a betrayal like that from Cam… I mean Olivia."

Joshua thought for a moment. He didn't like the idea that Olivia was still out there. "You're going to find her, right? I mean, she buried Cassie alive and tried to do the same to Eldalyn."

"We are going to try," Cathey responded. "But this girl disappeared once, and she was damn good at it then, just as she may be now. She probably already had an all-new identity in preparation for when all this went down. And this time, she doesn't have the baggage of Tyler weighing her down."

Cathey closed his notepad and stood. "And she's got millions of dollars to get wherever she's going. After the ten or so test withdrawals she performed the past couple of years, I guess she decided that her grandmother really hadn't noticed the trust was being accessed. Olivia cleared out her entire trust fund the night before you showed up at The Wolf Pack, Eldalyn. Regardless of what went down that night, she had been planning to ditch Tyler anyways. Maybe she knew she would come up in the investigation and needed to dispose of him first, we aren't entirely sure." Cathey seemed to ponder for a minute, then turned to Joshua. "I need to take your official statement now, if you feel up to it, but Eldalyn can't be here for it. Eldalyn we will need your official statement, separately, regarding the kidnapping as well."

They both nodded, and Eldalyn leaned in for a quick kiss before standing and heading into the hallway with Officer Gutierrez. As soon as the door was closed he turned to Cathey. "I just wish this would be over."

"I know Joshua, but trust me when I say, it most likely is. Olivia has gone somewhere else to be someone else. She won't come back for you or Eldalyn. She wouldn't risk it." He took a deep breath. "I also can't say this for sure, but I have a feeling that Cam was a defense killer, only hurting or killing people when she felt her livelihood was threatened. I don't think she did it for sport."

Joshua shook his head. He wasn't so sure.

ELDALYN

SEPTEMBER 22, 2014

Eldalyn placed the dish she was washing on the drying rack next to the sink, wiping her hands on the towel that was hanging just below it. She heard the shower shut off in the bathroom.

"Hurry up! We're going to be late!" she shouted as she turned to shut off the lights in the living room. She was interrupted when a slippery pair of arms wrapped around her mid-section.

"Late for what?" Joshua whispered in her ear.

"Hiking with Miki and Marc—now cut it out! Now I have to change my shirt." Eldalyn looked down at the quick dry spandex top she was wearing, debating on if she really did have to change or not. Joshua retreated to the bedroom to finish getting dressed. Deciding that she really would be uncomfortable in the wet shirt, she headed to the bedroom to change, running into Joshua who had just exited the bathroom.

"Ow!" Joshua grabbed her before she fell, but winced, as his shoulder had not yet completely healed.

"You sure you're okay to go hiking?" Eldalyn asked with a concerned look on her face. The doctor had said some light activity was fine, but she was starting to worry it was too much too soon.

"I'm fine babe. Now let's get going so we can get you home in time for work."

Eldalyn smiled and grabbed her purse and bottle of water, her thoughts of changing the shirt completely forgotten.

She had recently been hired as a server at a local restaurant. It was only a temporary job, but the hours were flexible, which is what she needed in order to finish school. Joshua had helped her enroll in the local community college where she was currently taking classes in computer science. It was tough, but she knew it was a stepping stone to improving her position in life.

"You got the day of the wedding off, right?" Joshua asked as they walked out the door.

"Of course. I would never let Liam or Rita down," Eldalyn smiled. She and Rita had formed a sort of bond, replacing the hole left in Eldalyn's heart by Cam. They weren't nearly as close and didn't share everything like Eldalyn and Cam had, but they usually met once a week for lunch and discussed the happenings in their lives. Honestly, it was nice to have a girlfriend again.

In the meantime, Joshua and Eldalyn's relationship had flourished. Joshua had insisted that Eldalyn move in to his apartment, and she was currently in the process of selling the property where her house had once stood. In light of the damage caused during the attack, the realtor had recommended they raze the building. They were presently considering an offer by an apartment complex company who saw the large amount of land as an investment opportunity. If the deal went through, Eldalyn was set to make just over two hundred thousand dollars.

As they climbed into the car, Joshua leaned across the center console and kissed Eldalyn lightly on the lips. "Shall we?" She nodded.

They sped out of the parking garage and down the street in Joshua's Prius. During the course of the investigation, the cops had recovered Eldalyn's car from Tyler; however, she felt the memories attached to it were too much to bear and had sold it almost immediately. She had been in the market for another car but had not yet decided what type she wanted. Sharing a car with Joshua was tough at times, now that he too was back at work, but she knew it was only a matter of time before she found one she liked.

Joshua was working on rekindling his relationship with his family. Although meetings with his parents still seemed a bit tense, the two of them had obviously been trying hard to treat Joshua as an adult with his own life.

Eldalyn had suggested that he try hanging out with his siblings without the overbearing presence of his parents, and he had liked that idea. Recently they had taken Juni and Miki to go see a new cartoon movie that had been in theaters. Marc had argued that he was too old to see it, so Eldalyn had suggested he come hiking with them another time. He had agreed.

Eldalyn looked out the window as the city passed by. Her memory had almost fully returned. There were still a few holes surrounding the actual attack, but she figured she didn't need to remember those parts anyways. Her body had healed perfectly; she was back to pre-attack condition with no lasting effects. Her heart, however, was another matter entirely.

After a two-month investigation, Cassie had finally been laid to rest. Eldalyn had met Cassie's mom at the funeral, and she had been inconsolable at the loss of her only child. In the days and weeks following, Eldalyn had been visiting and calling her regularly, worried that she may lose the will to live. It had turned out to be to both of their benefits; Eldalyn found that she could confide in her about anything, as it was often hard to discuss her feelings regarding Cam's betrayal with Joshua. Eldalyn couldn't blame him though; men were known to give advice rather than sympathy. Luckily for all parties involved, Tyler had indeed pled guilty and saved them all the stress of a trial.

No leads on Eldalyn's father had come to light during the investigation. As it turned out, Eldalyn had been on his health insurance plan from when he had lost his job and applied for government-provided medical insurance. Because of her age and the fact that they still showed her at the same address where she had resided with her father, Eldalyn had continued to maintain coverage as his child. The cops had spent a day or two trying to trace his truck and subsequent actions. But Mr. Wren was either deceased or didn't want to be found. Officer Gutierrez had called and apologized, but Eldalyn understood they couldn't keep spending as much time on her case. All in all, it had mostly come to a close, and there were other cases in the city that needed attention. And at this point, Eldalyn had come to accept her life without her father, and honestly, him being found wouldn't affect her life in the least. If he had wanted anything to do with her, he had known all along where he could find her.

As Joshua turned the corner and stopped at a crosswalk, Eldalyn watched as the walk symbol turned white and a group of pedestrians on the other side began to cross. It was while this was occurring that Eldalyn's eyes were drawn to a particular red head in the crowd. Her nose was thin, lips full, and the skin tone was familiar. She couldn't help but try to picture the woman with the brunette hair that she had known her to have. At that very instant, it was as if the woman sensed she was being inspected and stopped briefly to glance up. Eldalyn gasped.

It was her.

As briefly as she had glanced up, the woman quickly looked back down, turning the corner and fading out of sight, almost as if she had never been there at all.

ABOUT THE AUTHOR

Deceptive Perfection is Hope's first novel. While she isn't writing, she is busy traveling the world, trying new foods, or hanging out with friends. A graduate from Metropolitan State University, Hope grew up in Colorado but currently calls Nevada her home. To find out information on future novels, follow Hope on twitter: @thehopeopera.

84353471R00166

Made in the USA
San Bernardino, CA
08 August 2018